Copyright 2022

Version 1.0
1 July 2022

ISBN: 978-1-7344700-5-5
Library of Congress Control Number: 2022911364

waynegoodman**books**

waynegoodmanbooks@gmail.com
Twitter: @Wgoodmanbooks

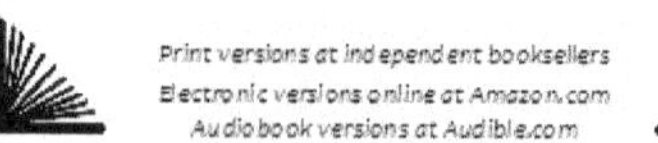

DEDICATION

First, and most importantly, my partner, Richard May. His support and valuable input along the way helped me complete this work.

Second, the wonderful Benicia Outlaws Writing Group. My skills have grown immensely since I started participating with them a few years back.

Also, I wish to mention author Jude Tresswell, who inspired me to consider crafting a story with an asexual protagonist.

This book would not have been possible without the creative genius and artistic contributions of Pyotr Ilyich Tchaikovsky, Lev Nikolayevich Tolstoy, Modest Petrovich Mussorgsky, Mikhail Alekseevich Kuzmin, as well as the women who supported them, and all the other denizens of 19th Century St. Petersburg who inspired me.

Table of Contents

1

As I scanned the layout of fortune-telling cards on the table, several images jumped out: the ring, the crown, a castle. I didn't need these pasteboard squares to tell my client's future, but this pretense of foretelling someone's destiny facilitated the fantasy I portrayed.

Next to me sat Catherine Dolgorukov, a handsome woman in her early thirties, daughter of impoverished Prince Mikhail. She had joined the House of Romanov staff as a young woman, serving as lady-in-waiting to Tsaritsa Maria Alexandrovna. When the Empress took ill, Tsar Alexander II turned his affections to Catherine—a 30-year age difference—who served as his most favored mistress.

"Katya," I addressed my client, "you have asked me to provide a cure for your current affliction." My hand pointed to the cards. "I have determined you will soon regain your previous health, especially when you hear the news I have for you."

She turned her sad eyes to my face. "Yes. Please help me, Rodya. I know only you can."

I assumed the name Rodion Fyodorovich Propok when I first reached St. Petersburg. Whenever circumstances encouraged relocation to a new town, I chose a different title for myself once my prior existence ended. Having read Dostoevsky, I favored the Christian name of his protagonist in *Crime and Punishment*, added the appropriate Patronymic, and Propok merely sounded like "prophet."

Several hundred years ago I had succumbed to what I thought was the plague. Almost everyone around me had died from this mysterious illness, and when I lost consciousness one evening, I just assumed it had gotten me as well. When I woke the next day, surprised at remaining alive, I took it as a blessing and left my little hometown on the first carriage available.

Years passed, but I never appeared to age. Disease did not seem to affect me. Wounds mended and disappeared within days. I later dubbed myself 'Lazarus' and began chronicling my journeys. After several years, I would need to leave wherever I dwelled and select another town to call home before others discovered my secret longevity.

"My dearest Catherine Mikhailovna, the arrangement before us clearly displays what I know—with all certainty—shall come to pass." I swept an arm above the array of decorative illustrations.

Another gift I had received from my brush with death was the ability to see into the future. Not very far, a few weeks, a month or two at best. I could look at a person and know what would happen to them in the days to come. Having the foreknowledge of all humanity's outcome might have been too overwhelming for the son of a poor farmer from a small village. This precognition only worked on others, though. I could not see my own way ahead.

It took me a while to discover how to make a living with this talent, but, in due course, I determined the role of healer paid quite well. Most people preferred healers to doctors. For some reason, the mumbo-jumbo we spewed comforted them more than medicinal science. The more flim-flammery we provided, the more smiles and praises we garnered.

My clients always turned out the way I foretold. The ones who recovered from their infirmities demonstrated generous appreciation with gifts of food, livestock, or money.

Why would I not put such a marvelous capacity to work for the good of all people? A valid concern. However, Sir Thomas Browne wrote, "how shall we expect charity towards others, when we are uncharitable to ourselves? *'Charity begins at home,'* is the voice of the world." The man I regarded in the mirror agreed.

"Tell me more, Rodya." Catherine brushed her long black curls aside, displaying her ashen complexion as she studied the columns and rows. "I must know."

Over the years, I developed a passion for books and reading. As for other methods of artistic entertainment, I knew how things would turn out a few minutes into an opera or stage play. However, a book—much like a brick—felt opaque and impenetrable. It held secrets I could not predict. The more twisting and meandering the plot, the better. I preferred lengthy tomes with a cast of hundreds. In fact, part of my decision to move to the center of Russian culture hinged on the incredible literary scene.

After my arrival in St. Petersburg during late 1879, it did not take long for news of my talent to reach the Romanov palace. Several members of the royal family sought out my services, but Catherine made the most of my attentions.

On my first visit a few months back, she showed me these cards, claiming an old Gypsy woman named Minditsi had given them to her years ago. I picked one up and rotated it a quarter turn. This joined the two halves of the dagger image, which I then indicated with a flourish of my fingers. "The Empress will soon be no more."

She jolted upright, the color returning to her pallid features. "My mistress is to *die?*"

I nodded the confirmation as I pushed the fallen sleeve back into place.

"Oh!" squealed Catherine. "Oh…" she repeated, facing downward. "She has been in ill health as of late. Sashka has called me his secret queen, and he promised we would marry when Maria Alexandrovna–bless her soul–left this Earth." She hugged herself as her revitalized rosy lips pursed into a tiny smile.

The ends of my mouth levitated without intention in response to my client's volte-face in health.

"When, Rodya, when?" Catherine panted.

"Please calm yourself, my lady." I motioned with open hands. "You do not want to bring about another attack of the vapors."

"You are correct, Rodya. I brought you here to calm my nerves, not to foster further excitement."

And by *here*, the lady-in-waiting referred to her chambers at the royal palace. The sitting room itself measured at least five meters on each side, large enough to provide housing for several Russian peasant families at the same time. Furnishings came from the world's best: Chippendale, Kimbel and Cabus, Hepplewhite, Thomas Sheraton. A small Boisselot & Fils upright piano stood in a corner. These sumptuous appointments seemed on par with the rest of what I had observed at the palace. I cannot imagine what marvels occupied the bedchamber behind that closed set of hand carved doors at the far end of the room.

I moved to stand, but Catherine grasped my hand in the manner of a clinging vine. "My work here is complete, my dear lady. I'm sure you have your duties to perform," I murmured.

"The Tsaritsa is visiting her brother at Schloß Heiligenberg." She glanced up at me, her eyes, moist with tears, suggesting my payment might not have been food, livestock, nor money. Possibly a passport to the inner chamber. "Please stay with me."

The final phenomenon–for I would call it neither gift nor blessing– from my near death by plague happened to be a total inability to perform my manly duties. At first, I found it frustrating and disappointing, but, in due course, I accepted this downside in conjunction with prescience and prolonged existence. Many have tested me, both women and men, but every time, alas, the same impotent result. Even though I consider myself only mildly attractive at best, people have often expressed their physical desires for me throughout my existence. Perhaps it was the intimate knowledge of their days to come that drew them to me.

I plucked the lady's hand from my arm. "While I am flattered by your affections, madame, they cannot pay for my flat in Nevsky Prospekt nor my various accounts."

She shuffled through various velvet covered objects on a nearby table. Her hand reappeared with a five-ruble gold coin clenched between her thumb and forefinger. "Here," she spat. "If you prefer money to love, then take *this*." Catherine placed the piece in my palm. She reached into the same bag and retrieved another. "You might want this as well. It does nothing for me."

I grabbed the coin with my free hand and started toward the way out. "I shall see you again next week for more particulars of your story, my lady."

I knew the Tsaritsa would be dead in a few days and that the grieving Tsar would marry this blood-sucking parasite the month following. Nevertheless, it would be better for me to reveal only little bits of this tale at a time. More visits meant more gold. More gold meant more books. And–who knows–I might be able to afford a wingback Hepplewhite or Chippendale of my own someday.

ONE of my favorite patrons, Nadezhda Von Meck, had requested another home visit. A financially comfortable widow whose husband had struck it rich in the Russian railway business, she hardly ever left her small mansion in the Liteinaya district. Those who had risen above the rest or who had ties to the Royal family built their homes in that particular enclave of the city.

Following a healthy luncheon of borscht and toast at home, I caught a *konka*—a horse-drawn tram—on Nevsky Prospekt. An illustrative cross-section of St. Petersburg residents rode these carts. Elegant ladies with furs and jewels sat next to dock workers and shopgirls.

Various aromas from the travelers' bags announced their next meals. Fresh garlic, boiled cabbage, and citrus filled my nose. Unfortunately, I could also smell rotting meat, an odor that very much disturbed me.

Having to be in close quarters with others caused me occasional spiritual distress, as I would peer into their futures without intending to do so. Every so often, I would gasp or wince when sensing someone's bad omens. People would turn to me with unspoken questions. "Gout," I would say and point to my healthy feet.

At Liteyny Street, I boarded the northbound streetcar and rode it to Zakharevskaya Street. Within a minute's walk, I stood before the Von Meck home, a brownstone three-story residence with a plain façade.

The entryway opened into a large sitting room with a high, arched, carved-wood ceiling. From the center hung a sparkling chandelier as large as a grand piano. A parqueted floor revealed an intricate, maze-like pattern. Large tapestries hung between the double doors along the side walls. At the far end of the room, a young fellow with dark, unkempt hair sat playing parlor music quietly. His blank expression and pursed lips suggested a desire to be elsewhere. My senses informed me he would have an easier time in the Von Meck home if he desisted from pursuing one of the family's six daughters.

"Rodya," my hostess chimed as she entered through one set of doors. Still fetching at nearly fifty years, she wore a powder-blue frilly frock with a crinoline hoop skirt. Her cropped hair accentuated the inherently masculine features.

"Madame Von Meck," I muttered as I bowed.

"Please, I have invited you to call me Nadya." She touched a teardrop sapphire necklace at the base of her neck with several fingertips. "All my friends do."

"Thank you for that permission, madam; however, due to the professional nature of our acquaintance, I would prefer to maintain a more suitable quality of communication." My head turned toward the musical instrument. "Who is your student?"

Nadya tittered like a schoolgirl, touching one hand to her lips before returning it to the necklace. "That is *not* a student, Mr. Propok, but rather the young man I have engaged to instruct my daughters on the pianoforte." She stepped toward the instrument. "Would you like to hear us play?"

"Of course." While music never interested me much as an art form, I did not wish to insult my patron.

"Move over, Achille. We shall play the Glinka four-hand for our guest."

The sullen young man slid to the left as Nadya settled herself on the remainder of the bench, sweeping the clacking hoops to her right. This bothersome skirt style had never appealed to me, and I hoped that such fashion might change in the near future.

"This is *Capriccio on Russian Themes*. I hope you enjoy it."

The two of them pounded with impassioned intensity upon the keys for the next 15 minutes or so. Fragments of Slavic melodies floated throughout the large, resonant room. After the finale, resplendent with repetitive arpeggios and flourishes, Madame Von Meck stood, narrowed her eyes, and patted her accompanist on the shoulder.

"Keep practicing, Achille. You will soon achieve the proficiency you so desire." She turned to me. "I hope you found that a pleasant experience."

"Of course. Quite refreshing and invigorating."

"Shall we?" My hostess indicated our way out.

We strolled into a narrow hallway. She stopped at one of the many doors, opened it, and indicated I should enter. The small, windowless study smelled of smoldering lamp oil, which caused me to cough several times. Of all the things humans have used over the centuries to bring light into the darkness, burning whale blubber smelled the worst. Much of the civilized world had begun to install electrified lighting, but provincial, old-fashioned St. Petersburg had yet to move toward that modernity.

My hostess pointed to one of two decorative chairs, and I sat. A small, hand-carved table stood between us with a pot and two small cups.

"Coffee?" she offered.

"No, thank you."

"Mind if I do?"

"Not at all." The aroma of the brewed beverage helped to offset the stench of lamp oil. A chemical compound in coffee affected me the opposite way of most other people. It made me very sleepy.

After taking a bit from her demi-tasse, Madame Von Meck looked away, as if gazing through a large window at an endless landscape. "Mr. Propok,"–she faced me–"Rodya, if I may."

I nodded.

"You know how I feel trapped in this house, unable to set foot outside. Following my husband's death four years ago, nothing has motivated me to leave. I have even foregone the weddings of my daughters because I cannot work up the courage to depart this home. Despite this dread of the outside world, I have still managed to maintain my contacts within the community by hosting several societal events here each month."

She took another sip of coffee, set the cup on its saucer, and dabbed at the corner of her mouth with an embroidered napkin.

"As we have discussed in previous sessions, I believe I am very unsympathetic in my personal relations because I lack femininity. Despite being a mother, I know not how to evoke compassion in my breast. Perhaps I am afraid to be affected or sentimental, causing the majority of my relationships to be somewhat comradely."

She looked down at her clasped hands in her lap.

"I have never believed in a supreme being, and no one has ever attempted to dissuade me from that opinion." Madame Von Meck raised her head, extending her neck. "However, I turn to you today to inquire whether I should attend a church service or two, make amends with society, and ask for forgiveness."

She locked gazes with me, and I experienced a cold shiver. Eyes are the mirror of a heart, and hers felt fairly frosty. My head snapped to the side.

When your life extends over a few centuries, you have the time to consider the possibilities of whether a power greater than yourself directs the actions of this universe. I have contemplated the motives behind why a benevolent–or a mean-spirited–overlord would have taken interest in one poor peasant and given him this longevity. The notion of an indifferent divinity makes little sense.

There is an old Russian saying, "It's not the gods who burn our pots." This left me to wonder who burnt mine.

I have watched people survive and succumb, prosper and perish, develop and decline. No pattern of existence has made itself clear to me; therefore, I practiced no devotions to a deity.

Looking into my client's future, I saw no changes, no improvement, no decay. Her choices, in reality, would have no effect.

"My dear lady"—I reached across the table and grasped her cold, sallow hand—"your actions in this matter cannot affect an outcome, whichever path you choose. Your sustained good health is of the utmost concern to me, and if you should leave the safety of your home, it is uncertain what suffering might beget your spirit, even if the journey should be to the nearest house of worship."

Her head bobbed a few times.

"It is my firm belief the most prudent course of action would be to remain true to your initial presentiments and keep to your stronghold here."

She squeezed my hand before withdrawing. "That was my sense as well. In the past few years, I have begun to rely upon my innermost thoughts less and less, but I feel much better now that you have corroborated my natural feelings."

"Of course. Calming people's fears and anxieties should be what a good healer can perform for his clients."

"Thank you, Rodya. I knew I could count on you."

I stood, and she handed me a small purse as I left. At least I knew I could afford adequate meals for the next week or so. And, perhaps, a new book.

THE next morning, I caught the Nevsky tram to Liteyny Street. Fewer people rode in the morning, and I thought I might be spared the spiritual onslaught of other people's lives. However, one woman sitting by herself in the corner carried so much distress that I found it difficult not to feel her anguish.

Her husband had died at the palace the night of the most recent attempt on our Tsar's life. A revolutionist had placed a delayed-fuse bomb beneath the dining hall, but due to the late arrival of a guest, dinner did not begin at the scheduled time. No members of the royal family sustained injuries, but several guards and house servants perished. This proud woman held her head with dignity and kept the tears inside. She planned to take the train to Tula and return to her parents' home, where she would deliver the young couple's unborn child.

When the *konka* reached my destination, I could not step down fast enough. Such tragedies and sufferings unnerved me. I found it best to distance myself from the unfortunate soul as quickly as possible.

I walked one block to Italyanska Street and turned east. My route took me past the *Novoe Vremya* newspaper offices, but it was their publishing department around the corner on Ertelev Alley that I sought.

The proprietor, Alexey Sergeyevich Suvorin, greeted me at the door. He dressed in a long, black cassock and groomed himself in the manner of an Orthodox priest, though he rarely attended religious services. A stringy beard wrapped around his face from chin to ears, and a gray streak in the center of his combed-back hair suggested middle age.

Suvorin had dedicated his journalistic endeavors to loyalist, Tsarist principles; however, the novels and books he printed had a much broader appeal. He maintained a close friendship with one of my favorite authors, Dostoyevsky, a man with whom Suvorin shared similar political ideals. I have been a regular customer, and my arrival portended book sales.

"Rodya, how good to see you!" His smile spread the hairy fringe. "What brings you to my humble shop?"

I had encountered that smile several times before. From his joy, I could tell he had something special he wanted to share with me, that he would first offer it at a price higher than I would be willing to pay, and we would bargain to an agreement.

Following him inside, I responded, "It is good to see you as well. I have just recently finished *The Idiot* by your Fyodor Mikhailovich, and I would be interested in finding another set of volumes to satisfy my thirst for fine literature. What might you have, old friend?"

He opened the door of a nearby chest and withdrew two dented pewter cups and an unmarked clear bottle filled with a golden, glowing liquid.

"Let us first deal with your thirst before we discuss literature, no?"

"Is that your kvass?"

"Yes. Made the way my old granny taught me. I believe she got the recipe from Baba Yaga herself!" He filled both containers halfway and handed one to me.

We lifted our drinks toward each other. "To our health!" I declared.

"To books!" Suvorin responded before we both swallowed our share.

"To books!" I echoed, holding out my cup for a refill.

"*The Idiot.* A good tale. One of Dostoyevsky's most splendid pieces." As he poured, he asked, "What did you think?"

I shrugged. "What is there to say, Alexey Sergeyevich? It is brilliant. It is madness. I found the character of Myshkin difficult to believe. The man who is not tempted by power nor money does not exist."

"Perhaps that is why it is a fiction, no?" His shoulders and hands raised as one.

"True, but I need to cultivate a solid connection with the people of the book. How else would I care to read more?"

One of his bushy eyebrows arched. "Was there *anyone* who fascinated you?"

"Of course. The young man, Ippolit, who attempts to kill himself because of ill health." My head bobbed twice. "I found him rather sympathetic."

"*Sympathetic?* The man was an atheist and a coward!"

"Perhaps"—I raised a finger—"but he provided the necessary balance to the ludicrous Prince Myshkin."

"Nevertheless… you finished reading it, yes?"

"Yes, I did because I enjoy lengthy books with many, many characters. Something protracted and profound, such as *War and Peace*, suits me just fine."

"Ahhhhh!" he sang in the manner of a sacred chant. "I am happy for you to have mentioned the illustrious Mr. Tolstoy." The joyous smile returned.

I could tell his pride bristled, having shepherded me to the very subject he wished to discuss. "And why is that, Suvorin?"

"You have heard of his latest work, *Anna Karenina*, yes?"

"Yes. The *Messenger* had been printing it but stopped before delivering the final installment."

Suvorin waved a hand to one side. "Tolstoy had a disagreement with Katkov about how it should be presented. Did you read any of it?"

"No. Without a conclusion, I would not want to spend any effort on such a futile undertaking."

"Then, I have just the thing for you, my friend." He moved to a standing cabinet, opened it, and retrieved a three-volume set of books. "*Anna Karenina*!" Suvorin placed them on the chest near the kvass and slapped the top book.

"Why would someone publish a story with no ending?"

"Ahhhhhh." Another hymn-like melody. "What if I tell you this edition includes the missing section?"

That would be something. If it were anything like his last work, it would contain innumerable names and places, something to keep my keen mind honed.

The gold-embossed, soft leather binding appeared rather expensive. "Even so, I doubt I could afford something so finely-made."

"A bargain at 10 rubles! No?"

"*10 rubles*? That's half a month's wages for common laborers!"

"But, come, Propok, you are not common, and you are certainly not a laborer by any means. You siphon off the coins of the well-to-do by whispering auspicious words into their depraved ears." The heat of his mind burned within his eyes.

"Even so, Suvorin, you would accept my silver all the same, would you not?"

"Of course! If you have what it takes."

I took a deep breath. "Perhaps we could strike a bargain."

"A bargain worth more than the money itself?" He slammed a hand on the chest, causing the bottle of kvass to quiver.

Distracted by the literary discussion, I had not bothered to peer into the publisher's days ahead. Once I probed his condition, I could tell he had been worrying about a carbuncle on his lower right leg. This temporary affliction would disappear in a week's time.

"My dearest friend, your bloated boil will not fester." I pointed to the corresponding spot on my body. "Keep it clean, and it will fade away within a fortnight."

"But how did you *know*…?" His eyes grew bigger. "Did I limp? Have I touched the tender spot? What did you see, mister healer?"

I let my lips curl in amusement. "You have given me no indication of your condition, my friend. A good healer understands the suffering of his clients and can provide—as you described them—auspicious words."

Suvorin glanced heavenward. "God help me hold onto my good mind."

As if such a celestial being would pay attention or respond to the entreaties of one middling man. "Four rubles for the books," I offered.

"That is less than they cost me! I have not caught you stealing"—he jabbed a finger in my direction—"yet you speak like a thief. Seven-and-a-half, yes?"

"Five, and not one kopek more. I just saved you from a week of worries." I tilted my head and raised my brows. "They say fear has great eyes."

His head shifted one way, his eyes the other. Two and a half seconds later, he lowered his chin and wagged it a few times, sweeping the scant beard across his tunic. "Oh, Rodya! You should have been a merchant with your unconventional negotiating skills."

No, I tried that a few centuries back and lost everything in the tulip market. I fished one of the gold coins Catherine Mikhailovna had given me from my vest pocket and slipped it to Suvorin.

He replenished the cups. "To books!" the publisher proposed with an upstretched arm.

"To your health!" I responded.

I left the store carrying the wrapped volumes under my arm, eager to irrigate my dry desert of distractions.

LATER that evening, a furious storm drenched the city. I heard the booming thwack of the front door knocker as I sat in the study reading my newly acquired copy of *Anna Karenina*. A clap of thunder resounded throughout the room. Or was it the knocker again?

"You have a visitor, sir," my manservant, Dmitri, proclaimed. Tall and lanky, his shadow darkened the pages.

Without looking up, I responded, "Not tonight, Dima. This book has captured my attentions."

I had just reached the part where Count Vronsky first noticed Anna at Nikolaevsky train station in Moscow.

Dmitri did not move. "The lady seems quite insistent upon seeing you."

"Tell her to go away and return in the morning."

"But, sir, she has brought a child with her."

I slammed poor *Anna* closed with a thump. Given my inability to reproduce, I suspected the unforeseen visitor had not come to beg for paternal patronage. And if she had, I could contend that argument with no difficulty. What possible business could a strange woman have with me, especially at this late hour during a furious tempest? My curiosity intensified.

"Show them in," I ordered, dropping the last word's pitch to indicate my reluctance.

"Yes, sir."

After placing the book on a side table, I stood and pulled the quilted banyan tighter around me. The air had gotten colder, and I moved to the fireplace. When the aroma of damp cloth and the slosh of wet feet triggered my senses, I turned about to confront my callers.

"Your guests, sir," Dmitri announced and withdrew.

Before me stood a woman, not young, but not very old. The rain-soaked kerchief hid most of her hair, but what I could see appeared black with a few streaks of gray. Her face displayed the beginnings of a mother's wrinkles, and her eyes focused on the floor.

I knew we had never met. However, my senses told me she would be returning to her peasant village without the child.

Beside her, a boy, about age ten or so, removed his cap, a *kartuz*, allowing water to drip on the wooden planks below. His dark hair retained the shape of the hat, and his serious, dark brown eyes targeted me the way a marksman might.

As with the woman, I had no memory of meeting such a lad, but I also had no sense of his future. Where I would, as a rule, perceive a story unfolding when first encountering someone, I could not detect anything from him. In all my hundreds of years, I had never confronted a person whom I could not read. This lack of capability quite intrigued me.

"What brings you here on such an inauspicious evening?" I inquired.

The woman took a half-step forward, bent a little at the waist, and raised her dark eyes to me. "I am Anna Vasilyevna, and this is my son, Grigori Yefimovich." She reached for his hand.

Her son crossed his arms and took one step toward me, threadbare shoes skimming across the floor. His chin rose and his head tilted, as if measuring me up for his own personal services.

"We have come from Pokrovskoye to seek you, Mr. Propok. Your reputation as a successful *znakhar* has reached far out to our little town in Siberia."

I flinched at the use of *znakhar* in reference to my services. People of that ilk employ bogus witchcraft artifices to enhance any natural healing skills they may possess. While chanting ineffectual incantations, they cast melted wax onto a bowl of water, pretending to interpret the clotted patterns. I would have never stooped to such ridiculous theatrics. However, I could understand how these silly behaviors provided purposeful diversions.

"Madam, my restorative skills do not make use of those performances and postures. I prefer to call myself a healer and have my own ways of commanding the healing arts." My wrists flicked with slight embellishments.

"Yes, of course, Mr. Propok." She repeated the slight bow. "It is because of my little Grishka that I entreat your services. Perhaps you could mentor him. I believe he has great powers for curing others."

One of my eyebrows raised at this claim. "Can you provide an example, please."

"Of course, sir." She wiped at the water on her face with a wet gloved hand. "My son had a pet mouse that took ill, and he nursed it to health."

Another glance at the boy's intense eyes suggested he most likely caused the little creature's illness through premeditated mistreatment. Cessation of his hostile actions doubtless allowed the hapless rodent to convalesce.

A fusillade of wind-swept raindrops strafed the windows as a flash of lightning illuminated the gem-like beads of water scattered about the room.

"Has he helped *people?*" I wanted to know more about this blind spot in my paranormal perception.

"Oh, most certainly, Mr. Propok. Grishka helped my mother, his *babushka*, through her consumption. He applied dirt from a grave and bound her in a cow hide." She smiled at her son. "Mama recovered in a week."

This strange custom of introducing something from the dead to scare a disease away has been used by peasants for centuries. I hoped he hadn't tried smearing manure on his patrons.

"Well, young man, you come highly recommended." When my eyes met his, penetrating energy from the returned gaze forced my head to turn. The image of the woman leaving without her son nagged at me. "Do you wish to stay with me, Grigori Yefimovich?"

"He could learn much from you, Mr. Propok."

"I wasn't asking *you*," I blurted as another peal of thunder exploded, rocking the building. "Please let the little fellow speak for himself."

The boy faced his mother and nodded four times. "I believe I can work with Mr. Propok." His voice sounded raspy and dry, as if he had gargled with sand. "Do you believe you can work with *me?*" He turned his tilted head in my direction, his eyes thin slits.

Even after a few more tries at viewing his future, I failed to sense a picture. Like a book, I could not foretell his tale.

"Let me be the first to admit I have never taken an apprentice before," I inhaled, the damp air sticking to my lungs. "However, you have traveled a great distance to meet me, and I consider that quite admirable. But —"

"Grishka can pull his own weight," Anna Vasilyevna cut in. "He can do chores and provide for his own needs."

I coughed into my fist before speaking. "Madam, I have a manservant and do not require another. Your son will need to find some other way to recompense me for his food and lodging, not to mention the tutelage."

"You like books, don't you?" Grigori snarled, his focus on me. "They fascinate you. Am I correct?"

How could he possibly know or deduce that? Only the new Tolstoy volumes lay out. While I had no interest in schooling someone, this boy had prowess, and I wanted to tap into it.

"Why don't you both stay the night, and we can discuss this further in the morning when we are all rested. I imagine your long journey must have been wearing." I turned to the archway and called, "Dima!"

"Yes, sir?"

"Please show our visitors to the guest bedroom. The three of us will break our fast together in the morning."

The manservant squinted, implying that he disagreed with my request. "Very good, sir. Right this way, ma'am." He spun on a heel and walked out.

Before leaving the room, young Grigori faced back to me and nodded four times in a slow cadence.

Outside my flat, the storm raged on, splashing rain, flashing lighting, and crashing thunder.

I took a few deep breaths before returning to my reading chair. When I resumed the story, Count Vronsky approached the lovely woman he had espied, and a railway worker fell from the platform in front of an oncoming train. Anna Karenina construed the mishap as a "bad omen."

I had an eerie impression I just encountered my own "bad omen." Much like with *Anna Karenina*, I will have to wait for the long, long story to unfold.

BY morning the rain had stopped. Water droplets dangling from the eaves outside my bedroom window served as the only remnants from last evening's storm. My table clock indicated the hour as six. I have always believed the gods served those who rose early, and I chose to return to the study for more of *Anna Karenina* before the morning meal.

Dmitri had set the fire, and crackling flames filled the room with warmth. He knew me well enough to predict my daybreak habits. I sat in the reading chair and opened Tolstoy's volume.

Continuing my reading, I discovered Count Vronsky donated two hundred rubles to the slain man's family in response to the railway worker's accidental death. This act of discretionary generosity swayed Anna Karenina, who then felt better about leaving her young son at home.

The Anna resting in my guest room had made the difficult decision to entrust me with her own child. They had traveled over 2,000 kilometers just to entreat me with the boy's training. How my name and repute breeched that distance, I could not imagine.

Anna Karenina visited the home of her brother, Prince Oblonsky, casually known as Stiva, and his wife, Dolly. Upon reaching the scene where Anna and Dolly discussed, over a light meal, Stiva's presumed dalliance with the governess, my belly grumbled. I set the book on the side table and went to the dining room.

Grigori sat poking a bowl of kasha with a large spoon.

"Good morning. Do you not like kasha?"

His nose wrinkled. "It tastes like manure."

My eyebrows rose. "You have tasted manure before?"

He stared at me with those piercing, yet murky eyes.

After a half-second pause, I continued, "I prefer mine with a slab of butter and sprinkle of salt. Perhaps you should try that before dismissing it. Where is your mother?"

"Where are the sausages? I thought all rich people ate sausages."

"I am not rich, and we do not eat meat in this household." I felt my distaste for flesh as I spoke the words. Chewing on beef or pork felt like grinding my teeth against sinewy strips of metal, and I had discontinued the practice a long time ago.

"No meat? How do you sustain your health?" He poked at the kasha a few more times. "I'm going to starve."

"Is your mother readying herself in the guest room?"

"No. She left early this morning."

Such news did not bode well for the boy. "Are you upset how she abandoned you?"

"I sent her away."

A lump caught in my throat, and I swallowed to clear it. "What if I do not agree to take you on as an apprentice?"

"I do not foresee that happening." He stood and went to the samovar on the side table. "Would you like me to pour you some coffee?"

His nonchalance regarding the absent parent who had accompanied him across Russia to my home felt alarming. However, this freely offered act of service gave me hope that the young beast might have some glimmer of civilization within him.

"It is tea, and, yes, I would like some. Thank you."

He reached up, grabbed the pot, and sniffed at it. "It does not smell like tea."

"You should give it a taste. It is an infusion of rosebuds. Some chemical compound in coffee and China tea makes me quite sleepy."

Dima placed a plateful of kasha before me. I stirred the sweet, yellow block, with a sprinkle of salt, into the gelatinous gruel.

Grigory set the cup of tea next to my bowl.

"Thank you, Grishka." I said.

He grimaced. "Do not call me by that name. Only my mother uses it."

"I see. What do you prefer I say?"

"Grigori... is quite adequate." He returned to his seat in short, faltering motions, as if his muscles had stiffened.

A slight grin curled my mouth. "Not Grigori Yefimovich?"

He shook his head. "I prefer not to invoke my father."

"Grigori it is."

After taking a spoonful of kasha, I washed it down with a mouthful of tea.

The boy sat staring at me, implying I had the most fascinating face in the world. "How long have you been alive?" he asked in unfluctuating tones.

I took another sip of tea. "Whatever do you mean?"

"You should be dead right now."

"I believe I am... in good health." The kasha tasted delightful. Perhaps Dima had doled out a bit more butter this morning. "What are you insinuating?"

He narrowed his eyes. "I put a dose of inheritance powder in your cup before filling it with that brown water you call tea. It should have dispatched you straightaway."

"*What!?*" I recoiled. For all my many lives, no one has caught me off guard like this. Because I could not pierce his wall of thought, Grigori managed to surprise me in a most distressing and dreadful manner. With such extensive experience, I should have been able to guess this possibility.

"I had my suspicions about you, and now I can be certain. You are not fully human."

Instinct caused me to cough into my balled fist a few times. "Do you mean to say you laced my tea with arsenic in an attempt to try my humanity? What if I had died?"

Grigori's expression remained placid, "You would have failed the test."

"And then what would you have done? You said your mother has already left."

"Do not worry about me, Mr. Propok"–his head angled down a bit–"or whatever your name really is. I shall always find my way. I survive."

I squinted as I surveyed the boy anew. "And do you customarily carry poisons as a rule?"

"You never know when you might need to… slay someone." One corner of his mouth curved up.

"How do I know you will not attempt a prank like that again?"

"There is no need… now that I know I cannot kill you."

"Yes, I guess there is some truth in that." I allowed my head to bob as I considered my options.

"Are you acquainted with the expression, 'live for a century, learn for a century'? How many centuries have *you* been learning?" He opened his eyes full.

This boy had a gift. If I were not blessed–or cursed, if you prefer–with longevity, I would fear for my life in his company.

"It has been a few hundred years now"–I waved a dismissive hand–"but that is none of your concern."

"Perhaps, but *your* concern should be that I now know your secret."

No one had ever challenged me this way before. It made me wonder what other exceptional talents this little parcel contained that I could turn to my own advantage.

"I believe your mother had a good idea. We should work together. You could learn quite a bit."

"And what exactly do you suppose you can teach *me*, Mr. Propok?"

I had never considered this question before. Up until that point, my entire existence revolved around earning sufficient funds to secure a comfortable living. My inability to perceive Grigori's future continued to perplex me. Perhaps, given enough time, I could bend this alder-tree of a boy toward becoming a respectable, beneficial member of society.

"That is something I am not prepared to answer at this moment, but I believe, over time, we shall discover our mutual advantages together."

He nodded his head four times. "I do not respect immodest people. Your humility serves us well."

I stood and went to the samovar.

"What are you doing?" he inquired.

"I would like some proper tea."

"And I would like some proper sausage."

After a few seconds of consideration, I responded, "How about a meat pie later?"

"What did you have in mind, sir?"

"On our morning walk in the park, peddlers line the sidewalks. I will purchase for you a meat pie while we observe the pedestrians parade."

The look in his eyes suggested a mental licking of the lips. "That sounds reasonable." He stabbed at the kasha.

"Dima, please bring our young master some butter and salt."

The barest of smiles crossed the boy's face.

Following our silent meal, I returned to the study to read a bit further into the Tolstoy. Anna Karenina assured Dolly that her unfaithful husband still loved her, and that forgiveness might be the correct path. The conversation then turned to a visit by the debutante Kitty, object of Count Vronsky's affections despite the imminent proposal by his long-time friend Levin. Preparations began for a formal ball to be held that evening.

As I prepared for our constitutional, I considered the many pathways before me regarding my enigmatic guest. Should Grigori choose to remain with me, he would elevate from a poor, peasant life to one where everything is chocolate. Things might come too easily for him, which could foster indolence and carelessness. To maintain operational order, I would need to develop ways of administering effective constraints upon his extraordinary behaviors.

I suspected his goals included presenting me an unhealthy bowlful of comeuppance. Several people in the past have endeavored to show me where the crawfish hibernate. None succeeded.

ON our walk to the Summer Garden, we strolled past rows of sedate, stately brownstone residences along Nevsky Prospekt. Many of these homes belonged to the rising merchant class. Several faces could be seen through gauze-draped windows along the top floors. Idle womenfolk having little to do occupied themselves with the business of others.

"Where is your wife?" Grigori posed.

After a pause to consider, I responded, "I have no wife."

"No wife? Ever?" His voice squeezed out the last word.

"Never."

"Do you not like women?" The boy looked up at me with wide eyes. "Do you prefer men?"

I allowed a slight smile to adorn my lips. "So many questions."

We rounded the corner onto Garden Street. "Do you have any children?" Grigori persisted in pressing for information.

"I am sure you have figured out by now that I must relocate every few years so that others do not learn of my longevity."

"Of course."

"That would make for difficult relations with a woman—or a man—for that matter."

"But you could still father children, no?"

"No, truly not." A leaden, pensive sigh fell from my mouth. "One shortfall of this longevity is the inability to engage in intimate, child-creating behavior."

"Hence, the lack of descendants." He nodded his head four times. "I can see that now."

We traversed the bridge across the Moika River that led to the Summer Garden. Several vendors stood bellowing descriptions of their wares along the embankment.

"Meat pies! Meat pies! Hot, fresh meat pies!" a middle-aged, pot-bellied, balding, unshaven fellow with bright eyes and bushy brows called as he waved a pale lump of dough in the air.

From my first impressions, I could tell the fellow would attempt to cheat us, but as far as a resolution, nothing apparent surfaced. The introduction of Grigori into a situation seemed to fog my vatic vision. Much like with a book, I would have to endure and discover the outcome in due course.

"Propok," Grigori addressed me without using an appropriate title. How audacious of him to speak to me so. "I would very much like a meat pie now." He looked up at me, his pinched expression suggested hunger.

"Did you mean to say, 'Mr. Propok'?" I glanced down my nose at him.

"Of course. What was I thinking?" He scraped a tattered shoe along the embankment.

A scowl formed on my face. "As long as you are in my care, I would prefer if you spoke to me with proper respect." The scowl transformed to an amused smile. "When you achieve the same station as me, you can then drop the honorific. Do you understand?"

"Yes, *Mr.* Propok." His eyes darted about as a tiny drop of drool formed at one corner of his mouth. "But that day will come sooner than you would like."

"Perhaps, but I caution you not to jump above your head."

His hand went to his midsection.

"You want one from *that* fellow?" I pointed at the disreputable-looking vendor.

"Yes. Please."

Ah. At least he has learned to use a polite word.

"How much?" I asked the peddler.

"For you, sir?" That seemed an odd question. What matters who ate his pie?

"No, for my"–I paused while attempting to find a suitable word– "friend." My outstretched arm indicated Grigori.

"Five kopecks. And you won't find a better meat pie in all of Petersburg!" His smile displayed a few missing teeth. The remainder flashed yellow and brown stains.

I reached into my pocket for a coin and handed it to the vendor. The fellow pulled a glob of browned dough from a burlap sack. He chuckled as he handed the pie to Grigori. "Enjoy, young master."

"It feels neither hot nor fresh," Grigori whispered. He took a hungry bite, as if he hadn't eaten in a week. When he pulled his clenched teeth away, a strip of dark cloth waggled from his mouth.

My sense of dishonesty proved correct. It remained to see how Grigori would handle this knave's deceit.

The boy yanked the soggy bit of fabric from his lips and waved it at the pie vendor. "What is the meaning of this?" he demanded.

The man laughed, and his bulbous belly shook. "For five kopecks, what did you expect, silver brocade?" He continued to chortle as Grigori and I exchanged looks. The boy put his free hand in a pocket and turned to the salesman. Grigori's eyes grew larger as he stared.

The vendor's eyes also bulged, and he gasped for breath, as if an unseen hand crushed his thick, bristly throat. He dropped the sample pie.

"Either you return my friend's coin, or you give me a proper meat pie." Grigori hissed in a deep and dark tone. "Do you understand me?"

While rubbing at his neck with one hand, the vendor reached into the sack and retrieved a better-looking, better-smelling pie. "Here you go, young master. I apologize. I am sorry. I must have grabbed the wrong one."

Grigori returned the first pie as he took the second. "Yes, this one feels much better, thank you." He glowered at the man for a moment. "Come on, Propok—*Mr.* Propok. I believe I have gotten what you paid for." He took a bite as we walked off. "Delicious!" Grigori shouted back to the vendor as he chewed. "No better meat pie in all of St. Petersburg!"

"Is it really any better?" I asked.

He angled his head shoulder to shoulder. "It isn't any worse. That man swirls his tongue like a cow's tail."

"As twice two is four," I muttered.

Grigori took another bite of the pie. "This might be meat. I'm not sure what kind of meat, but meat it is."

We both laughed together at his little joke as we stepped toward an open-arched diminutive commemorative chapel. Behind my laughter lay fear of this boy's potential powers. I had just witnessed him nearly killing someone over a spurious meat pie. Beads of sweat formed around my collar.

Grigori halted. "Something bad happened here. Did it not?"

While I lived elsewhere at the time, I had read of the unpleasantness. "An assassination attempt on the Tsar. He survived. The people took it as a sign from Providence and built this memorial."

"I can feel the residual dread resonating."

My senses only worked on people, excluding my present companion. This unexpected ability to perceive vibrations from inanimate objects fascinated me. The incident in question happened almost fifteen years before. "Can you explain to me what—or how, rather—you observe these phenomena?"

His head tilted a few times before responding. "I wish I could put it into words for you, but it is only a thought, an instantaneous flash of an idea, that floods my mind." He closed his eyes. "I just *feel* it."

His voracious chewing continued, and the meat pie disappeared a few bites later. During this time, Grigori appeared focused on—and absorbed with—eating. I could feel my heart reduce its pace and my breath slow. Perhaps the discovery of his gustatory distraction will assist me in the days yet to be.

A ring of crumbs and brown sauce ringed the boy's mouth. I offered my pocket square with one hand and drew a circle about my lips with the other. He took the handkerchief and wiped at his face, checking the cloth with each dab.

I glanced up at the formidable wrought iron fence. Its ornate curlicues and involuted whorls exhibited prophetic patterns, possible portents of disquieting times ahead with my apprentice. I pondered, who would learn more from whom?

We passed through the Summer Garden gate and stepped onto the gravel path.

"WHAT is that big book in your study?" Grigori asked as we ambled into the garden. His head turned side-to-side as he took in the manicured park.

"*Anna Karenina*? It's Tolstoy's latest."

"Who is this Tolstoy?"

"Have you not heard of *War and Peace*?"

"I have not yet experienced war, and I presume we are experiencing peace currently."

His innocent reflection triggered a chuckle. "It's the chronicle of several Russian families during the Patriotic War of 1812. I have always been a reader, and I prefer larger, longer stories, like the ones Mr. Tolstoy writes."

He angled his head and squinted. "Did they even *have* books when you were born?"

I moderated my initial impulse to slap him by taking a few deep breaths. "Books have been around for thousands of years in some form or other. In my earliest days, they were quite expensive and rare, but with time, they have become much more common."

"I see." Grigori nodded a few times then faced me. "Did you find my mother attractive?"

"It was difficult to determine because her hair dripped with rain under the damp head covering. Perhaps if you had not sent her away so soon, I could have had a better look."

Grigori pointed at a young couple standing on the Swan Bridge holding hands. "What about her?"

"I'm sure she is attractive to many." Especially her fellow, who would soon convince her to grant the physical intimacy he craved. She would bear the burden of that encounter.

"But not you. What about him?"

I shook my head in disbelief and held up my palm. "I believe it is my turn to ask a question."

"That seems only fair."

"What did you do to the meat pie vendor?"

"I did nothing. He tried to sell me a second-rate pie."

"Which upset you." I put a hand to my neck. "The fellow began choking before he swapped pies."

Grigori's gaze fell to the path. From his pants he withdrew a dark nugget about the size of a thumb. The surface had many pockmarks, like tiny craters. He held it up to the sun. The little rock seemed more like dark green glass with bright light behind it.

"This is my magic stone. One day, I was chasing a deer in the forest. I heard a loud sizzling noise and a splash behind me. When I turned about, I saw smoke rising from the stream and leaves smoldering above. I reached into the water and pulled out this rock, still hot. Whenever I squeeze it, things happen." He slipped it back into his pocket.

"And you believe this 'magic stone' gives you power?"

"That has been my experience so far."

I scratched at my head. "How did you figure out its use?"

"It was a cold day, and I warmed my hand with it. When I looked up, the deer I had been tracking stood before me." His eyes narrowed, as if reliving the experience. "I squeezed tighter, and the animal fell over."

The boy attributed his unusual abilities to this dark rock. Given such a coincidence, I might have arrived at the same conclusion. "How often have you used its power?"

Rather than respond to my question, he asked, "Don't you have something to assist you with your *znakhar* practice?"

"As I said last evening, I am a healer, not a *znakhar*. I do not employ needless devices nor illusionist's tricks to heal my patients."

"You have extraordinary powers?"

"It might be difficult to explain, but please, just accept the fact that I am able to sense people's outcomes."

"Perhaps you should have chosen to be a fortune teller instead."

"There is something to be said for that. However, people don't generally trust such spurious gypsies and witches. Besides, older women are much better suited for playing that role."

"Then, how do you heal people?" Grigori looked up at me. "Do you use powders, potions, and tinctures?"

"So many questions…" I indicated the path to the right.

He adjusted his cap. "They don't hit your nose for asking."

Perhaps not, but the desire might develop. "That's what they say."

"I am apprenticed to you so that I may learn the craft of healing. I don't understand how you can cure your patients without using medicine."

"And speaking of apprenticeship, you have not made it clear how you plan to pay for my tutelage and still support yourself."

"I am working on that. You haven't answered my question about how you heal people. I want to know."

"It's not a simple answer." I stopped walking and faced him. "I do not actually *heal* anyone. I can look at a person and know what the next week or so holds for them. Most people will recuperate on their own. If I get a sense their health is going to improve, I tell them, and they pay me for that good news."

He looked up at me with one eye. "People actually give you money for doing nothing?"

"I provide reassurance at a time of uncertainty."

"And that's all?" he whined.

"That's all."

Grigori shook his head. "But what if you know someone is going to die? What do you say then?"

I inhaled and exhaled, raising my chin. "I do not take on those clients."

"You just let them die?"

"If there is nothing I can do for them, what good is offering false hope?" I rested a hand on his shoulder.

"You could tell them they will recover and take their money anyway."

I pulled my hand away and rubbed a finger on my chin. "Yes, I guess I could, but then word might spread that I am not a very good healer."

"Unless they die before telling anyone." He pulled a smirk. "You could be making more money at this, Mr. Propok."

"Look at that couple on the bridge." I indicated the two young lovers. We had gotten closer and could almost overhear their intimate conversation. "What do you make of them?"

Grigori shut his eyes and cocked his head. "The man loves the lady… but she loves him even more."

"That's very good. How did you come to that conclusion?"

"Because that is the way it always is in a relationship. At least that is what my mother has told me."

I laughed. "That is usually the case, yes. But see if you can tell what will happen to them in the coming days."

He put a hand to his forehead. "If I make the man jump off the bridge and drown in the river, the woman would lead a better life, I believe."

"That might be true, but I don't understand why you would want the man to kill himself."

"It's just something I feel."

"Now that I think of it, you tried to kill *me* this morning with arsenic powder."

"I wanted to test my theory." Grigori's smirk returned.

"You have quite a preoccupation with death."

His shoulders raised and dropped. "Everything dies."

"I thought you wanted to learn the craft of healing."

"No, that was my mother's desire for me. I just wanted to get away from home."

I stopped walking and faced him. "If you're not interested in studying with me, and you cannot afford your meals, perhaps I should just take you back on the next train to Pokrovskoye."

"Please, do not! I never want to see those filthy peasants again." A tear trailed down one cheek.

I had found a truth that hurt his eyes. "Would you prefer to live on your own?"

"We are not like two drops of water, but I prefer your home."

"Even without meat?" I posed.

"Even without meat." He nodded.

If I could find some way to reshape this boy's obsession with mortality, to bend this budding alder-tree toward the light and away from the dark, it might preserve the rest of us.

"All right, then. If you wish to remain here in Peter with me, we will need to find you a position where you can earn your keep, preferably without killing people."

He raised and lowered his head as if it had gained ten kilos. "I agree."

A thought occurred to me. "Do you like music?"

Grigori's face snapped toward me, the additional weight vanishing as quickly as it had arrived. "I have never played an instrument, but the idea fascinates me. Why do you ask?"

"Let us walk to the Conservatory. Perhaps we can find you a position there."

While I did not favor harmony myself, one of my clients taught at the school. It might be possible that Grigori could make himself useful. Such responsibility might provide the needed structure and discipline I could not.

"You mean a *job*?"

"Yes. That is how people earn money. Unless you want to return to your mother in Siberia, follow me."

I started off, back the way we came. Glancing over my shoulder, I saw the boy put a hand in his pocket.

I knew it would be a long walk from the Summer Garden to the Conservatory. No streetcar lines ran along the route. I hoped the exertion would tire young Grigori, or, at the least, make him easier to handle.

Several wide, short boats floated near us as we strolled along the Moika riverbank. The low bridges restricted water traffic height. Sprays of brackish water reached my nostrils. Colorful, blocky buildings lined the embankments. St. Petersburg had its charms.

"What made you choose to be a healer, rather than a doctor?" the boy asked after a long silence.

"It has been my experience that most people prefer a more traditional approach to illness and health, as opposed to a scientific, medical professional."

"Because doctors chop off your diseased body parts?" He wielded a rather mischievous grin while performing a swift hacking motion with one hand.

"Well, that used to be how things were until the Battle for the Holy Places. Pirogov initiated the use of anesthetics and more precise surgery techniques. They say we lost the war but won in medical research."

"Perhaps I should study to be a doctor. Do they make big money?"

My shoulders hunched. "I'm sure they do, but I believe it would take several years of formal schooling."

Grigori scowled. "That does not sound like fun. Who are your clients? Rich, famous people?"

"We will be meeting with one of them soon. He teaches music classes at the Conservatory."

"Would I know of him?" the boy questioned.

"Nikolai Andreyevich Rimsky-Korsakov." It sounded so grand to recite his full name. "He wrote *Sadko* and *The Maid of Pskov*."

"Never heard of them."

"He is a great composer and instructor. You might learn something from him."

Grigori crossed his hands and swept them apart. "I am not interested in learning, only earning my keep."

This boy is still young, I reminded myself. When I was his age, my family had already apprenticed me to a stained-glass master. He started me with maintaining the oven. My responsibility involved keeping the fuel constant and working the giant bellows when the master required more heat. After a year of sweating my way through the day, he began teaching me the art of creating glass, how to add potash to lower the melting temperature and lime for more stability. After a while, he taught me to add various pot metal powders to create the various colors. I had begun crafting my own master piece when the plague struck our village. Even if I should live another thousand years, I never want to work with glass again.

So much knowledge and life experience resides within my skull. I must bear in mind to eat the mushroom pie and keep the tongue behind my teeth.

After nearly four kilometers and an hour of walking, we approached the Conservatory, a squarish, brownstone building, somewhat lacking in detail. For all the amazing things that happened inside, the exterior wanted more finery.

As we strode into the open entrance hall, students wearing red shirts with black trim nodded to me. Unseen musicians practiced their lessons, as strains of folk melodies and finger exercises blended in a cacophonous concerto.

We went to the office of Nikolai Andreyevich and entered. A man in his mid-thirties with side-parted black hair sat behind a small wooden desk focused on a large sheet of lined paper. Shelves overflowing with musical scores lined each wall.

"Kolya," I beckoned.

He raised his head and peered at me over his round-rim eyeglasses. "Rodya! Do come in. Who is your friend?"

Grigori and I entered the small room. The boy's head angled around, gawking at the profusion of papers cascading from the folders surrounding the room.

"Is all of this *your* music?" the boy asked, jaw hanging slack.

Korsakov smiled. "No, son. Much of it is the work of my pupils. I keep my own scores in a safer, less-cluttered location."

I placed my hand on Grigori's back and edged him forward. "Nikolai Andreyevich, this is Grigori Yefimovich, my... charge."

The teacher stood, scraping the chair on the wide wooden slats and stepped from behind his desk to grasp the boy's hand. "Master Grigori. A pleasure to make your acquaintance." He shook twice, consulted the clock, and returned to sitting behind his desk. "It appears I have a few minutes before my next lecture. What brings you here today, Rodya? Did we have an appointment I seem to have forgotten?"

Nikolai had started writing music before he had learned formal theory. Conservatory staff pointed out his deficiencies, and he took classes to improve his works. Never satisfied with completed pieces, he constantly revised as he acquired more knowledge. That kind of determination made him a formidable composer. He had quite a few admirable qualities.

When I gazed into his outlook, I could see he had started working on a new operatic composition. My original thought for the boy had been as a maintenance worker, but I could sense other avenues of opportunities.

"My ward is interested in learning about music, and I know you are the best teacher in all of St. Petersburg."

Korsakov blushed and lowered his head. "I believe you are overstating my qualifications, sir. How can I be of assistance?"

"I see that *May Night* is still playing at the Mariinsky. Do you have any plans for a new work?"

The teacher shuffled some of the papers before him. "As a matter of fact, I have just begun preliminary sketches for a new piece based on Ostrovsky's *Snow Maiden*. Also, I am writing the libretto again, and it is turning out to be much more effort than I had anticipated." He looked at Grigori through the round lenses. "Young man, do you have any experience copying music notation?"

The boy looked up at me, as if I knew the correct response.

"He is a bright thing, Kolya. Given your teaching abilities, I would imagine it would not take long to train him."

"Can you read and write, young master?"

"Yes, sir." The boy assumed a rigid posture, as if for military inspection. "My mother insisted I attend gymnasium. I took top marks."

"Let me see an example." Korsakov cleared a corner of his desk, placed there a scrap of paper, and handed Grigori a pencil.

The young fellow grabbed it and examined the slender wooden rod from all angles. "What is this? Where is the ink?"

Korsakov chuckled. "I do not use pen and ink, as it makes revision difficult. The object you hold is a Faber stick. When you strike it upon the page, it leaves a mark that can be removed with a piece of rubber. Give it a try."

Grigori scraped the stick along the paper, leaving a nearly invisible mark. On his next attempt, he pressed too hard and broke the pencil's point, producing a messy splotch.

"Oh, my fine Siberian graphite. Let me have it." The instructor extracted a pocketknife from his desk drawer and sharpened the writing instrument's tip. Shavings wafted to the floor, dancing in rhythm with his honing. "This time, try to be more gentle, as if it were a very expensive ink pen."

The boy took the pencil and scrawled his Christian name:

Korsakov glanced over at the page. "Grigori. Yes, I can read that quite clearly. And your abilities will only improve with practice."

"Then you can provide the lad with some work?" I prompted.

"If he can write this plainly, it should not be difficult. I can set him up with rehearsal scores, and he can copy them while I am in classes."

Grigori's head snapped. "You are studying still?"

Kolya pursed his lips. "No, I instruct the music students. However, I like to say being a teacher probably makes me the best pupil at the Conservatory."

The boy nodded four times.

I had a sense this collaboration would function well. Still unable to penetrate the mind of my little visitor, no negative outcomes, however, emanated from the composer. "Grigori, I am delighted you are interested in assisting Mr. Rimsky-Korsakov."

"You will have to resume your regular studies in the mornings–the Second Gymnasium is not far from here–and you can assist me in the afternoon. I will give you… mmmmm…"–the teacher glanced at his desk-top, then up again–"a silver quarter ruble each day."

If he agreed to what Korsakov proposed, it would, indeed, pay for his meals. "That sounds reasonable," I concurred.

"Well, what do you think, Master Grigori? Would you like to work with me?"

"Yes, I would, Mister Rimsky-Korsakov." He reached out a hand. "And, please, call me Grishka."

Grishka? He did not permit *me* to call him that.

As we promenaded along the southern shore of the river, Grigori hummed a tune. I could not determine the name, and I asked.

"Oh, it is but a little song my mother taught me. A tiny nothing. We used to sing it at school sometimes."

He seemed almost happy.

"It appears that you enjoyed meeting the music instructor."

"Yes! I imagine I can learn quite a bit from Professor Rimsky-Korsakov. However, I believe I shall require some..." He stopped, one foot not quite touching the ground. His head snapped to the right, then pivoted toward me. "What is that place?"

I followed his finger to the grand building just ahead on our right, Moika Palace. The bland, squarish, golden yellow structure, nearly a quarter kilometer wide, dominated the embankment. On our walk to the Conservatory earlier, we had traversed the northern shore, and did not come close to this fusty structure.

"It is the home of Prince Yusupov. He has assembled a vast collection of paintings and art. If you like, I can arrange a tour."

The other foot landed, and he looked up at the colossus. They say fear has large eyes, and I had never seen the boy's grow this big before. A rumbling growl emanated from his throat. "There is something about this place I do not like. Is it possible for us to proceed in a different direction?"

I found it peculiar that something distressed Grigori. From the moment of our meeting, he presented himself as fearless and confident. Nothing appeared to upset him. Here, outside one of the oldest palaces in the city, he blanched and whimpered. As I could not read his future, it may well remain a mystery.

"I suppose if we walk back the other way"–I pointed behind us–"we could catch the streetcar."

"Yes, please."

Every worm has a weak point, I reminded myself.

A *konka* rounded the corner of Glinka Street, and we hopped on. Fortunate for me, very few other passengers had boarded. This allowed me to relax a bit as my mind would not be bombarded by their outlooks. Once we had chosen seats, I turned to my traveling companion. "Can you tell me what happened back there?"

"Is there some place in your little village where I might purchase a few notebooks and some of those writing sticks?"

"School supplies?"

"Oh, yes. That as well."

The sun had reached its zenith, and grumblings in my belly marked the hour.

"We could ride to the Passazh, get a meal, and find you your wares."

"What is this Passazh?"

"It is on Nevsky Prospekt, not far from my home. A long hall with selling stalls along the sides." The throng of midday shoppers might possibly be too much for my senses; however, procuring something constructive for the boy would most certainly be a good reason to tempt the gods who burn my pots. "And were you having a go at pulling my goat's beard by calling St. Petersburg a 'little village'?"

One corner of his mouth rose and fell. "I am not sure how to describe this accurately, but I will give it my best. When I saw that large building, my insides turned cold. Worse than when I fell into the Mius River in November. As if my very heart had frozen."

Having lived the equivalent of many lifetimes, eluding death time and again, very little upset me to this level of anguish. However, I felt it important to say something to demonstrate some sympathy. "That sounds frightful."

"Something about that palace portends darkness for me, but I am not quite sure what it might be."

"You had a sense about the chapel near the Summer Garden where something bad happened." My eyebrows raised. "Perhaps something terrible occurred at Moika Palace as well. I'm not sure what it would have been."

"No. It's not in the past. It is a foreboding of… well, I am not sure."

His expression went blank, as if he had gotten drawn deep into some internal bottomless pit. I attempted to assure him. "We need not go by there again."

"You might not, but I *must*… at some point."

We sat silent in our own thoughts until the streetcar arrived at the Passazh. Grigori followed me through the entrance of the brownstone façade. Sunlight drizzled through the overhead skylight running the building's entire span. The recent storm had deposited stray leaves and branches upon it, which presented intriguing bits of shadow on the tiled flooring.

"Perhaps we should seek out Dostoevsky's crocodile," I suggested, in hopes of bringing my companion back to this reality. "I believe it's one of the stalls to the rear."

"His *what?*"

"Crocodile." I spread my arms. "A large African reptile that eats people when they're not looking."

The color returned to his face. "Yes! That sounds delightful. Where is it?" His head turned in all directions.

I put a hand to my mouth to stifle a laugh. "If only such a creature existed. It was the subject of one of his stories, and it may–or may not–be real."

Grigori's shoulders drooped at the unfortunate news.

Hawkers at the front of the various stalls called out for us to purchase their wares. We marched past the onslaught of tonal taunts and toward the small café. I ordered a bowl of borscht, a few boiled potatoes, and a bublik for myself. Grigori requested two piroshki.

As I sipped my soup and nibbled at the potatoes, I glanced at my dining companion. He sat motionless, I presumed in contemplation. If only I could have had some insight into what absorbed his awareness so deeply.

I broke the bublik in half and held up one piece. "Would you like some?"

He shook his head and picked up one of the little pies. The sound of his chewing let me know that he had begun to focus on the outside world.

Once we had finished our meals, I led him past the jewelers and haberdashers to the stationery stall. He chose a few notebooks and a box of Faber graphite sticks.

"Do you want one of these American pencil sharpeners?" I held up the metal device resembling a tiny bell.

"No, thank you. I will use my knife, the way professor Rimsky-Korsakov demonstrated."

"The professor? What is it about him that you regard so?"

Grigori cocked his head in thought. "Hmmmm. I do believe there is something in his soul that I find appealing."

"Ah." I nodded. "Because *he* has a soul, and I do not."

"You have a soul, Mr. Propok, but it just is not as fresh as his."

"I suppose there is something to be said for *that*." The total came to one ruble, and I handed the clerk a coin.

"But understand, sir, I still wish to learn from you as well."

"Of course." I wagged a finger. "Please confirm to me that you will not attempt to test *his* mortality as you did with me."

"Oh, no! Certainly not. He has been the first thing in this city I have truly enjoyed. I would never want to end his existence."

My client appeared to have left quite an impression on the boy. It would be for the good of all if Kolya could influence Grigori and infuse him with more utilitarian beliefs. Perhaps Korsakov's tutelage in music scribing–and humanity–would supplement my mentoring in the healing arts. At that point in time, I could not predict with any accuracy how things would work out for the lad. We wrote our days on flowing waters with a pitchfork.

Upon returning to my apartment, Dima stood waiting by the door standing on one foot then the other. He held a piece of paper in one trembling hand. The other wiped beads of sweat from his forehead. I did not require my special senses to recognize he had something important to tell me.

"What is it, Dima?"

He presented the perfumed stationery with a slight bow. "Her ladyship requests a prompt response."

I broke the seal and glanced at the note. Catherine Dolgorukov wanted to see me as soon as possible. As if I could move faster than my own shadow. When this woman becomes Tsaritsa, I can only imagine how difficult she will make life for everyone around her.

My own desire for the afternoon had been to lock myself in the study with *Anna Karenina*. It appeared I would end up in another chamber with a very different lady.

At my writing desk, I scribbled out a response, stating I would be at her apartments later in the afternoon and that my apprentice would accompany me. After refolding and sealing the missive, I handed it to Dima, who dashed away.

Grigori sat at the dining table practicing writing with his new acquisitions. His hand moved with jagged motions interspersed with bold, snaking embellishments. Writing in Russian had to be one of the most arduous labors ever conceived. Most other European writing systems consisted of fluid lines and gently sloping arcs.

He looked up, and our eyes met. For the first time since I had encountered the lad, a twinkle of satisfaction greeted me.

"You are doing quite well with your exercises. If you can execute music writing with the same proficiency, Master Rimsky-Korsakov will be most impressed."

One side of his mouth rose in a smile, then he returned to the paper.

"I must attend to one of my clients, and I would like you to accompany me. This will provide an opportunity for you to observe my craft."

His head sprang to attention. "Is it someone I might have heard of?"

"Not really. She is a lady-in-waiting. Nothing special." I did not want to reveal whom Catherine served. Grigori had already displayed some odd behavior regarding the royal family: his sensing the assassination attempt near the Summer Garden and the perplexing premonition at Moika Palace.

"I see. What is her condition?"

Now, *that* question might have been one with no good answer. I could not explain to a child that this manipulative parvenu craved constant attentions. "At this point, I am uncertain. Her message did not include such information."

His head tipped at various angles before responding. "Yes, I believe I shall join you."

I stared at him without speaking.

"Thank you," came the belated courtesy.

My heart lightened as I observed the rigid alder-tree beginning to bow, if even in the slightest.

We stepped out onto the busy pavement. Seeing no streetcars, we walked down Nevsky Prospekt to the palace grounds. To ensure secrecy, I brought us through the rear gate. Grigori gave no indication of knowing who lived in this grand building.

The guards recognized me and allowed us entry. One of the chambermaids ushered us into Catherine's outer quarters. The door at the far end of the room opened, and my client breezed through, followed by a young fellow about Grigori's age and height wearing a child's sailor suit.

"Rodya," she purred, "How grand of you to grant me your company." Light from the window flickered through her gauzy gown, imparting a hazy silhouette of the woman's curves. She extended her right hand.

I moved forward, taking the offer with the gentlest grip possible and applied my lips using the gentlest touch possible. "Nay, my lady, I believe you summoned me here." I stepped back. "What is the nature of your urgency?"

Her head turned to Grigori. "This is your apprentice? Not what I had expected at all." She huddled the sheer fabric of her gown close to her body.

"Catherine Mikhailovna, may I present Grigori Yefimovich of Pokrovskoye." I placed my hand on the boy's shoulder, giving a slight forward push in hopes of him demonstrating respect. He obliged with a slight bend at the waist.

"She is so pretty," Grigori blurted.

A rosy blush came to Catherine's cheeks. "Thank you, young master." She swung her arm out to the fourth occupant of the room. "Come, darling."

The boy in the sailor suit inched forward with delicate and cautious steps. He stopped next to the lady and put an arm about her waist.

I could sense little of the child as he had misgivings about this meeting. Our presence put him on edge, but he seemed to find Grigori of interest.

"Our little Kolen'ka has had difficulties with his father of late. Isn't that so, darling?" She glanced down as the boy nodded his head a few times. "I do not like how that callous fellow torments the boy. Can you work your magic so that he can stand up to the old man, Rodya?" A grim smile grew as she moved her palms in small, circular patterns.

Magic? There is no magic in my repertoire. That gypsy woman, Minditsi, must have sowed those seeds quite well. However, I have heard it said, "Those who act artfully eat doubly."

"Kolen'ka?" I inquired. "Do I have permission to call you that?"

He nodded.

"What does your father do that you would prefer he discontinue?"

He looked into the corners of the room and blinked. "He… wants me to be… exceedingly *manly*…" The voice sounded angelic and pure, as if heaven spoke through him. "Like one of his… soldiers."

"Do you not want that?"

The boy's head shook.

My brows gathered. "What would *you* like, Kolen'ka?"

With that question, his mind and soul opened to me. This young fellow had literary and artistic interests. He dreamed of sculpting and writing poetry. Within a week, his mother would present him a blank book in which to commit his thoughts and memories.

"I would like him to stop calling me a 'girly girl,' sir," he stated with a raised chin.

Grigori giggled. A stern glance from me caused a retreat into stillness.

"Yes, my boy," I encouraged, "a man can be a poet or an artist and still be manly."

"Exactly!" Catherine acknowledged.

I crouched in front of the lad. "Do you believe it might be helpful to write your sentiments and moods down on paper?"

His eyes wandered and, at times, caught the soft light from the window. "Yes, sir, I do believe that would be of great assistance."

"Well, Kolen'ka, I have some good news. In the next few days, you will receive a book with empty pages. It will be your job—or assignment, if you will—to fill them with lovely and wonderful things. How does that sound?"

The boy's lips formed a slight upward arch, and his eyes gleamed. "I like that very much, sir. Very much. Thank you, sir. Thank you."

"I enjoy writing," Grigori spoke in a flat tone.

"Of course." I stood. "My apprentice here will soon be assisting Master Rimsky-Korsakov at the Conservatory." I rested a hand on his shoulder. "He has been practicing his letters all day."

"It would be my pleasure, and an honor, to perform lessons with you," my apprentice offered.

"Perhaps we could carry out our penmanship exercises together." Kolen'ka looked up at Catherine.

"Not today, my darling. I think it best if you return to your rooms now." She stepped to a table and rang a crystal bell. The chambermaid reappeared and guided the boy out.

Three of us stood observing their exit. Kolen'ka never looked back as he left.

"Well, Rodya, you have certainly earned your pay today. I have never seen my Sashka's grandson so cheerful and enthusiastic." She opened a drawer and retrieved a gold coin. "Here you go."

Grigori's eyes grew like inflating toy balloons as the money changed hands.

Our hostess turned to my companion. "Would you like a treat, young master? I could have something sent in from the kitchen."

"I should like a graphite stick, ma'am."

"I have never heard of such a sweet before. Is that something from your homeland?"

With a suppressed smile, I responded, "A writing instrument, my lady. Requires no ink."

"No ink?" She reached for the bell and rang it again. "What ever will they think of next?"

The chambermaid escorted us out the way we entered. I considered how much information to divulge to Grigori regarding the people we had just engaged. However, I did need to inquire into his interpretation of the interview.

Once we had put a few meters between us and the tall metal fence, I posed, "What did you think of the boy? What feelings could you sense?"

He stroked his chin before responding. "There is much conflict within his heart. He has obligations he does not wish to fulfill." Grigori's eyes narrowed. "Regrettably, he will come to a bad end. Who was he exactly?"

"You did not recognize him?"

"No. Should I have? And who is Sashka?"

"The boy was Nikolai Alexandrovich. Lady Catherine uses 'Sashka' as a pet name for the lad's grandsire, His Imperial Majesty, Alexander."

He whistled the first line of "God Save the Tsar."

Upon our return home, Grigori went back to his writing exercises. I resumed reading in my study.

Anticipating something along the lines of *War and Peace, Anna Karenina* had turned out in a much different way than I expected. Rather than a mere historical accounting of several families' hardships during the war, this newer work incorporated intrigue and subterfuge.

I should probably mention that I may not have related dear Anna's tale in the proper order. Items I focused on meant something specific at the time of my own story. Tolstoy took pages and pages to reveal minutiae of his characters, including details too inconsequential to include here. It amazed me how the author's mind labored to come up with all those little particulars. My own brain functioned best when it browsed in the heads of others.

With an impassioned speech, Anna convinced Dolly that Stiva loved her very much, despite his liaisons with other women. Dolly, swayed by her friend's argument, decided to forgive her wayward husband. It amused me how Tolstoy wallowed in trivial particulars. Much the way he delighted relating the inner workings of the Bezukhov family in *War and Peace.*

A debutante named Kitty had arrived to attend a ball in her honor. She found Anna beautiful and captivating, as did Count Vronsky. Stiva's friend Kostya proposed to Kitty, but she turned him down because her mother favored Vronsky (as did Kitty). Her father preferred she marry Kostya.

The story had begun to get thick and murky, much the way I preferred my reading diversions. With all the people involved and the situations described, I could not make any guesses as to how everything would work out.

Just as I started the section describing preparations for the debutante's ball, Dima announced dinner. I set the book aside and made my way to the dining room.

Grigori sat writing. Pages of scribbles covered the table. The servant threw up his hands as he looked at me.

"I applaud your tenacity, young master, but the time has come for our evening meal. Please collect your work so that Dima can present his feast."

When Grigori raised his head, wide eyes darker than night confronted me. Unlike with others, I could not sense the boy's future, and determining his state of mind proved difficult. Several times in my long life have I experienced such intensity, and, as far as I could remember, none of them had positive outcomes.

Without speaking, he swiped the papers from around him into a messy pile.

Unable to determine his state by thoughts, I resorted to questions. "Are you hungry? You've had a very busy afternoon."

"My hunger is not an aunt who brings pies," he responded, lowering his gaze to the table.

Dima had prepared one of my favorite meals, cabbage rolls. He had learned to make them foregoing the usual meats used by most everyone else. A combination of peppers, onions, and rice worked quite well.

Grigori poked at the pair of rolls on his platter with a fork, moving them about in little circles. "There is no meat in these things?"

I nodded. "Quite correct. I do not allow such flesh in my home."

The boy scrunched his nose, picked up the knife, and began sawing away at the hapless filled leaves.

As I chewed on my most delicious and savory portion, I observed Grigori making attempts at chewing small bites of his. The sour look on his face suggested displeasure. If only I could sense his thoughts.

"Are they not to your taste?" I inquired.

His wrinkled lips smoothed, and his tongue darted out to sweep up some stray filling. "Actually, I find them adequate. If you had not told me they lacked meat, I might not have known." He sliced another section and chewed on it with the hint of a smile.

"My Dima has learned how to cook within these distinctive constraints and still provide delicious meals. You agree, no?"

His nodding and chewing stopped a second later. Grigori grabbed his abdomen with his left hand and put the right up to his head. "Ohhhhh… I feel unwell. My toes are tingling."

With other people, I would have been able to get a glimpse of their outcome; however, this lad remained a veiled mystery. Much like *Anna Karenina*, this story had become murky as well.

As I observed his face, his normally pale skin seemed even more ashen. Several wispy, bluish veins appeared on his cheeks and neck.

Dima approached. "If I may suggest, sir, a physician lives across the hall."

"Of course. Thank you." Many skilled professionals lodged in our building. I had not been very social with my neighbors, but I presumed the house staff discussed their masters' business on the back stairs.

I scooped up the boy into my arms and walked to the front. Dima opened the door ahead of me and knocked on the one opposite.

A round-faced fellow approaching middle age appeared. "Yes? May I be of assistance?"

"Hello. I am Rodion Propok from across the hall." I turned back to see my manservant standing in the doorway, waving. "My young apprentice suddenly took sick at dinner. I have been told you are a doctor. Can you help?"

The neighbor assessed Grigori from several angles. "Yes, I am a physician. Please, call me Yuri. I believe I have heard you are a healer." He took one of the boy's hands in his and dropped it within a second. "What were you eating?"

"Cabbage rolls," I answered. "There was no meat in them. I choose not to eat meat."

Yuri continued to examine the lad in my arms. "And you could not use your healing talents to mend the lad?"

"He had taken a bite and then clutched his stomach and head, saying that his toes tingled," I expounded.

"This appears more like arsenic poisoning," the doctor reported, bobbing his head. "However, *you* seem quite well. Therefore, I do not suspect the cabbage rolls to be the culprit."

My eyes had expanded at the mention of arsenic. "Grigori, what have you done with your powders?"

"Uhhhhhh," came the unintelligible reply.

"Give him plenty of water to drink. Or, perhaps, some tea. The excess fluids will help to rid his system of the noxious substance." The physician addressed me directly, "What was this boy doing with arsenic powder?"

A quick scan of Yuri informed me that he had no intention of alerting the authorities. My pulse slowed and my breathing resumed a more leisurely rhythm.

"He is learning my healing craft, and he brought some of the compound with him from his home in Siberia, where it is in common use for many household matters."

"Such as getting rid of…"–Yuri's eyebrows arched–"rats?"

"Yes, that as well, I suppose." I set Grigori on his feet, maintaining a hold on his shoulders. "Can you walk?"

He responded with slight up and down movements of his head.

"Thank you, Yuri. How can we repay you for your time?"

The doctor rubbed a stubby thumb along his chin. "I have not yet taken my evening meal, and those cabbage rolls do smell particularly good…"

"Dima, give our good neighbor four… no, six… of your rolls," I ordered.

Yuri smiled.

I escorted my charge back into our rooms and sat him at the dinner table. From the sideboard, I grabbed the water pitcher and filled his glass.

"Drink up!"

Grigori took small gulps.

"What kind of foolishness is this? How did you expose yourself to the arsenic?"

"When I moved my packets from one place to another, I must have gotten some dust on my hand without knowing it." He swallowed more water.

"Perhaps you should be a bit more careful when handling your powders." I had not meant to sound parental, but the situation called for strong language. "Believe me, I do not wish to be the bearer of sad news to your mother."

His head shifted upward, eyes still a bit glassy. "If I can build up a tolerance now, I will be less susceptible to the poison in the future, should anyone wish me gone."

Several times his mind has demonstrated a knack for dark forebodings. Perhaps he had an inkling of his own future I could not access.

With my hand on his shoulder, a half-smile formed on my face. "Well, when it comes to such matters, it appears you are not nearly as ironclad as I am."

THE following morning, I sat alone at the dining table. When Dima appeared, my face displayed an unspoken question.

"The young master left quite early with his writing equipment."

I had hoped to accompany him on his first day to the Gymnasium. That might have been a bit too parental. Never having had children myself, I had no standard to compare against.

The morning passed with more Tolstoy, and I saw several clients in the afternoon.

Grigori returned in the crepuscular light just before sunset. I sat sipping my *klotski*—a broth with potato dumplings—and called as he whizzed past the table, "Feeling better? Have you taken your supper?"

He returned to the dining room and announced, "I should like some soup."

A soupçon of the warm liquid from the spoon went down my windpipe as I gasped. Coughing ensued.

"I should like some soup… please," the youth rephrased.

My head rose and fell as I continued to whoop. Dima brought a bowl and spoon for the boy, who began slurping up the warm liquid without looking in my direction.

When the last bit of errant soup had cleared, I waved a hand in the air. "Don't worry about me. I'll be all right."

Grigori slurped a helping of broth before responding. "I need never worry about you, Mr. Propok. You are indestructible."

A grin appeared on my face without willing it. It astonished me how the boy had reckoned my immortality within hours of meeting.

"How was your first day at the Gymnasium?" I questioned.

He halted his gulping to respond. "I am farther ahead in my studies than the others."

It seemed odd that a small, provincial school in Siberia could be more advanced than our Gymnasium in St. Petersburg. Perhaps having fewer students allowed for accelerated progress. On the other hand, he could be precocious. His actions indicated advanced perception for one his age.

The rapid and repetitive clinking of his spoon against the bowl irritated my ears like smoke in the eyes. "Did they not feed you?"

Grigori shook his head as he continued to soak up the soup. He held the empty bowl aloft.

"If you would like a second helping, you must ask properly. We will *not* hit you in the nose."

I have felt the urge to administer such discipline at times, especially when he makes perplexing requests.

"Mr. Dima, may I please have some more soup?" the boy managed to mumble.

As the servant fulfilled the request, I continued my inquiry. "And how was your time with Rimsky-Korsakov?"

Following a few more mouthfuls of dumplings, he answered, "The Master began instruction for the musical notation he requires. He provided lessons for copying the manuscripts. I will practice after my meal." He returned to the bowl. Using his free hand, he withdrew a scrap of paper from a pocket. "The Conservatory will host a charity concert tomorrow. The Master's roommate has lost his chair-warming government job and requires assistance."

"And who is this roommate?" I attended Korsakov for nearly a year, and he never mentioned he shared his lodgings.

Grigori squinted one eye. "One of the other composers." He shook his head. "I cannot recall the name."

"I see. And who will be performing?"

"I do not know, but I believe this unfortunate fellow will be one of them."

"As it is for a good cause, we shall attend."

"You must go on your own. I and some of the students will be assisting with arrangements."

Following the meal, I retired to my study and resumed *Anna Karenina*.

The following afternoon I walked across St. Petersburg to the Conservatory. As I approached the building, a small crowd of gray men with gray beards in gray coats stood huddled near the entrance.

I stopped and watched people in more colorful spring wardrobes queue up. Two students wearing traditional red shirts with black trim greeted the attendees and collected money. I plunged my hand into a pocket to make certain I had a few coins to contribute.

"Are you a pederast?"

My head swiveled about to find the questioner. Grigori stood just out of my line of sight behind me wearing a student uniform. "How do you mean? What are you saying?"

"That fat fellow over there"–he pointed to one of the gray men–"said that Tolstoy was most assuredly one because of two soldiers from that book in your study."

It took a few seconds to recall the passage referred to. At one point Count Vronski ate his morning meal in the regimental mess. Tolstoy described two of the other officers in such a way that a reader could interpret as epicene or effeminate. Of course, it would take someone with a debauched mind to reach such a conclusion.

Someone such as Aleksey Nikolayevich Apukhtin, the man Grigori had indicated. Romantic poet, staunch patriot, and poison-tongued critic, but not necessarily in any particular order. That put things into perspective for me.

"Ah! Now I understand. He advocates men loving other men, and he sees it everywhere, whether it exists or no." Churches and governments– which generally teemed with such people–tended to focus on squelching that behavior. However, I had no opinion on who should love whom or not. "Some people refer to those men as *pederasts*–based on the Ancient Greek practice of mature men with younger ones–but I believe I do not fall into that category, despite what *you* may suppose."

I reached into my pocket, retrieved two rubles, and gave the donation to Grigori. As I walked away and into the building, I considered how others may have observed my unmarried status and assumed I had a predilection for men. As mentioned before, as a consequence of my longevity, I harbor no romantic attractions to anyone.

Once inside, I remained at the rear of the hall because I did not want to get too close to others' minds. Most of the chairs in the room had occupants.

When I turned back to the entrance, a tall, slender fop with a bushy light-brown beard dressed in a gold-braided tunic entered accompanied by a strikingly-handsome blond fellow. Grand Duke Sergei Alexandrovich, son of the current tsar, had appeared in public with his male consort many times. They could have been the model for the two army officers in *Anna Karenina* who titillated Apukhtin.

One of the tall, gray men from outside, a fellow with a deeply receded hairline, stepped to the piano. "Welcome. I am Vladimir Vasilievich Stasov. My friends, thank you for joining us today to honor our greatest living Russian composer, Modest Petrovich Mussorgsky." Polite applause arose from the audience. "But before we hear from our featured performer, there are a few people who wish to share their talents with you."

He stood next to a well-polished walnut grand piano and motioned to someone in the front row. "Our first piece today will be presented by our esteemed comrade, Alexander Porfiryevich Borodin."

While the audience clapped, a rather plain-looking fellow in his late 40s stepped up as Stasov took a seat. Borodin had more the appearance of a banker or undertaker than composer and pianist. Without saying a word, he sat and began playing. If I had a better appreciation of music, I might have been able to describe his performance. To me, it sounded like typical, moody, Slavic strains.

Tchaikovsky, Cui, and several others followed. Next, a group, including Borodin and my client Rimsky-Korsakov, stood around the piano taking turns in duets playing the humorous *Paraphrases on the Celebrated Chop Waltz*. An annoying little tune on its own, these musical masters brought fun and frivolity to the occasion while they bounced about, pulling comical faces as they performed.

With no introduction, a crumpled and disheveled man—Mussorgsky, more likely than not—shuffled to the piano. His hair looked as if it had not been combed in a week, and the whiskers on his face appeared the same. His fingers flew and the instrument sang. I had never heard such exquisite music before. Rather than long, laborious variations on a theme, he played short vignettes interposed with a repeated interlude. As I listened, I could picture various scenes playing out before me. Some of the pieces reveled in cacophony as the composer's fingers twiddled away in rushed tempi. Several featured slow, sonorous chords, evoking darkness and fear. The final run concluded in a vaulting of hands as they flew back and forth, louder than an empty vessel, from east to west, again and again, imitating end-of-war church chimes resounding raucous celebration.

When echoes of the final booming bass notes faded throughout the hall's hushed haze, the audience rose as one with protracted and generous applause. The composer sat on the bench mopping his sweaty brow, appearing unaware of the adulation bestowed upon him.

Stasov rushed up, shook Mussorgsky's shoulder, and indicated the ovation. "Come greet your patrons, Modest. Heaven knows, Jesus himself suffered more than you." The other performers guided the broken pitcher of a man toward the rear.

Rimsky-Korsakov approached the disheveled performer near where I stood. "Modest Petrovich! You must write out *Pictures at an Exhibition* before it is too late! Your addled memory will soon fail. We do not wish to lose this national treasure."

Pictures at an Exhibition? That seemed a suitable title for this compilation of musical poetry. As Mussorgsky passed by, I could sense his exhaustion, his confusion, but worst of all, his imminent mortality.

I found it sad that brilliant artists, such as Mozart and this fellow, live doomed, shortened existences, while I continued on, scarcely contributing to society's advancement.

I had looked forward to a relaxing afternoon reading more Tolstoy. I reached the section where Anna's husband contemplated divorce due to her dalliance with Count Vronski. However, to receive a dissolution, the guilty party must confess to wrongdoing, which would have caused Anna to besmirch her reputation. She nearly died giving birth to an illegitimate daughter, but her husband forgave her. The situation had become truly murky. Such intrigue gripped my interest.

A knock at the study door broke my concentration.

"Yes?"

"Sorry to interrupt, sir," Dima announced, "but you have an urgent message from Lady Catherine."

"Bring it here." I placed Tolstoy on a side table. The citrus-scented missive requested my immediate appearance at the palace for undisclosed matters. Given one of my previous sessions with Lady Catherine, I surmised that the Tsaritsa had died, and she wanted a blessing or some advice on how to proceed.

Following a deep, downhill sigh, I stood. Dima had retrieved my coat and assisted me into it.

As I stepped outside, I saw a tram approaching and trotted to meet it. I concentrated on the clip-clop of horse hooves in an attempt to block out the others' thoughts.

Loud shouting erupted on the paths near the palace as I stepped off the *konka*. A group of People's Will protestors chanting "Land and liberty!" marched in circles with placards. From what I had read in newspapers, they wanted to overthrow the tsarist government in favor of populist rule. Men in dark uniforms approached and circled the group in an attempt to suppress the activity. I had heard about the formation of a Secret Police to safeguard the Tsar following the most recent assassination attempt. The activists chanted even louder, and several took swings at the officers with their signs. I circumvented the skirmish and headed toward the palace's rear entrance.

House staff guided me to Catherine's chambers, and I stood waiting in the outer room. Situated on the writing table, next to a packet of paper and a crystal ink pen, I spied a bottle of Spider Lily, the perfume she had used to scent the summons. A few minutes later, her private apartment door opened, and she wafted through, a silhouette in black, complete with mourning veil.

"Oh, Rodya. So good of you to come." Her lace-covered head turned side-to-side. "Where is your little shadow?"

"Grigori Yefimovich spends his afternoons assisting Master Rimsky-Korsakov at the Conservatory." I lowered my gaze to the luxurious royal blue Persian carpet. "How can I be of assistance, my lady?"

"That is too bad. I had looked forward to spending more time with the charming boy. He made quite an impression on our Kolen'ka."

"I will inform my apprentice of your appreciations." I made a slight bow. "How is his young highness fairing? I trust our chat emboldened him."

"As you envisaged, his mother gifted him a journal, and he has written enthusiastically in it every day. At times we must pry it from his hands to get him to do anything else."

"It makes me happy to hear the little prince has found writing to be an outlet." I cleared my throat. Her bereavement garb indicated a recent death. "But that is not why you requested my presence, is it?"

I had difficulty reading her thoughts as they jumbled and raced. However, I sensed something unfortunate transpired that she took as advantageous. The gates would soon open, I supposed.

"Rodya," she gasped, pausing with a hand to her forehead. "It finally happened. Empress Maria Alexandrovna has succumbed to her drawn-out consumptive suffering."

Not a surprise to me. "Your news brings sadness, my lady."

"You previously mentioned her death would be imminent. We knew the time drew near, but no one could have foretold the exact moment." Her head angled in my direction. "Perhaps *you* could have."

"I am a healer, not a haruspex." Perhaps divining the future through entrails should be another skill for me to study.

"Of course, of course, but that is not why I have invited you here." We stood for a minute or so just looking at each other. "What I need from you is guidance regarding the interval between Maria's death and our marriage."

"Your marriage?"

"To my Sashka, the Tsar. He had promised to legitimize our liaison when he could."

"I see. Are there not established guidelines for such an occurrence? Surely, this cannot be the first time a sitting empress has died."

"The priests have advised me that it is customary to wait—at minimum—forty days before the emperor should remarry."

"Forty days? That sounds rather biblical."

"Yes, it is. Noah's flood, Moses fasting on Mount Sinai, Jesus wandering in the wilderness, and so forth…" One hand waved through the air, spreading a trail of perfume. "We must eat that horrid *koliva*"—she shuddered—"and place a decanter of water with a towel by the window."

"You do not like buckwheat?"

"*That* is peasant food."

"But I sense you want to proceed with the wedding before the forty days. It seems only right to give the departed soul suitable time for journey and judgment. You have waited all these years to marry. Why disregard tradition?"

"I want the children he has fathered to be recognized." Her head tilted back at a slight angle.

"They will become heirs to the throne?"

"Oh, no!" She stamped. "Maria saw to it that our left-handed marriage would not allow for succession through *me*."

My eyebrows raised. "Yet you still want to marry Alexander."

"Of course! What woman would not want to be Tsaritsa?"

This woman certainly did, no matter what it took. With her mind open, I could see she would force the issue, Alexander would relent, and the wedding would take place before the end of the proper mourning period.

"How can I be of assistance today, my lady?"

Her hand went to her chest. "My bosom is uneasy, Rodya. Can we use the cards and bring a gift of sight to comfort and calm me?"

Even with the black lace covering, I felt the intensity of her eyes. "Whatever I can do to help."

She went to the drawer that held the square bits of pasteboard. With both hands, she spread the cards on a nearby table and arranged them into a five-by-five matrix. We both stared at the array in silence.

"There!" Catherine pointed at a matched pair. "The diamond ring. I knew it! This is a sure sign I should marry the Tsar at the first opportunity."

I squinted as I attempted to locate the cards she specified. "But is not the design feet over head? Does that not suggest the opposite?"

"Feet over head?" She studied the arrangement for a moment, lifted the two cards that formed a ring and rotated the pair topsy-turvy. "How can you tell which direction is up? It could go either way."

Diamond against diamond. My scythe had hit a stone. "I caution you, Lady Catherine. If you marry the Tsar before the end of the forty-day period of mourning, you run the risk of upsetting the order of all things." Unfortunately, it did not matter how I responded because I knew she would be Tsaritsa half-way through that interval.

"Your healing gifts have temporarily escaped you, Rodya. You know not of what you speak." Her head tilted to the side. "The eyes may have fear, but the hands know what to do. I wish you to leave now." She stepped to the crystal bell and shook it with fury until a chambermaid appeared. "Escort the gentleman out," Lady Catherine ordered.

I had taken the risk of telling someone what they *needed* to hear rather than what they *wanted* to hear. That resulted in early dismissal with no compensation for my time and effort.

By the time I reached Nevsky Prospekt, the anti-tsarist protest had dissipated. With no *konka* in sight, I walked home, my mind abuzz.

When Catherine gained control of Alexander's elderly ear, *Anna Karenina* might seem more like a children's Petrushka puppet play. I had survived the rise and fall of nations many times, and with each historical turning point, I chose not to interfere. This gift of vision only worked on one person at a time. Determining the fate of an entire country lay beyond my limited capabilities. In any case, whatever happened, *I* would survive.

This time, however, I had developed an emotional attachment to the remarkable city of St. Petersburg and its talented artisans. The music, literature, sculpture, and art created here eclipsed much of bygone days. For once, I truly cared about the people and the place. If I didn't need to change my identity every so often, I would consider settling down here.

The 62-year-old Tsar had overseen major social reforms and eluded several assassination attempts. I dreaded these hurried nuptials would finally bring down Alexander.

And St. Petersburg with him.

I returned home to the enchanting aroma of roasting potatoes. The fragrances of garlic, onion, and mushroom also caught my nose. Dima knew how to prepare meals better than any other servant I've ever known. And that's several centuries of kitchen help.

In my room, I washed the day's dust and disappointment from my hands while I revisited the episode at the palace. No good could come from Catherine rushing Tsar Alexander to marry her.

A knock at the door derailed my train of thought. "Yes?"

"Pardon, sir, but the doctor from across the hall has paid a call and wishes to speak with you."

Yuri? That is odd. We have been neighbors for a year or so, and he has never made any attempt at socializing until this moment. "Have you prepared sufficient food?"

The servant's eyes levitated upward. "That depends on the young master's appetite."

I walked into the dining room to see Dr. Yuri standing next to Grigori.

As we shook hands, I addressed him. "So good to see you again. As you have probably surmised, your patient's health has improved. Thank you again for your benevolent treatment."

"Not a problem."

As he bent forward, I noticed the rear of his head exhibited a circular bald spot.

"What brings you to our home this evening, doctor?"

He inhaled with the sound of rushing air, widening his nostrils. "Aside from the marvelous aroma of your impending meal, I have a favor to ask of you."

"A favor? Of *me*?" My hand went to my chest. "How could I possibly help *you*?"

"Well… this may take some time to explain. Perhaps I should leave you to your supper and return later."

I glanced at Dima and his chin shifted up and down with the slightest movement.

"Why don't you join us? We can discuss your matter over food, as civilized people do."

He made another slight bow, and I caught sight of the bare scalp again. "Thank you very much. That is quite gracious of you, Mr. Propok."

"Please, call me, Rodion."

"And I am Yuri. Just let me return to my rooms for a moment. If I am to dine with you, I feel it only proper that I contribute something to the table."

Grigori and I exchanged questioning glances as our guest departed. He shrugged and sat at his place.

Upon his return, the good doctor held a bottle of clear liquid in one hand. "I have been saving this Smirnoff for the right occasion, and I believe this to be the one!" He landed it on the table with a clunk.

"Dima, will you bring us two glasses?" Grigori tilted his head and bulged his eyes at me. "Well… make that three glasses." The boy straightened up and smiled, nodding his head four times.

The servant brought a tray with one single and two double glasses. Yuri opened the vodka and poured.

"To our health!" he toasted before swallowing his share in one swift gulp.

I tipped my head back and duplicated the abrupt drinking maneuver.

Grigori sniffed at the liquor in his smaller glass, wrinkling his nose as if he smelled rotting manure.

"It's an acquired taste," I advised.

Instead of drinking it, the boy dipped the tip of his tongue into the liquid. "Bleh!" he proclaimed.

Yuri's chin snapped up and his nostrils flared. My facial reaction, while not as brutal, displayed mild amusement.

From the fruit bowl on a side table, I grabbed a lemon and sliced into it with my knife. "Perhaps a little flavoring might help." He held the glass up and I squeezed some juice into it.

The doctor replenished our cups, and we drank once more.

The boy sipped at his. "Better," he acknowledged.

Dima set a sumptuous platter teeming with roasted potatoes before us. He served our guest first, then me, leaving Grigori for last.

"Roasted potatoes?" Yuri confronted me. "No meat, Rodion? You can't tell me you are too poor to afford such comforts if you reside in *this* building."

"Yes, I could have purchased some animal flesh if I so chose, Yuri. However, my preference is not to eat from another creature's bones. Whether that creature be a cow, a pig, or a lamb."

He laughed in a boisterous manner, as if I had told an amusing story. "Instead of dining on the grazer, you eat the grass itself, cutting out the middleman, I suppose." A finger wagged in my direction. "You are a man of principles, Rodion, and a principled man is not easily found these days."

In my experience, truly principled men hardly existed. "Thank you, my friend."

Grigori stopped munching on his portion and looked up. He gazed at Yuri and me, in turn, a few times before resuming his rumination.

"Let me tell you why I have called upon you, good neighbor." He took a few bites of the potatoes. "Oh, my! This is even better than your cabbage rolls."

A stifled, "Thank you, sir," shot out from the kitchen.

"I have a patient laid up at Kirov Hospital on the Vyborg Side who has proven himself resistant to treatment."

"You mean you cannot heal him?"

"No, I mean he resists any medical advice we provide. Would you consider paying him a visit? It would help me immensely if you could use whatever magic charms you have to readjust his thinking so that he participates in his own well-being."

Magic? It continues to annoy me that people still believe I perform some sort of sorcery. "I am not sure what services I can offer, Yuri."

"I asked around and have discovered that you are highly regarded as a healer for some of St. Petersburg's finest citizens." He winked at me as if we had conspired together. "Including a particular lady at the Winter Palace, no?"

A particularly impatient lady who would soon be Tsaritsa, no less. "I am happy to hear that my reputation has garnered such praise." Flattery makes friends. Truth makes enemies.

"In fact, your apprentice here"—he indicated Grigori with his free hand—"attends the gentleman regularly."

My eyes enlarged as I turned to the boy.

"Master Rimsky-Korsakov asked me to take musical dictation from the composer." A thin smile crossed Grigori's face. "He makes me laugh."

Memories of the concert at the Conservatory played in my mind. I recalled Korsakov's plea to write down *Pictures at an Exhibition* before it became too late. "Are you referring to that Mussorgsky fellow?"

"Modest Petrovich himself!"

"And he's in hospital? We just saw him perform the other day."

"A sudden turn of health." The doctor shook his head in dismay. "I have ordered him to remain in bed and abstain from alcohol and tobacco, but somehow he manages to continue the use of both. Someone"—he stabbed a chunk of potato with a clink—"has been smuggling these things into the room."

Grigori's head lowered over his food.

As the composer passed me in the concert hall, I had glimpsed his failing health. He would not live much longer. I made it a point not to accept as clients such people for whom death loomed.

"I am afraid I cannot undertake your request, Yuri. I believe the gentleman is too nigh on his demise for my talents to make a difference."

"The eyes may be afraid, but still the hands work!"

That phrase hounded me yet once more.

The doctor filled our glasses again. "To Mussorgsky!" he charged and downed the Smirnoff.

"Mussorgsky," I muttered before swigging.

When my hand came to rest on the table, our neighbor reached over and covered it with his own. My spine stiffened. I hadn't looked into his thoughts before, but this action prompted me to pry. The drink may have clouded both our minds; however, I did get the distinct impression that he found me appealing. I did not feel the same toward him. A friendly fellow, yes, but friendship would have been all I could offer.

"Russia's greatest living composer." Yuri hummed the promenade from *Pictures at an Exhibition*. "Tomorrow afternoon might be just the thing, you know," he suggested while patting the back of my hand. "It would mean a great deal to me."

I looked across the table at his fluttering eyes, moist and glistening in the gaslight. Even though I shared no attraction for him, the admiration, nonetheless, felt good.

"Yes. Of course, I will attend him." I don't know if sympathy, curiosity, or vodka spoke for me.

T HE Nevsky tram connected with the Liteyny line, and I rode a *konka* over the Neva River to the Vyborg Side. Kirov Hospital stood nearby, and I arrived at Mussorgsky's room a few minutes later.

"No! No! *No!*" a gruff baritone wailed. "The line is down a major second, up a major fourth, another major second, followed by a perfect *fourth*. Not a perfect *fifth*." Mussorgsky's hair and beard looked just as unkempt as when I saw him perform. He lay under a single sheet wearing a faded, ragged, silk dressing gown.

Grigori sat in a chair next to the bed, scribbling on some lined paper. He showed a page to the patient.

"Yes, yes. That is it. Let us continue." Mussorgsky hummed a few bars. "Did you catch that, my boy?"

"I brought something for your health, Modest." A tall man entered holding a greenish-yellow apple in his outstretched hand. I remembered him as Vladimir Stasov, the host of the charity concert at the Conservatory.

From under the bedsheets, Mussorgsky produced a fist-sized bottle containing a reddish-brown liquid. "When it comes to my health, I prefer cognac, thank you." He uncorked it with his teeth, spat the stopper, and took a swig.

"Modest!" Stasov protested. "You might have another attack if you continue to disobey the doctor's orders."

"I paid good money to get this in here." The composer patted Grigori on the shoulder. "Twenty-five rubles! Are you thirsty, Vovochka?" He held the flask up.

"No! Give that to me." When Stasov reached for the offered drink, Mussorgsky snatched it away. He returned the bottle to his lips, swallowed the remains in one gulp, and slipped the drained vessel beneath the covers.

"Shrovetide lasts but a day. Soon Lent arrives." He belched, and it echoed around the room. The fruity, sweet aroma of cheap cognac filled the air. "I do find myself rather famished. Bring that here."

Stasov placed the apple in his friend's grasping hand. Mussorgsky gnawed at it as if he had not eaten in a week.

"You must take better care of yourself if you want to complete your project." Stasov pointed to the stack of papers in Grigori's lap. "Korsakov will be very disappointed if you do not."

"What?" the composer mumbled in response, his mouth full of apple. He cupped his free hand to an ear. "The hungry belly has no ears, you know." He chomped another chunk of the fruit.

Stasov turned to me. "And you are?"

"Rodion Propok. The gentleman's physician requested my presence."

"Ah. You are also a doctor, then?"

"No, sir, a healer."

He jutted his chin before uttering a curt, "Oh."

Many people preferred healers over physicians because we generally brought good news, and doctors, bad. It appeared Stasov did not share that predilection. While his mind flooded with social events and parties, the scene inside Mussorgky's head turned volcanic with pain and agony. The great composer went limp, then twitched and convulsed.

"Doctors!" Stasov shouted. "Modest! What have you done?"

Mussorgky sobbed and cried between spasms, "Ah, I am a wretch!" His body trembled. "It is all over." He lay back, arms flopping to his side. The apple core dropped to the floor and rolled a few centimeters.

I made an attempt to access his thoughts, but saw nothing, much the way I experienced Grigori. However, I felt a small ping in my skull. A fleeting flash. No pain, just a passing spark.

"The first of my Mighty Five to succumb. A great loss," Stasov declared. "A great loss to us all."

Yuri appeared at the door, but the patient lay silent and still. It had been many years since I witnessed the death of another. My mind froze with inertia, and I had the sensation that my heart within its casing ceased to beat. I felt faint and, by instinct, reached for the door frame to steady myself before losing consciousness.

"Rodion, you and Grigori can leave now." The doctor's voice whispered.

My eyelids felt melted together, and I struggled to open them. When, at last, I pried them apart, I could see a dim hallway. Yuri's arm supported my own, as if I had required guidance. I had no memory of how we got there.

"There is no more to be done here. I appreciate your attempts."

I looked up into his reddened eyes. When I attempted to sense his future, instead of the expected view of patients and treatments, I saw blackness. Not even dinner on my table. "But how —?"

He placed a finger on my lips. "Just go now. Please. I will call upon you later when I return home." The doctor withdrew back into the room we had just exited.

"Come. I'll take us to the *konka*," Grigori muttered.

The boy led me with his small, cool hand out into the open air. We stood waiting for the next tram without saying anything. I felt clammy sweat in my collar, worried that my inestimable immortality had also departed. Or worse, physical interest in other humans returned.

Once we boarded and found seats, he turned to me. "What happened?"

"How do you mean?"

"In Mussorgsky's room. You went blank. Yuri had to shuffle you out into the hallway."

"I don't know. I honestly don't know." I shook my head. "In all my centuries, this has never happened."

For once, I actively sought out the minds of those around me. Nothing. Most days, I endeavored to avoid getting too close to people in order to evade their stray thoughts. My mind perceived naught from other passengers.

"Things die, Mr. Propok." I believed Grigori attempted to console me. "Things die."

"Yes. Yes. I know that. I have witnessed more death than anyone alive today." I struggled to make sense of the situation. "Somehow, this time it is different."

"How so?"

"I cannot sense the futures of others around me."

"Neither can I."

"No. No." I waved a hand. "My healing properties come from being able to sense someone's coming days and whether they might live or die."

Grigori arched one eyebrow. "You do not accept clients whom you know will die?"

"That is correct."

"Very smart. Hmmmmm. Very smart, indeed. You do not climb the mountain but, rather, sidestep it."

"I guess one could say that. But losing that ability frightens me." Visions of my own incapacity and death passed before me. I teared up and felt immobilized.

My companion broke the contemplation, "Do you think it might be something specific to the composer?"

His foreshortened life, like that of Mozart, might have affected me in ways I had not considered. Both failed to complete their final endeavor. A thought-provoking juxtaposition. "That is possible," I whispered.

It occurred to me I had attempted to look into the mind of someone who had just passed. I could not remember performing such an undertaking before. Perhaps that disrupted my ability to sense others.

As we transferred to the Nevsky line, one of the passengers bumped my arm while boarding. She touched my face with her hand. "I am so sorry, young man. Please accept my apologies."

In an instant, I saw her times ahead. All rather pedestrian, but, at that moment, a marvel to me.

I grinned. "Not at all, madam. Not at all."

As we took our seats, the boy asked, "What are you smiling about, Mr. Propok?"

"I saw it! Her future. When she caressed my cheek." My face flushed. "This is marvelous! No longer must I suffer the onslaught of stray thoughts from people nearby. It seems I must make physical contact with them to see into their coming days."

I reached over to touch Grigori's cold, sallow face. Nothing. Still nothing.

"What did you see?"

While I could not envisage the boy's outlook, perhaps I saw a glimpse of mine. I resolved to make something of this long life I have been granted and contribute to the common good. Along the lines of Mozart or Mussorgsky, but with many more years to accomplish whatever goals I chose.

Aside from my fledgling days at the glass foundry, the only skill I applied with any regularity has been my healing act. Over the years, I have ready many, many books, and it might be time to put this experience to good use. And authors, should they be successful at their craft, do earn sufficient money to subsist.

Given that—in my belief—I had risen from the dead, I chose the pen name Lazarus and decided I should chronicle the times I have lived and the people I've met. At least that way I could leave something behind for others to discover and enjoy. While not beautiful and inspiring music, my words and works might move people, nonetheless.

Grigori tugged at my sleeve. "Mr. Propok, what did you see?"

"The future, dear boy. *My* future."

I looked at the coins sitting on my desk and questioned, "What is this?"

Grigori entered the study. "My contribution to the household. You said you wanted me to help pay for meals and such."

"And where did you get *six rubles*?" My voice, as well as my eyebrows arched. "Master Korsakov pays you only a quarter ruble each day."

"Mussorgsky." A bemused smile budged the boy's mouth. "He gave me money to bring him… things."

My eyes closed. I inhaled to the count of six and let out the air at the same pace. "It might have been the brandy that killed him."

"I do not think so." A slight shrug punctuated his refutation. "He would have died without it all the same."

"And how do you know this?"

"He told me his death approached quickly, and he preferred to die comfortably. Should we not attempt to ease our friends' pain?"

My eyes puffed out and I imagined my forehead reddened. "Did you consider that he may have lied to you to get those *things* his doctor prohibited?"

Grigori's head tilted to one side then the other. "Why would such a person tell untruths?"

A medium sigh emerged from my throat. "You have *much* to learn about the human condition, my boy. People *lie*. Especially when they want something they're not supposed to have."

"Are we not taught, 'Eat bread and salt, and speak the truth'?"

"Yes, but not everyone subscribes to that proverb." I closed my eyes for an instant. "What made you do this?"

"I wished him to survive. And if not, no tricks could help him, and he should be able to live comfortably." Grigori sounded sincere.

The memory of the meat pie vendor outside the Summer Garden passed before me. "Did you do anything–*anything*–to Mussorgsky that might have hastened his death?"

The boy shook his head a few times.

My eyes shifted heavenward, and I let out another sigh. "I would like to believe that he died a *natural* death."

"I am certain that up until those last few moments, he was happy. I enjoyed working with him."

"Perhaps our neighbor will enlighten us as to the poor fellow's final medical state."

"Dr. Yuri for you, sir," Dima announced.

"Well, speak of the gray one…" I muttered. To the servant I ordered, "Please show the good doctor to the dining room. We will join him in a minute."

"He does show up at suppertime, does he not?" Grigori suggested.

A half smile bent my lips. "Bread and salt, bread and salt," I reminded myself.

We stepped into the dining room. Our neighbor stood with hands clasped and his head hanging.

"Yuri," I greeted him.

"Rodion," he responded. "I wanted to thank you for attending my patient. Yes, the timing could have been better, but you did make the effort, and I wanted to express my gratitude for that."

"Of course. Of course." I rested my hand on Grigori's shoulder. "You cared for my apprentice here, and I appreciate that."

"As would anyone, I suppose," my neighbor responded.

Awkward silence permeated the room. I ventured forward. "Can you tell us what ended the great composer's life?"

"Ah, yes. Poor Modest. A grand mal seizure brought on his end. He had not taken the bromide I prescribed, and that allowed for the fit of apoplexy you witnessed, regrettably."

"And so young, too. Such a shame."

"He had just reached his forty-second year the week before." Yuri's gaze settled on my face. "May we speak in private?"

The question troubled me. I had no idea of his intentions because we had yet to touch. Having asked for a fingernail, he may want the elbow. I attempted to maintain a calm expression. "Please join me in the study." My outstretched hand indicated the way.

Once I closed the door behind us, he began. "Rodion, it makes me sad that we had not met previously. You are an exemplary fellow, and one I should be honored to have as a friend."

"Thank you, Yuri. I believe I can return the compliment." I wanted to reach out and make contact so that I could read his future, but he might have misinterpreted such an action. "What is it you wish to discuss?"

He scuffed a foot on the floor, he fiddled with his fingers, and he scratched at his beard before speaking. "I get the sense that you might…

hmmmmmm… find me attractive." His eyes widened and appeared to search mine for a response.

A situation I had not anticipated. From our first encounter, I had an inkling he might have been interested in *me*. As far as I knew, I had not given him any indication of my feelings toward him, which consisted of friendship alone. With renewed eyes, I examined his face. I felt sweat on my palms and a pulse in my ear. Relief came as no feelings of desire arose from my bosom.

"Yuri, my friend," I blurted as I attempted to find words to express myself. "I am not certain how my actions could have driven you to such a conclusion. My intentions toward you are as a friend and neighbor. Nothing more."

His expression drooped, shifting from desire to dispirited. "I thought I had experienced a shared interest, but I must have misjudged the circumstances." A tear appeared on his cheek, and he looked down. "I apologize if I offended you. Perhaps I should speak less. That might be smarter."

This gave me the opportunity to grasp his hand. I sensed his sadness at losing Mussorgsky. I mourned that loss as well. As far as Yuri's days ahead, I saw him treating others in hospital, but no signs of me.

"No offense. No offense, indeed. I am flattered by your attentions." While I did not find his looks appealing, some might. I smiled and squeezed his hand. "It is not every day a handsome doctor finds you appealing."

He pulled away. "Now I am embarrassed by my actions. I hope we can still be friends, Rodion."

"Yes. Yes! Good neighbors and good friends. Both."

"This demonstrates how you got such a good reputation. You are a noble and honorable man, and I can tell your healing powers are strong." He smiled. "Pardon for the interruption. I shall leave you to your evening now. So long."

"Did you not want to stay for supper?" I took a few sniffs at the air. "My servant usually prepares enough for three or four people, although I have no idea of what it might be tonight."

"No, I have burdened you with my presence enough for one day. Thank you. We will have that meal another time."

As nice a person as I found Yuri, I knew that in a few years I would have to leave St. Petersburg. Everyone else would age, but I would not. That made maintaining intimate relationships impracticable. I took it as a blessing that I did not crave the affections of others.

"As you wish." I opened the door and called, "Dima!" When he arrived, I instructed, "Please show our guest out. I shall dine here in the study this evening. Provide the young master his choice of meal."

The servant ushered our neighbor from the room. I sat in my chair and took up the Tolstoy. One element of reading would include studying the writing style so that I could, perchance, employ some of his art to my own forthcoming story, which promised to be an enormous enterprise. Modest Mussorgsky's early death inspired me to value my own life experiences to a much greater extent.

The intriguing wiles of Anna, her infidelity with Vronsky, Stiva's matchmaking, and Kitty's romance with Levin could not divert me. My interview with Yuri kept circling in my head, eclipsing Tolstoy's various yarns as I struggled to make sense of my own particular social complications.

As much as I wished to study the author's craft, I could not shake our neighbor's efforts at probing interpersonal interests. It came as a pleasant surprise that I had no romantic attraction for Yuri. Given that I lost some of my ability to sense people's futures, I had worried how that incident at the hospital may have affected other aspects of my existence.

My mind kept drifting as I struggled to resume *Anna*. The book thumped when I slammed it closed. I placed it on the side table and opened my diary to check over the appointments for the week ahead.

As if a universal force cosmically coordinated my affairs, I had scheduled to visit Avdotya Panaeva the following afternoon. One of St. Petersburg's foremost authors, she also hosted a regular literary salon. Instead of requesting monetary remuneration, I could press the lady for some suggestions on the techniques of writing. Call it fate, fortune, chance, or providence, I felt the timing rather opportune.

"HAVE you ever wanted to die, Mr. Propok?" Grigori put to me as I sat drinking my morning tea.

After choking on some of the infusion, I responded, "Such a question." No one had asked that before.

"After all, you have lived—what—hundreds of years? Don't you get to a point where you no longer wish to go on?"

I felt my apprentice had demonstrated progress of late, the alder-tree bending a bit. Now this. "What inspired your peculiar question?"

"I have been thinking lately about your situation. If I had been granted longevity as you have, I don't know that I would want to live so many lifetimes."

"You have barely lived one. How can you reach judicious judgments with your very limited experience?"

He crossed his arms and shifted his weight to one leg. "Answer the question."

Such impertinence. "There are so many things I have yet to do: places to visit, people to meet. I never tire of all the new wonders I continue to find."

"You might not feel the same if you had lived as a *peasant*." His tone suggested spitting on the floor.

"That is how I started. A poor laborer working my bleeding fingers to nubs. If you add all my years of underpaid work, they would far outweigh what *you* have experienced so far. It took me several 'lifetimes'—as you put it—to develop the necessary skills for rising above serfdom."

"Then I find it difficult to believe that one peasant could achieve that same goal with only one lifetime."

I raised my eyebrows as I realized he did have a point.

"The rest of us live in fear of pain and death, Mr. Propok." Grigori focused his piercing gaze on me. "If you cannot *die*, what are you afraid of?"

"Do you not have to attend gymnasium?" I stamped my foot.

In the afternoon, I took a *konka* to Liteyny Prospekt. The experience proved delightful without the constant psychic bombardment of others'

lives. Perhaps I could look forward to outings where being in a crowd would not upset me the way it had in the past.

A servant led me to a modest sitting room overlooking the street. Sunlight illuminated various portraits above a vase of blue lobelia on a stand. I sat upon one of the carved, wooden chairs.

"Rodya," Avdotya Panaeva greeted me as she entered with another woman I did not recognize. "I hope you do not mind, but my very good friend, Yulia Zhadovskaya, has paid me a visit from her nest out in Kostroma." The two women sat on an upholstered bench.

"Of course not, madam." I rose, took my host's hand, and kissed it. The faint aroma of citrus caught my attention. Her days ahead held little surprise, I sensed, mostly consisting of writing and attending her salon. Even with white hair, she presented a comely countenance.

I moved to the guest and bent forward, taking notice she had no left arm. As she raised her right, I had to move even closer as it had not developed to full length. When she presented her hand, I could see she had but three fingers on it. Not wanting to display alarm or disgust, I grasped it as I would have any other woman's and gave it a delicate peck. I thought back to Grigori's earlier question regarding what fears I might have. This direct confrontation with deformity brought to the fore my own discomfort with debility. I felt fortunate in that moment to possess the standard complement of human extremities.

Visions of various gentlemen courting Yulia filled my mind. Apparently, her malformed presentation did little to dissuade amorous fellows. Indeed, it appeared to encourage their interest. Cats, however, have died from such abundance of curiosity.

Avdotya stood, hands clasped as if in prayer, and recited. "I still love him, it's crazy! At his name my soul shivers, Longing still squeezes my chest, And my gaze with a hot tear involuntarily shimmers." A profound sigh followed. "Isn't that divine?" She smiled at her guest. "Yulen'ka pens the most lovely quatrains, does she not?"

My distaste for music, drama, and opera pales in comparison to the antipathy I harbor toward poetry. *Words wasted*, I called it, as a rule. "Lovely, just lovely, my lady."

The poet grinned at me, her eyes pointing in different directions. "Dus'ka, he is just as charming as you had said." Her lopsided smile grew, as did my discomfort.

"My dear, I need to speak with my healer in private for just a moment. Please do excuse us." Madam Panaeva took me aside to a hallway alcove.

"I see that my guest demonstrated an interest in you. Do not trouble yourself, Rodya. She has a husband, but it is not a happy marriage."

Apparently, she found her happiness elsewhere. "Thank you. I appreciate you providing that knowledge, madam."

We returned to the room where Avdotya's guest sat.

As my client took her seat, she announced, "My dearest Yulen'ka, Mr. Propok will perform his regular healing with me. Please be patient."

Yulia nodded her assent.

"There is not much to say, Madam Panaeva," I began. "You are in excellent health. Nothing gives me any indication otherwise. Is there something concerning you?"

"No, Mr. Propok, but I do believe you have something to ask of *me*." She tucked her chin and batted her eyelashes.

In all the times I have attended her in the past, I had never gotten the sense that Avdotya possessed any ability to read thoughts. However, in this moment, she stated her feeling that I wished to consult *her*. Of course, I wanted to discuss my writing project. It might have been inadvertent facial movements that revealed my inner thoughts.

"Well, I am caught up short, madam," I blustered. "How could you know what I had on my mind?"

"Mr. Propok." She shook her head in tiny movements. "A good author learns to read people. I do not wish to give away my secrets, just as you would not want to divulge the mysteries of your healing powers."

"Yes, you are quite correct in that. On both accounts." I cocked my head and raised a finger. "There is, indeed, a subject on which I should like to deliberate."

"And is it something that can be discussed before my guest?" Her eyes slid toward the poet.

"I believe so." The noise emanating from my throat sounded louder than I had anticipated when I cleared it. "I… uh… have been considering writing down the events of my life."

"A worthy goal, indeed! I, myself, have begun the process of penning my own. What composition experience have you?"

"Although I have not written heretofore, I have read extensively, including various members of your salon: Dostoevsky, Tolstoy…"

"Well, Mr. Propok, you *must* attend my next writing circle. Are you available Thursday next?"

"I shall consult my diary, madam. It would be my honor to attend your salon, if only to breathe the air of such great literary luminaries."

"And, perhaps, to develop new clientele!" She laughed. "A debt repaid is beautiful, you know."

"The thought had not crossed my mind, madam. I only had intentions to develop my authoring skills."

Yulia sat observing me, her head tilted to one side. The position exaggerated its asymmetry even further. She reached her shortened arm to tap her friend's shoulder.

Avdotya leaned toward the poet. Yulia whispered into the proffered ear.

"Mr. Propok"–our host started as she straightened up–"my guest desires you to provide any healing guidance you can. She hardly ever gets to the city these days, and it would mean a great deal to me as well. We can double your charges, if you like."

"Madam, I had no intention of demanding any money for this visit because you have been so benevolent as to invite me to your writing salon. Twice naught remains naught."

"As you wish, Mr. Propok. What can you tell my dearest Yulen'ka?"

Having already seen a glimpse of her future, I did not wish to divulge my knowledge of her upcoming succession of engagements with several men. If Avdotya already knew, I would only be repeating something established beforehand. However, if unaware, I would not wish to be the instrument of unpleasant or unwelcome news.

I turned to face the Russian Jezebel. "Madam Zhadovskaya shall continue in as good as health possible, given her... corporeal challenges. I sense nothing ill-starred for your well-being in the near future." I nodded in her direction.

She returned the nod. "That is good to know. Thank you." Her bosom leaned toward me as she shifted in the seat. "It is unfortunate that I shall not see you again before I depart for the east. I have enjoyed meeting you." She winked the eye not pointing in my direction.

"The pleasure is mine, madam." I gave her the dignity of a bow.

As I exited the home, I thanked my lucky stars–or whatever providence provided me this life–that I did not turn out like this deformed, debauched, poet.

I walked to the Passazh and purchased some writing supplies to embark on the overwhelming undertaking of transcribing my chronicles. As I had the idea for the book here in St. Petersburg, I decided to begin with the current chapter of my life as it unfolded.

The penname Lazarus had stuck with me. I considered several other immortal characters, such as Ashvatthama from the *Mahabharata* (unfamiliar to most Europeans), Koschei from Russian folklore (a spell kept him from dying and he hid his soul in various objects for protection, which I did not), the Arthurian Legend's Merlin (I have not performed magic, as far as I know), Shakespeare's Oberon (but I couldn't see myself as the Færie King), and Struldbrug from Swift's *Gulliver's Travels* (which did not sound very friendly or healer-like). I preferred the resonance and biblical allusion of Lazarus.

I commenced with my arrival in this capricious city and set out to narrate my days attempting to establish myself. It had not occurred to me how difficult the task of putting together words could be. With a little patience and effort, I might make some progress. After a few sentences, my admiration for successful authors multiplied. However, I would not want to blame my egg basket for poor presentation, as a second-rate ballet dancer might.

Dima brought me the day's post. One piece looked like an invitation from Madame von Meck, and the other a letter from Grigori's mother. I took the opportunity to shirk my own scribing and read her missive.

> "Mr. Propok, I have not heard anything from you, and I am writing to inquire into my son's progress. Can you please provide me with details of his apprenticeship?"

Sometimes the easiest questions require the most difficult answers. I could have mentioned that her son had a thick malevolent streak, that he seemed to take pleasure in the misfortunes of others, and that he behaved more like a political anarchist than a ten-year-old schoolchild.

Grigori's mother had left him with me on the pretense of apprenticeship. At first, I had wondered if her mission more resembled abandonment. She might have had difficulties raising such a boy on her own in Siberia, but she wouldn't have made the long trip to Peter if she could have just as easily found him a placement closer to home. Or, perhaps, she might have wanted him as far away as possible with little hope of him ever finding his way back.

Despite some measurable progress, he still displayed flashes of his unpredictable nature from time to time. My inability to sense his thoughts filled me with both frustration and fascination.

I took one of my new, blank pieces of stationery and responded to Anna Vasilyevna, explaining how her son attended gymnasium each morning and assisted the music master in the afternoon. I hoped she would find satisfaction with that. As far as apprenticeship, I had to adopt a more diplomatic narrative. While I could not tell her the whole truth, I could demonstrate several instances along those lines. He did attend at least one of my clients with me.

This might have been a good opportunity for me to ask the mother to retrieve her son, leaving me to my life as it had been before. I could have pled how his being farther from her sight made him closer to her heart. However, a feeling nagged at me that I still had more to learn from him, despite having given up hope that *I* could ever teach *him* anything. Rimsky-Korsakov had captured the boy's interests, which I welcomed. He seemed eager to attend the master's bidding every day. If only I could have gained Grigori's veneration as well.

Madame Nadezhda von Meck's envelope included an invitation to the unveiling of a portrait by Ilya Repin memorializing the recently departed composer, Mussorgsky. She frequently held public events in her home due to fears of going outside. All of St. Petersburg's finest would attend because she commanded the attention of the city's upper crust with the opulence she afforded from her dead husband's profitable railroad investments.

By then, Catherine Dolgorukov should have wedded the Tsar and would, most likely, want to make an appearance as Tsaritsa. Nadya liked nothing more than to play hostess to royalty and rub her bony elbows with dignitaries.

After dispatching the post, I decided to spend more time reading on my own. The futile attempts I had made at writing exhausted my mind.

In *Anna Karenina*, I began to realize Tolstoy had painted the female companions as stifling, smothering lovers. It made me wonder if that was how he saw women. I have known several who wished to put me on a lead and keep me close, but, for good or ill, I am not drawn to such liaisons.

When Grigori returned from his time at the Conservatory, he joined me in my study, and I mentioned the invitation from Madame von Meck.

"Oh, yes, I know all about that," he responded. "Are we attending?"

The boy seemed very well informed. "How did you find out about the event?"

"Madame von Meck's young fellow—the piano player, Claude—told me. He attends the music school and says he wants to teach me to play."

I suppose I should not be surprised regarding Grigori's advanced knowledge of the presentation. It appeared he made good use of his time at the Conservatory. "Are you interested in learning?"

He nestled his chin between the thumb and first finger of his left hand. "I am not sure I would want to spend that much time mastering an instrument you cannot carry about with you."

So practical for one so young. "Is Master Korsakov providing enough tasks to keep you busy?"

"Oh, yes." He brandished his puckish smile. "I work hard and have learned much from him."

A twinge of what I can only describe as jealousy caused me to shiver. "More than what *I* have taught you?"

He cocked his head. "It is different. From you I learn by observing. From him I learn by direct instruction and doing."

Several days after he first arrived, I no longer wanted the boy around and felt relieved when Korsakov took him on. Hearing his delight with the other man's guidance produced a disheartening emotional response I had not anticipated. I picked up the correspondence from my desk. "A letter from your mother arrived today requesting information on how well you are doing."

His head moved up and down four times. "Is she in good health?"

"She gave no indication otherwise. Her concern centered on how you have been treating me and whether you have been able to pay for your upkeep."

Grigori's eyes expanded. "I hope you are not planning to tell her about that business at breakfast the first morning when I served you that tainted tea."

"No, I do not believe she needs to read that. However, I do plan to mention what happened to the meat pie vendor outside Summer Garden."

"You *what*?!"

Even though I had not thought about including that information, I pretended I had to see how Grigori would react. I received my answer.

However, I could not help but smirk. "Of course, not. I just said that to see how you would respond."

"That was not funny!" He stamped.

"No. No. How silly of me." I attempted to suppress the grin but had no success. "And how are your studies at the gymnasium progressing?"

He threw his head back. "Ugh! Repetition, repetition, repetition, repetition. The mother of all learning. It makes no sense to me. They lecture the same things over and over and over again. And then they ask us to repeat it back *ad nauseum*." His head rotated side to side. "Once you have told me something, I know it forever."

"But not everyone is as quick as you, Grigori."

The boy tapped his left palm with his right index finger. "Learning by rote may work for others, but it infuriates me."

"You know one cannot pull a fish from the pond without any effort."

The barest hint of a smile appeared on Grigori's face. "I thought you did not eat fish."

"That is true." I nodded. "Neither fish nor meat. It is an old aphorism."

"Speaking of food, would you want me to invite Dr. Yuri to dine with us?" the boy asked with a leer. "I believe he fancies you."

Again, another male he regarded above me. I had not realized how much I valued Grigori's attention. I made sure I took a full breath and exhaled before responding. "You need not concern yourself with my interpersonal affairs. I believe if the good doctor wished to dine with us, he would have already made his intentions known. He is a friend—a good friend, indeed—but no —"

A loud knocking at the door interrupted my speech.

"Dʀ. Yuri to see you, sir," Dima announced.

As Grigori had observed, the neighbor did seem to show up at dinner time.

"Please, show him in. Thank you," came my response. "What could he want?" I mused.

"Cabbage rolls," Grigori suggested.

My eyebrows raised at his implication. "You could be right."

Yuri strode into my den as if it were his own, at a swift pace and leaning slightly forward. Perhaps our apartments had similar layouts.

"Doctor," I addressed him.

"Please… I have asked you to call me Yuri."

"Of course. Do come in." I indicated a chair.

He crossed his arms. "I prefer to stand, thank you. I don't believe I shall take up much of your valuable time."

It is possible he did not come in search of Dima's flavorsome food after all. "How can we be of service?"

"Mmmmmmmm." He hummed and nodded. "I take it you also received the invitation from Nadya von Meck for her art display."

I turned and picked up the envelope. "As a matter of fact, yes, I did."

"Are you planning to attend?"

Grigori gazed toward me with one eye opened a bit wider.

"Yes. I believe we are."

The boy moved his head up and down in agreement.

"Ah. Good. I wanted to ask if you would like to go together."

"*Go together?* I'm not sure what you mean. Are you suggesting we … like a couple?" My head cocked. "Are you proposing to *court* me, Yuri?"

"No. *No!*" His hands waved before him. "I believe I have muddled my meaning. What I meant to ask is: How do you plan to travel there?"

For some reason, seeing him flustered amused me. "I usually take the *konka*. Why?"

"Well." The doctor pulled at the hem of his jacket. "I plan to hire a *droski* for the evening. As it is supposed to be an elegant event, I figured we should arrive in style." He brought his hands together in front of his chest. "Would you care to join me?"

I turned to Grigori. "My apprentice is planning to attend as well. Will there be sufficient room for him?"

"Oh, dear. It is a carriage for two"–he scratched at his chin–"but I imagine he could sit with the driver, if that is permitted."

The boy volunteered, "I could just as easily walk."

"That would not be necessary," the doctor asserted.

"I shall walk." Grigori raised his chin a bit. "You two ride."

My eyes shifted toward the boy without moving my head.

"Please, Grigori. Do not make this more difficult than it needs to be. If the good doctor wishes to transport us to the event in his hired coach, we will honor his invitation."

The boy pursed his lips and glowered.

"And won't it be fun to sit up behind the draw horse?" I posed with a smile, encouraging him to join us.

Grigori trained his eyes on me. "If you fancy that so much, why don't *you* sit there?"

Hearing the unkind words of my apprentice, my heart paused. It resumed a beat later, slightly bruised.

"I did not mean to bring conflict into your home, Rodion." Yuri offered, "My apologies."

"No apology needed, my friend. At times, the boy speaks his mind without concern to how others might feel."

The doctor nodded. "I see. I have not been in the company of young people for quite a while, and I am not accustomed to their particular behaviors." He swallowed. "Mmmmm. By the way, what do you make of Madame von Meck?"

The question caught me on the hop. "How do you mean?"

"Well… I attend her as a physician, and there is nothing wrong with her, theoretically… physically. You see her as a healer, and I suspect she has some spiritual wounds that want tending."

"I prefer not to discuss the intimate details of my clients' lives. Should anything I say ever get back to her, my career is ruined!" I jabbed a finger skyward. It surprised me that the doctor did not have familiarity with Madame von Meck's fear of leaving her home.

"But you can trust *me*, Rodion." He touched his chest with the fingers of one hand. "I'm a doctor."

I looked to Grigori. He lowered his eyes.

"Dear neighbor"–I coughed into a fist–"I shall be pleased to attend Madame von Meck's affair with you, but I cannot disclose her private, personal matters. I hope you understand."

"Yes. Perhaps I should not have asked such a question. How unprofessional of me."

What an unusual concept. Yuri, as a doctor, spent years in schools learning his craft. I, on the other hand, conjured up my skills from life experiences and a special gift from the universe. If anyone here could be labeled "unprofessional," it would be me.

When I glanced at Grigori, he stood looking up at the doctor, smiling. A green fire ignited in my chest. The boy should be venerating *me*, the honest one who continues to pay for his upkeep, not the gossiping neighbor who saved his life.

My burning eyes faced the boy, and I pointed at our neighbor. "You indulge this *trouble-maker*, and *you* are just as bad!" Once I heard the time-worn saying depart my lips, I gasped and covered my mouth with both hands. How unfortunate spoken words cannot be little birds one can recapture once set free.

When I glanced at my neighbor, his rumpled eyebrows expressed the pain I had caused with my callous remark. I could only hope my sentiment-soaked brain would figure out how to undo any potential damage.

In all my years, I could not remember an incident where I allowed my passion to burst forth so unreservedly. Not getting involved in interpersonal relationships had relieved me of such emotional entanglements. Perhaps the recent change in my ability to perceive others sparked this bewildering outburst. No longer did I suffer the stray thoughts of those around me unless I made physical contact. This newfound aggression might have been the unsolicited replacement for my loss of sensitivity.

"Perhaps I should see myself out," the wounded doctor suggested, his reddening eyes dampened, tantamount to tears. Nobody moved. "Well, good night, then." He turned to leave.

Grigori tugged at my sleeve. My mind reopened. "Oh, would you… like to… stay and… dine with us? I'm not sure what Dima has prepared, but he always makes extra."

Yuri pointed toward the kitchen. "I believe I caught a whiff of those delicious cabbage rolls, like the ones he prepared last week."

The boy's face pulled a smirk. "Cabbage rolls," he whispered in my direction.

"Please. Stay. Make yourself at home," I invited.

Our neighbor faced me and grinned. "*Your* home is the best place." He stepped to me and took my hand. A quick glimpse of his days ahead revealed no reason to be suspicious. However, the doctor's forward action, again, caught me by surprise. I pulled away from him.

He blurted, "I didn't mean to —"

I interrupted, feeling red in the face. "Of course not. I did not mean to either."

"Would you still like to accompany me to Madame von Meck's?" His eyes searched my face.

"Of course, my friend. Of course."

"Mmmmmm. Shall I call for you an hour before the event?" Yuri murmured.

"Yes, that seems proper." I figured it best to agree to his request. For now. "Quite proper, indeed."

The three of us walked to the dining room. Yuri led the way.

FOR the next few days, life fell into a predictable rhythm. Grigori attended gymnasium each morning and assisted Korsakov at the Conservatory in the afternoons. Several evenings, Dr. Yuri dined with us. We avoided discussing the spiritual health of our clients.

While I did not find our neighbor particularly physically attractive, over time, I began to realize he possessed many qualities that would make him a good husband. Level-headed and confident, learned and successful at his craft, he could have been a fine catch for any Russian woman seeking to rise in social status. However, he demonstrated more of an attraction for other men. And me, in particular.

Flattering as it might have been, my life circumstances dictated I remain free from intimate relationships. Desiring only friendship with him and nothing more, these shared meals gave us the chance to learn more about each other.

My emotional flare-up did not recur. Grigori's actions could rile me, and I resisted the urge to react in the hot moment and considered several interpretations of his actions before deciding upon the least offensive one.

As much as I would have liked to just ignore the boy and hope he decided to take up lodgings elsewhere, I continued to feel a responsibility to his mother. She deposited him with me and took the time to write a letter inquiring into his condition. I agreed to take responsibility for him, and he must stay with me. For the time being.

One thing occurred to me I had not considered before. At first, I imagined Grigori had some conscious power over other people. It might be possible that he did not, and just being close to him caused unpredictable behavior modifications with no deliberate effort. Almost the opposite of my sensing ability. This would be something to observe. At least I knew from the meat pie incident he could be controlled best when hungry.

During some free time, I made several attempts at capturing my St. Petersburg life in words. There must have been more than a dozen leaves of paper I tore up in frustration with my amateurish writing. When I scrawled the pen across the page, the phrases resounded like the lyrical peal of a church bell in my mind. However, upon reading what I had written aloud, my self-assessment brought me to exasperation more often than elation.

By Thursday, I had filled several sheets not destined for the dust bin. I rolled and bound them, tucking the scroll into my jacket before racing to meet the *konka* toward Liteyny Street. Madame Panaeva's housemaid ushered me into the library, where several gentlemen sat sipping beverages, poking fingers into the air, and conversing.

"Vodka or kvass?" the woman asked me.

"Kvass, please," I responded. "Thank you."

"No need to be so polite to the servants, young man," one of the older fellows chided me through a bush of white hair surrounding his mouth. It never ceased to amuse me when people referred to me as 'young man.'

"Oh, Vanya, quiet down or you'll scare off our guest," admonished one of the others, whose graying beard reached halfway down his chest.

Our hostess breezed into the room, and the menfolk rose in greeting. "Pardon the delay, gentlemen, one of the grandchildren seems to think he belongs here with us." She reached behind a writing desk and pulled the hand of a young boy. "Come on, little one. You may join our group when you've penned your first novel." From the doorway she directed, "Rodya, introduce yourself while I return the child to his rightful place."

The maid handed me a glass as the other guests returned to their seats. "Your kvass, sir."

"Thank you," I said as I took the crystal goblet.

"He is so polite," the fellow with a drooping moustache and oval eyeglasses proclaimed.

"Gentlemen, to our hostess." I raised my glass in toast, and we all drank. "My name is Rodion Propok, and I am healer to Madame Panaeva. At our last visit, I mentioned I am considering writing about my time in St. Petersburg, and she invited me to your salon." I looked at each of these men, whom I assumed were famous authors, and wiped a moistening palm on my trousers. "I can only aspire to rise to your level of art as I have but barely begun."

"If you enjoy riding a sled, you must be willing to drag it back up the hill as well," quoted a fellow with a trimmed white beard and far-reaching forehead. "And do you believe you are prepared to commit to the hard work we have undertaken and, perhaps, someday, become a writer worthy of our station?" He set his glass on a table and began touching the fingertips of his hands together in order.

"Yes! I mean, no. *No*, of course not. You are all accomplished in your field, and I... well..."

Madame Panaeva returned, relieving my anxieties of drowning in this lake of literary luminaries. "Have you made your introductions, Rodya?"

I took a breath to calm myself. "Just, madam."

"Ah, good." She waved a hand about as she indicated, "That is Ivan Alexandrovich, Nikolai Gavrilovich, Ivan Sergeyevich, and Lev Nikolayevich."

"Tolstoy..." I mumbled to myself with eyes agog.

"Yes?" the fellow with the long beard asked.

"Oh, nothing. Nothing. I have read several of your books and am currently working on *Anna Karenina*."

"It is good that you are, sir. I worked on her for far too many years and am *finished*." He wiped his palms as if ridding himself of the title character. The others chuckled.

In an attempt to impress him, I decried, "I have the complete version, which I purchased directly from Suvorin."

"Ah, then you will be with her for quite a while longer, I suspect." He laughed at his own judgment. "Have you read any of Turgenev's labors?" Tolstoy's eyes shifted toward the fellow with the bushy white beard.

Like Tolstoy, he had written a novel with an overly complicated plot and a plethora of interconnected characters. "Oh, yes. I enjoyed *Fathers and Sons* immensely, and your *Virgin Soil* is a populist manifesto."

"Finally!" Turgenev turned his head and smiled. "Someone with good taste has joined our little group."

"I, for one, did not particularly enjoy the taste of your latest work, my dear Vanya." Tolstoy announced with a snicker. "I found the dry pages lacked sufficient moisture for a good palate." He smacked his lips.

"You weren't supposed to eat it..." cautioned Turgenev as he patted his friend's protruding abdomen.

"And do I understand correctly, Levushka, that *you* have a bit of your work-in-progress to share with us?" our hostess hinted.

"More, Lev?" teased the fellow with the receding hairline. "Haven't you given us plenty enough already?"

"Do hush, Goncharov." Madame Panaeva reproached. "*You* haven't published anything in ten years! When will you do us the honor of a *new* work?"

"I would have submitted material long before, but some people"–he turned a jaded eye at Turgenev–"have found it profitable to steal my words and put them into their own mouths!"

"That I would consider your inept writings worthy of plagiarism is pure folly, old man,"

Goncharov glared at his tormentor. "Ivan Sergeyevich, you managed to scare off Dostoevsky, but you will not bully *me* from this circle!" He emptied his glass and slammed it down.

"Gentlemen, please," cooed our hostess. "We are here to celebrate words, not cross them like swords." She looked at the two hot-tempered authors in turn. "Should you both want to continue your argument, please take it out onto the street, should anyone notice or care!" Her finger pointed the way.

The fellow with the eyeglasses spoke, "Lev Nikolayevich, you have written so many, many… many words. What is there left for you to say?"

"Oh, Chernyshevsky." Tolstoy inhaled loud enough for all to hear. "Lately I've been wrestling with the purpose of life." He groaned. "Someone once told me, you can never understand its meaning, so do not think about it, just live. I can no longer do that. I have already done it for so long now that I cannot help but see day and night going round and bringing me closer to death. That alone is true. All else is false." His eyes turned to each of us.

Tolstoy had been graced with over sixty years to observe human behavior. The purpose of life has been a concept I have struggled to understand for centuries.

"But, Tolstoy, you are the youngest of us assembled here." Goncharov bleated and turned to me. "With the exception of this fellow. What is all this talk about living for so long and being brought to your death?"

I chuckled to myself regarding ages. While I might have appeared younger, the truth would have to remain concealed with me.

"Yes, Levushka," Madame Panaeva articulated, "it is far too early for you to be designing your own sunset."

"I have written of war, peace, country, politics, positions, poverty, charity, religion, and faith." A loud sigh echoed. "I now choose to write about death."

None of us spoke while his gloomy words hovered in the heavy atmosphere.

"Death must surely come to us all in turn," Turgenev broke the gloomy silence. "But it seems to those of us–some of whom are at least ten years your senior–that time is quite far off."

Tolstoy nodded. "I believe you misunderstood, my friends. I am not planning to write about *my* death, but, rather, the process that we all must face at some point, determining whether our lives have been authentic or artificial."

"I, myself, have been wrestling with those concepts of late." We all turned to face Goncharov. "After all, I am the oldest one here."

Our hostess beamed at Tolstoy. "Perhaps we should ask our dear companion to recite from his new work, and then we can provide some appreciation and critique."

"Yes, of course, *Levushka*, do recite for us," Turgenev taunted.

"I shall read, despite your goading, *Van'ka*." Tolstoy reached inside his coat pocket and produced a folded sheet. Upon unwrapping and rotating it to the correct orientation, he delivered his words.

> In the great Law Courts building, during a recess, members of the court met in Ivan Yegorovich Shebek's office, and the conversation turned to the famous Krasov case.
>
> Fyodor Vasilyevich argued passionately it was beyond their jurisdiction, Ivan Yegorovich stood his conflicting ground, while Pyotr Ivanovich, who did not take part in the argument, perused the just delivered Gazette.
>
> "Gentlemen!" he said, "Ivan Ilyich has died."
>
> "Really?"
>
> "Here, read it," he told Fyodor Vasilyevich, handing him the newspaper.

None of us said anything, as I, for one, expected more words from the great author. Honestly, I had hoped for a few literary gems, but he provided mere grist.

After a minute or so of silence, Goncharov asked, "And what is to be the title of this new book?"

"*Ivan Ilyich has died*. Pyotr Ivanovich, himself, articulates it when he reads the headline."

"Hmmmmmm," Chernyshevsky hummed. "Do you not think it would have more vigor if you changed it to *The Death of Ivan Ilyich*? That way the subject is the death and not Mr. Ilyich, whoever he might have been."

"I see your point, Nikolai. I shall consider that suggestion."

"Personally, I had hoped for more than a few sentences from you, Lev," Turgenev stated. "Given what you have shared with us, I have several comments."

Tolstoy wiggled a few fingers. "Please, proceed."

"First off, it's no 'All happy families are alike.' The first sentence here does not draw us into the story adequately. Who cares about a court recess? I would have liked more information about what leads to this discussion and its significance." He threw his hands up. "What trial is it? And for that matter, was it just the court or had others joined the conversation? I wanted more. Much more to fire up my interest."

Tolstoy pulled a pencil from his pocket and scribbled on the paper.

Madame Panaeva sat up tall. "You used the word, 'passionately,' to describe the action of Fyodor Vasilyevich. Would it not be preferable to depict his behavior frankly rather than deprive us with a parsimonious adverb?"

"Was this Ilyich a tall man or a short one?" Chernyshevsky asked. "Bald? Clean-shaven? I want more details so that I can picture your characters in my mind."

"And my senses were not at all activated from this excerpt. No sounds nor smells, nothing to excite the reader's feelings," Goncharov added.

"May I give it another go?" Tolstoy looked at Madame Panaeva, who nodded. He wrote a bit more, cleared his throat, and examined the paper for a few seconds before reading:

> In the great Law Courts building, during a recess in the proceedings of the Melvinsky trial, members of the court met with the prosecutor in Ivan Yegorovich Shebek's office, and the conversation turned to the famous Krasov case.
>
> Fyodor Vasilyevich, hot with excitement, argued it was beyond their jurisdiction, Ivan Yegorovich stood his conflicting ground, while Pyotr Ivanovich, who did not take part in the argument, perused the just delivered *Gazette*.
>
> "Gentlemen!" he said, "Ivan Ilyich has died."
>
> "Really?"
>
> "Here, read it," he told Fyodor Vasilyevich, handing him the newspaper, still warm and smelling of printer's ink.

"Much better," Turgenev appraised. "But I still miss the biting opening of your *Anna*."

"I like the feel and smell of the *Gazette. We* never receive it in that condition," Goncharov said with a scowl.

"Yes, I concur with our other authors," the hostess articulated. "Much better. I await the continuation with anticipation." She turned to me. "Mr. Propok, have you prepared something for us to consider?"

"I have, but I am hesitant to recite before such remarkable authors."

"Nonsense!" barked Turgenev. "We are equals here. In a fist, all fingers are the same."

"And you don't really get to know someone until you've eaten a pound of salt together," Goncharov weighed in.

"Rodya," Madame Panaeva purred, "our little group has survived because we have developed a level of trust and honesty amongst ourselves. We understand this is your initial effort, and everyone knows the first pancake is never perfect."

Heads around the room nodded in agreement.

My sweaty palms managed to produce even more moisture. I could not remember being as nervous. "If you insist, madam." She winked at me. Better her than that depraved poet, Yulia Zhadovskaya. "It took many attempts before arriving at this opening passage."

"What is your book about, young fellow?" Tolstoy inquired. Just his asking me a question caused my heart to flutter.

"I… uh… want to tell people about my time in this wonderful city," I managed to squeak.

Turgenev raised one eyebrow. Chernyshevsky pursed his lips. My chest constricted.

"Do go on," our hostess prompted.

"Th… Thank you, Madame Panaeva for this… most incredible opportunity." I gave each of the others one last look before reading. All those eyes upon me spurred my anxieties, but I took a deep breath and began.

> St. Petersburg defies the reproach of its critics and detractors as a precariously improbable city that should never have been. Built upon the bones of laborers ordered to drain and fill the swamplands—and perched on the brink of inevitable disasters, either natural or human-caused—it fell and rose time after time. Floods, fires, and violent uprisings periodically devastated the well-ordered streets, crisp stone buildings, and

majestic metal monuments, but like Sisyphus or the Phoenix,
St. Petersburg persists.

At first, no one spoke. It felt as if time had paused. When I looked to each of the group members, they turned their heads away.

After thirty seconds or so, Madame Panaeva opened the discussion, "For a first-time author, I must say you have a very good grasp of writing."

My anxiety gave way to a flat smile. "If anything, I feel I should give credit to each of you, as I have read and studied your works. They have inspired me."

"Gentlemen," our hostess spoke, "I believe he has given you some very good praise."

"But would anyone really understand all those mythical references?" asked Goncharov.

"Too many unnecessary words," Chernyshevsky suggested. "For what you have to say, you could have accomplished your goal with about half as many."

Turgenev raised a finger, "And is your book to be about *you* or the city? From what you have read, one might mistake this for a travel guide. If you want to draw people into your story right off, begin with action—straightaway—with conflict and mystery. *That* is what pulls the reader in."

"I think you have sculpted a lovely preamble for your work." Tolstoy's grin parted his wispy beard. "Pray, continue your efforts."

"Perhaps you make a better healer than author. I, for one, suggest you follow your normal path and leave the writing to us." Turgenev indicated the assembled guests.

His brusqueness could have been what drove Dostoevsky from the ensemble. I should have paid more attention to Turgenev's writing style before committing my words to paper.

"Are you seeking his talents as healer, Vanya?" countered our hostess. "My friend Yulen'ka speaks very highly of him."

"Yes, well." I glanced at our hostess. "She and I don't exactly see eye-to-eye."

"Very few people do," Turgenev stated as he aimed two fingers in different directions.

"If you come so highly regarded, I should like to engage you, young man." He continued, "I am getting on in my years, but not as far as some of the others." His eyes settled on my face. "What do you make of *me?*"

I coughed into a closed fist before responding. "While I welcome your patronage, sir, I would prefer to consult with you in private. This setting is not conducive to proper healer practice."

"Of course." Turgenev extended a hand, and I took it, revealing the author's weeks ahead.

While most of his time to come involved writing, toward the end of the period, I sensed some unexpected bad news from his regular physician. The prognosis would reveal a long, slow decline.

With his free hand, he withdrew a calling card from his vest. "Here, you can attend me next week." As I reached out, he pulled it back a few centimeters. "Are Wednesdays good for you?"

22

"W HAT are White Nights?" Grigori asked, interrupting my reading. Levin and Kitty had traveled to Moscow in anticipation of Kitty giving birth. Stiva invited Levin to a club for gentlemen, where they encountered Vronsky. The count requested they visit Anna, who had taken in an orphaned girl from England. Complications upon complications upon complications.

"Where did you hear about White Nights?" I asked.

The boy scratched his head before responding, as if that would generate the proper answer. "Professor Rimsky-Korsakov mentioned he would be going this evening."

Grigori had come from the provinces, where this phenomenon did not take place. "In the summertime, sunset does not occur until late. To celebrate, the people of St. Petersburg socialize in the streets, mostly near the harbor. Ships with colorful sails float around. Sometimes there are fireworks." I could not read his blank expression. "Are you curious? Did you want to see it?"

He blinked a few times. "It sounds interesting."

In the past, I shied away from such gatherings, as the thoughts of thousands of people overwhelmed my mind. This time, I might be able to pass through the throngs without sensory overload. "Instead of eating dinner at home, we could find food vendors along the street."

"Meat pies…" He wiped a dribble of drool from his lips.

"I will inform Dima." After depositing *Anna Karenina* on the side table, I strode to the kitchen. "The young master and I shall be attending the White Night celebrations this evening. There is no need to prepare food for us."

"Whatever will the doctor do…?" he mumbled with a shift of his eyes away from me.

"Sorry. What was that?"

"Nothing, sir. Nothing. I trust you and the boy will enjoy yourselves."

"Would you care to join us?" Most of the time, people do not ask their house staff along, but I felt rather giddy about the event.

"Not this evening, sir. My days of White Nights are far behind me."

"As you will. I hope whatever you had been planning to prepare can keep for another day."

"I had not even begun to start the evening meal." The manservant displayed a tiny grin. "You have perfect timing, sir."

"Well, then, we shall see you on the morrow. Enjoy your time."

A knock at the door resounded through the rooms.

"Shall I get that, sir?"

"No, Dima. I can go."

Yuri stood in the hall wearing a long coat, not his usual mealtime attire. "Doctor?"

"Rodya. I am calling to let you know I shall not be dining with you this evening as I wish to attend the White Night festivities."

I looked over my shoulder to where Grigori should have been. "What a coincidence! The boy and I had just made our decision to go as well. Shall we travel together?"

Yuri glanced down and shuffled one foot before addressing me. "Yes… yes! The three of us can walk to the harbor, but I have… some business later in the evening."

It seemed odd that a doctor would have business to conduct on a White Night, but, perhaps, Yuri's unease indicated a potential personal encounter. I could have settled my curiosity with one touch but decided to leave my friend his privacy.

The three of us made our way down the stairs and into Nevsky Prospekt. As expected, throngs filled the street. I could hear folks singing "*Kalinka*" and "*Roumka Vodki na Stole*" in multiple keys and different tempi.

Café patrons spilled out onto the sidewalks. People, mostly in couples, strolled about. The pale orange rays of waning sunlight bathed the scene in a creamy sorbet, reminding me of those French Impressionist paintings, billowy and out-of-focus.

As we neared the *Passazh*, Yuri glanced around, as if searching for someone or something. I noticed a preponderance of younger men about. Some of them followed our movements with stares, smiles, or nods. I had heard tales of the shopping area after store hours developing into a meeting place for those of a particular passion.

Grigori looked up at me, the doctor, then back to me again. I waggled my head at the implication.

When we reached the harbor, ships with assorted solid, brightly colored sails drifted along. The water rippled, sending brackish sprays onto the walkway.

"It looks like a rainbow!" Grigori shouted, pointing at the little armada.

Rockets exploded along the shoreline, shooting fireworks into the evening sky. The three of us paused our progress to watch the dazzling display.

A wedding party scurried by. People shouted, "*Gorko!*" at the bride and groom as they passed. From various balconies, operatic arias burst forth into the evening air, seemingly oblivious to the other performances.

Grigori found a meat pie vendor and purchased his dinner. Nearby, I bought a potato on a stick. Yuri opted for a bowl of something I could not determine. At another cart, I got us each a glass of kvass.

Once he had consumed his meat pie and drank the kvass, Grigori proclaimed, "I am tired. Please continue without me. I appreciate you sharing this with me." He turned and walked back toward our building. Perhaps he worked harder than I assumed.

"Are you going to let the boy travel on his own? There are thieves and all sorts of rogues about," Yuri cautioned.

A smile spread across my face before I could even begin speaking. "I understand your concerns, my dear doctor. My experience with him has demonstrated he is quite capable of handling himself." We finished our food and drink. I indicated the pathway. "Shall we continue?"

The sun's disc touched the distant horizon, and the glow of another White Night began to fade. Drawn-out shadows inundated the street in an eerie chiaroscuro of dark and dusk.

"Rodion…" Yuri stopped and turned to me. "I am planning to visit Znamensky's. Would you wish to accompany me?" His eyes blinked a few times, as if hesitant.

"I am not familiar with that location." Its name evoked the club in Moscow Count Vronsky and his friends attended. "Is it an establishment for gentlemen?"

The doctor's eyebrows rose up his forehead. "You might say that." Beads of sweat glistened in the fading light.

"Is it nearby?"

"No, unfortunately. We would need to cross the Fontanka." His breathing deepened. "It's in the Rozhdestvensky district."

"Yes. That is a bit far for me, I'm afraid. As you pointed out, I should not leave Grigori alone for too long. Well." My hand took his, and I saw a flash of the hours ahead. He intended to visit a Turkish bath. I tried not to change my expression, as it would have been improper to judge him for his choices. My mouth articulated the only thing I could think of saying, "I hope you enjoy the rest of your evening."

He strolled off, I presumed in search of a tram. Perhaps taking care of his burning physical needs would lessen his attention to me.

As I walked back to our building, revelers warbled their bibulous and inharmonious songs out-of-tune. The smell of stale vodka permeated the nearly empty street.

After crossing to our home block, my nose hit the walk before me, and several hands held me down. When I attempted to move, the grips tightened.

"Give us your money, *znakhar*! None of your tricks," a voice hissed in my ear.

I didn't know if I was more upset about being mislabeled—once more—a *znakhar* or momentarily losing sight of my surroundings. If I still had the ability to sense those around me, this would not have happened.

"Gentlemen," I struggled to say, the side of my face forced onto the ground, "you must have mistaken me for another. I have little money. Just a few ruble coins, and you are welcome to them if you release me."

"We know who you are, Propok." Whoever held my head with gloved hands pressed down harder. "If we let you up, you will use your witch's powers to deprive us of your money."

Thieves are not known for their logic skills. "If I possess these 'witch's powers' you have ascribed to me"—my lips scraped on the ground as I attempted to speak—"could I not use them to release myself?"

"Remain silent! Your words are —"

Screams of pain rang out, and my captors sprang up and ran off. One of them shouted, "Your little crawfish has quite a mighty bite!"

When I rose to a sitting position, Grigori stood over me, reaching down a hand.

I stood on my own, brushed the dirt from my clothes, and wiped at my face. "Thank you. How did you know —?"

"I waited outside our building for you and saw what happened. You are welcome." He turned and walked toward the main entrance.

The little monster somehow effected my release, and for that I felt grateful. Perhaps he saw me as his own shirt and worthy of protection. However, I feared he might use this rescue episode in future attempts to exert influence over me.

My face felt wet, and I touched my cheek. Blood.

As they say, trouble has come, open the gate.

SLEEP eluded me. By the time my regular rising hour arrived, I couldn't remember shutting my eyes. The fear of further physical assault and theft of my money haunted me. Perspiration and heart pounding kept me awake.

The unforeseen attack from the previous evening troubled me worse than if the hoodlums had caused serious bodily injuries. Never before had someone surprised me like that. And this time, they knew my name!

If someone were out to get me, I wondered how far they would be willing to go. Also, I had no idea what the leader of this group might be after. I tried to keep a low profile, but somehow, my existence interested someone disreputable.

My ability to sense people had always alerted me so that I could prepare. This recent reduction in awareness of people around me had begun to demonstrate its downsides. The forays into public engagements of late without the onslaught of others' futures delighted me. Due to the crowds, I could have never attended the White Night celebration before. If given the option to restore my previous power, I don't know how I would choose.

Even though I have remained physically indestructible throughout my years, the surprise of this attack rattled my nerves. I wanted to retreat to my den with *Anna Karenina*, locking the door to stay secluded and safe the rest of the day. I needed to isolate myself until I could regain my previous composure.

By the time I went for my morning tea, Grigori had left for the day. We said nothing to each other since the unfortunate event. Because the assailants withdrew once my "apprentice" appeared, I wondered what part the boy might have played in the assault.

Dima did not speak to me, and I returned the favor. Thankfully, I had only two appointments and dispatched posts to cancel them.

Tolstoy distracted me for the remainder of the day. The drunken Levin, although married to a very pregnant Kitty, continued to pursue Anna. He asked Mr. Karinen to divorce her, but the husband refused, based on something mumbled in French by a clairvoyant in a dream-like trance. Vronsky ended the affair with Anna after a heated fight. Thinking back to her arrival in St. Petersburg, when an oncoming car crushed a railway worker, she went back to the station and propelled herself in front of a moving train's wheels.

That helped give me some perspective. No matter how tragic or overwhelming my life felt, Anna made things much worse for herself.

When Yuri did not appear at dinnertime, I poked my head out the door and surveyed the hall. Seeing no one else, I leapt over to my neighbor's door and knocked.

"Rodion," the doctor observed in a monotone.

"Yuri," I whispered, as if initiating a secret rite. "I desire your counsel." My head swiveled in both directions to check the emptiness of the hall again.

"Ah. Do come in." He opened the door, and I scurried into his apartment. The layout looked exactly like mine. However, the furnishings appeared more opulent than my meager pieces. I had wooden chairs; he had upholstered ones. Where I had plain wooden paneling, he had flock wallpaper and artwork. A fancy highboy occupied a corner that in my rooms sat empty. The crushed velvet divan looked like something on loan from a French bordello. "Please sit down." He indicated one of the overstuffed, leather, high-back chairs.

"I am so sorry to bother you, but I had hoped you might have joined us for dinner."

He pulled a set of keys from a coat pocket and dropped them on the Chippendale desk. "Yes. Well, my office hours ran later than I expected."

"And we did not get home until very late last night," I grumbled as I sat.

His eyes opened wide.

"Oh!" popped from my mouth. "I did not mean to impugn *you*, sir. My thoughts went to an incident that occurred right on our very street. A gang of ruffians tackled me and attempted a robbery!"

He took the chair opposite me. "My dear! Were you injured?"

"No, the young master came to my rescue, and the thieves scampered off before anything untoward happened. However, one of them said to me, 'We know who you are, Propok!' and that worries me they may try again or attempt to break into my home." I looked directly at him. "I have come to discuss matters of personal safety."

Yuri's head tilted to one side. "Yes?"

"You have lived in Peter much longer than I have." I glanced around the well-appointed room. "And you have financial comfort. Have you ever been attacked or robbed?"

He glanced down in thought. "Not that I can recall. My position as a doctor is fairly well known. Perhaps the profession—or my height—deters potential criminals."

"Are you not concerned that your… private affairs could attract the attention of others who might want to do you harm?"

His head shook a few times. "I'm not sure what you are endeavoring to ask, my friend."

"You know… your… your interest in men. Many people do not condone such behavior."

"I see." His brows knitted. "Are you such a person?"

"Not at all." I pointed a finger in the air. "As far as I am concerned, what you do with your time in private is your business and yours alone. Tastes should not be debated, you know."

"I am glad to hear. I was not sure where you stood on that matter."

"Do you feel safe in your apartment here?"

His questioning expression did not change. "I have never felt unsafe."

"I apologize. This whole episode has me very upset. I need to find a place where I can relax and not worry that someone might attack or rob me."

"Do you feel safe with me?"

"Yes, but I cannot have you or Grigori escort me everywhere."

"Then I might have a solution for you." Yuri displayed the hint of a smile. He cleared his throat. "If you recall, I attended a Turkish bath after we parted ways."

"Yes. You invited me to join you, but I declined. Do you feel safe inside that building?"

The doctor nodded a few times. "Are you asking me whether one can enjoy himself without fear of arrest?"

I waved my hands between us. "No, no, *no*! It's not *that* at all." My gaze fell to some of his collected porcelain statuettes on a shelf, most of them nearly naked men. "My body feels tight with tension. After the incident of last evening, I want to be somewhere I can feel secure and safe so that I might relax."

"Perhaps you could accompany me to Znamensky's and see for yourself."

"It seems I have avoided the wolf, but I don't wish to encounter the bear. My preference would be to spend some time in a cloistered space where I can feel sheltered and nameless. I have no interest in the specific activities within. Just safety from those who wish me harm."

He cocked his head. "Although I visited just last night, I suppose I could take advantage of its benefits again." His eyes narrowed. "However, your reaction to my previous invitation suggested a distaste for such places."

"Well, I know that in some villages, the bathhouse is the cleanest location in the town, and mothers go there to give birth."

"That is true. I, myself, was born in my little city's bath." The edges of his lips curled up. "But, aside from the 'specific activities' of which you implied, several of the attendants are quite skilled at massage and bathing. Very relaxing." His smile broadened. "In fact, I believe several appear as though they could be potential bodyguards."

"Massage…" I mumbled. "Attendants…" I had not considered any positive benefits to taking cover in a Turkish bath. It had been many years since I patronized such an establishment.

"Some of them are quite muscular but not very clever. Perhaps you could hire one of those fellows," Yuri suggested.

"When someone has physical strength, I don't believe they require intelligence." My chin rested in one hand as I considered the possibilities. Colleagues of the doctor's sort went there regularly, and I imagined it must have been quite secure. If they performed illegal acts inside its walls, and the business continued to prosper, either the police knew about it and some sort of arrangement kept them away, or the management understood how to keep unwanted folks out. I had not considered the advantages of engaging a personal bodyguard. "But is it not some distance from here?"

"The Nevsky *konka* will drop us off nearby."

I examined my sweaty palms and bolted from the chair. "When can we leave?"

"PLEASE, try to relax, Rodion," Yuri cooed.

My head kept rotating as I assessed each new passenger on the tram. Although I had never been in mortal danger, the surprise attack raised my level of vigilance. Everyone looked like a potential malefactor.

The doctor grasped my coat sleeve and I flinched. "I do not believe that grandmother will assault you."

"You never know. She could have hidden an awl in that sack."

He laughed. The sound of his amusement helped to diffuse my anxiety.

Our *konka* traversed the Anichkov Bridge, beautiful bronze horse statues guarding each of the four corners. We entered a part of St. Petersburg of which I had little knowledge. One block past Kalashnikovsky Prospekt, we alighted. I followed Yuri, swiveling about, looking for any sign of trouble.

He stopped at a bland, squarish building whose architect's motto must have been: Taste and color have no friends. One could pass by and not notice it. All the better for going into hiding.

Yuri guided me to an entrance not visible from the street. When he opened the door, the odors of pungent sour cabbage–prevalent in so many of St. Petersburg's older buildings–and musty Russian sweat greeted my nose. I felt like giving it a pinch but worried that might offend others.

An older, grizzled fellow greeted Yuri with open arms. "Again? So soon? You must enjoy this bathhouse very much, my dear friend!" He let loose a loud guffaw, peals reverberating from the walls dripping with condensation. His speech included the Old Church *yat*, suggesting Balkan ancestry.

Following a back-slapping hug, the doctor performed introductions. "This is Gavrilo, proprietor of the esteemed establishment, and this is my neighbor, a healer."

"A healer? We may have need of your services here if the steam gets too hot, you know!" He laughed again. "Come, let me show you who is available." The fellow led us to a table with a set of miniatures.

Sweat caused by the heat and humidity began to flow down my face, around my neck, and under my arms. I wiped my forehead with a sleeve.

After fingering through a dozen or so candidates, Yuri made his selection, a young man who bore a resemblance to me. I turned to him wide-eyed.

He shrugged. "Shall I select for *you?*" the doctor asked.

"Yes, please." I had no idea whom to choose. He probably knew most of the staff from previous visits.

Yuri pointed to one of the photos. I didn't want to look.

"Ah, Vasily!" Gavrilo bellowed and winked. "He has been one of our most popular attendants. You should consider yourself fortunate to have him tonight." He made hand gestures in the air, and man dressed in all white turned and walked away. "Be sure to tip him well if you want *special* services," he advised while poking an elbow into my side.

A moment later, a younger, leaner version of me appeared. "Igor," the doctor stated. Probably not the boy's real name. Yuri followed "Igor" down a hallway to a door, and they both disappeared.

"Sir," barked a tall muscular fellow. "I am Vasily. Please follow me."

I looked to Gavrilo, who winked at me again. This time with a smile.

The sweat I swam in could have come from my internal anxiety or the warmth of the building. Vasily led me past a communal pool full of men bathing each other with towels. Once inside our room, he parted curtains to a small parlor with a waist-high table in the center. The attendant indicated for me to enter, and I stepped in, happy to be away from probing eyes. Steam poured from vents around the baseboard, giving the place an aura of mystery and sensuality. It did not, however, cover the pervasive stench of sweat and sour cabbage. I heard moans of pleasure and groans of delight. I presumed other patrons received rubdowns, baths, and some slightly more personal care, depending on the tips.

Vasily placed a towel on the table. "You can hang your things there." He pointed to a set of pegs.

It had been quite a while since I undressed before another. Sensing nothing sinister from Vasily, I disrobed. The attendant patted his hand on the towel. I climbed up, and he pointed to one end.

"Please, lie face down and we can begin your bath."

I needed to review the situation before I could place myself in such a vulnerable position. If he wanted to do me harm, the opportunity already existed. So far, he treated me with professionalism and respect. My arms and legs trembled as I hoisted myself upon the table, but I felt safe with this young man.

Vasily began by swabbing my legs and arms with hot, moist towels. It felt so good to let my guard down and allow someone take care of me. When he made direct contact with my skin, I could read his modest and uncomplicated life. Married with a year-old baby girl, his wife expected another child, which he did not yet know. They lived in a small flat on the Petrograd side with many of the city's laborers. He possessed no ill intentions, nor did he know my identity.

After a few minutes, the lad nudged me to suggest I roll over. At that point, I had become so relaxed, it took quite an effort to rotate my body. Vasily continued to bathe me, and I felt like a spoiled infant. When his hands moved toward my hips, I grasped his wrist and uttered, "No, thank you."

The young man cocked his head and lowered his brows in question. This must be the part of the routine where attendants earn their big tips.

"But… but…" he sputtered.

"I am here to relax, not for any of *that* activity."

Vasily gasped. "Are you an inspector, sir?"

"No, no. I am a healer."

"A very commendable trade, but I need the money to support my family, sir."

I flapped one hand in a calm fashion. "Do not worry, my friend, I will tip you all the same for your services."

"Thank you, sir. Thank you very, very much."

As he handed me a towel, I could only imagine how this strapping chap helped to satisfy the needs of the St. Petersburg menfolk in one way or another. Once dry, I put my clothes back on.

"I am looking for a man, such as yourself, to provide me with protection against criminals. Might you be interested in serving me in that capacity?" I pulled out a few coins and placed them in his palm.

"For the proper price, I can be your man."

I snickered, thinking it might not have been the first time he uttered *that* phrase. "I could give you five rubles a day for your services, and my manservant is a marvelous cook." It felt like a generous offer. The stingy ones pay twice, they say. "And you would still be able to continue working here at night, earning whatever is your custom."

"Yes, I believe that is a good price."

"Can you accompany me home, this evening?"

"Would you want me to sleep over?" His eyes searched mine.

"That is not necessary. I only need you to escort me to my building in Nevsky Prospekt… uh, near the *Passazh*."

"Oh, I know that area. Of course."

Having seen the swarm of young, hungry men there during the White Night celebration, I could only imagine he knew it quite well. After all, he did have a family to support.

As I dressed, I told him, "I shall remain just inside the entrance."

The foul stench lingered as I waited for my neighbor and new bodyguard. Yuri appeared first. Igor followed him.

"I hope you feel more relaxed now, Rodion."

"Much better. Thank you."

The outside door opened and a slender man with a trimmed beard peered in. He reminded me of a frightened chipmunk, and his face seemed familiar.

"Pyotr Ilyich!" Yuri shouted.

"Shhhhh!" the timid fellow admonished. He entered and looked about with jerky movements. Perhaps someone pursued him as well.

"Oh, don't be silly, man." The doctor clapped him on the shoulder. "We are all comrades here."

"Please, keep your voice low. Unlike you... some of are not a mouse without a cat." He regarded me, then Igor. "Two?" He pointed fingers at both of us. We did share a resemblance.

Yuri shrugged and raised one eyebrow. Vasily emerged from a cloud of steam wearing a coat.

"Shall we?" I suggested.

The doctor raised the other brow while he held the door for me and my new companion.

Once outside I turned to my neighbor. "Who was that fellow? I believe I have seen him somewhere before."

He looked back over his shoulder at the building we just exited. "Him? That was Tchaikovsky. You can catch him here a few nights every week partaking these delights when he's not performing elsewhere."

"Ah. Yes! We saw him at the Music Conservatory for a charity concert. Quirky fellow."

Yuri glanced past me at Vasily. "You are full of surprises, my friend. I thought if anyone would be leaving this facility with another man on his arm this evening, it would have been me."

"DOES your residence have a new doorman?" Grigori asked as he entered my study.

I sat holding *Anna Karenina*, which I wanted to finish. The serialized version did not include the last section.

"Good afternoon. And how was your day, young master?" I decided to revert to decorum rather than answer his impertinent question straightaway.

"It was quite satisfactory. Who is that colossus standing outside our door?" He pointed toward the entrance to the apartment.

"You and I have not spoken recently, and I would like to keep abreast of your progress. Are you maintaining your studies at Gymnasium?"

"Indeed. My prior schooling still outpaces what your St. Petersburg classes teach here. Moreover, the marching exercises and theology lessons bore me."

"What about your Latin and Greek? Do you need help with them? I have some experience with those languages."

"Οχι ευχαριστώ. *Artes credo meae satis esse in utroque.*"

"I see." I inhaled and held my breath for a few seconds.

Footsteps announced a third person. "Dinner, sir," intoned Dima.

"Thank you." I turned to Grigori. "Shall we?" I set the book down and held out my arm. We followed the manservant to the dining room. Bright pink borscht and the smell of roasted potatoes whetted my appetite.

As we sat, I inquired, "How about your work with master Rimsky-Korsakov?"

"Do you truly care about my welfare, Mr. Propok?" His beady eyes focused on me like a Berdan rifle. "My mother left me in your somewhat questionable care, and you have all but abandoned me to the supervision of others. You were supposed to provide mentorship in your healer craft. So far, we have not had any lessons." He crossed his arms and leaned his elbows on the table.

It felt as if we had begun an imaginary game of chess. My moves followed the classic openings, but his aggressive tactics put me on defense.

"I had no idea you felt this way, Grigori. As I recall, you attempted to poison me the first morning."

He swung a knight out in front. "How else could I prove your immortality?"

"No one but you knows my condition." I advanced a pawn. "What signs gave you the idea?"

"Most people do not have the ability to sense things the way I do." He maneuvered a bishop across the board toward me. "I needed to establish whether I could trust you."

"That is how you assess for fidelity?!" I squinted at him. "It seemed to me you had little interest in my work and that Korsakov and our doctor neighbor provided more of the guidance you sought."

"Perhaps they do, but I live under *your* roof, pay *you* for these meatless meals"–he tapped his spoon on the soup bowl–"and that little room I sleep in. Has this been but a business arrangement for you, Mr. Propok?"

Since the moment we met, I found it difficult to read the boy. Perhaps I might have ignored and overlooked his interests. Like they say, devils dwell in a quiet lagoon. "It appeared to me you had no desire to learn my craft." I slid the salt cellar across the table like a rook.

Grigori folded his arms across his chest. "I wanted to learn from you, but it appeared to me you had no wish to teach."

Perhaps my desire to learn from him outweighed my interest in tutoring. "I did allow you to accompany me when I went to visit Lady Dolgorukov."

"That boy annoyed me. I wanted to be away from there as soon as possible."

Little Nikolai, the Tsar's grandson, required special attention because he lacked the social armor of his father and grandfather. "The sad part is, he will most likely grow up to sit on the Russian throne someday."

"That is sad." Grigori pointed toward the front door again. "You still haven't answered my question. Who is that man out there?"

"Vasily."

"You know his name?" He castled on the king's side with a twitch of his mouth. "Is he your paramour?"

"Such nonsense." I positioned my white bishop to threaten one of his black knights. "I have engaged him to protect me. After the attack on my return from White Night, I wanted some extra security."

"For yourself? I thought you were indestructible."

"Yes. I have not yet found anything that will kill me, but I would like to preserve what little money I have."

"You have no fear of pain"–he narrowed his eyes–"but you dread losing your riches."

One of my pawns reached the fifth row. "I fear pain as much as the next fellow…"

"But keeping your funds is more important to you."

"Very important." I banged a fist on the table. "Without capital, I—or we—could not occupy this splendid apartment in such a wonderful city. You cannot forbid living beautifully."

"Tsk. How bourgeois…" He took my forward pawn *en passant*.

"In a manner of speaking, it is… Who taught you that word? You most certainly did not learn it at gymnasium."

"Some of my friends say it in reference to people like you who prefer to use wealth to maintain their social position rather than help others in need." Grigori placed his bishop in line with my queen.

"I may lead a bourgeois life, but I believe I do help others in need." I moved a pawn to block the attack. "You, for example."

"You demand payment for me to live here."

"And who are these new friends of yours? Revolutionaries?"

"Not everyone loves His Imperial Majesty, you know." His queen placed my king in check.

"I am aware of that, but members of his house are my clients, and I cannot become associated with any anti-Tsarist activities." I took a spoonful of soup. "It's those people at the Conservatory, isn't it? Students always want political change without the responsibility of having to hold a job." I moved my king to safety.

"It's not just them, Mr. Propok. I have spoken with members of People's Will. Their ideas make sense to me. 'Land and liberty,' they say." He munched on a chunk of potato as he pushed a pawn forward.

From what I had learned, People's Will had plotted assassination attempts on government officials—including the Tsar—to thwart the autocracy. "I would prefer not to discuss politics at the dinner table, if you please." I captured the pawn with a knight.

He took it with a bishop, leaving his queen vulnerable. "As you please." His fork clanked as he stabbed at the plate.

Dima approached. "May I remind you, sir, the doctor will be calling soon. The three of you are to attend Madame von Meck's unveiling this evening."

"Thank you. That had slipped my mind." Given the events of the past few days, it amazed me I could remember my own assumed name. "Oh, before I forget, could you take some of the leftover food and give it to the chap outside our door. His name is Vasily."

One of the servant's eyebrows raised to its highest position. "Vasily. Of course, sir."

"Are you still planning to go with us?" I took Grigori's queen. "There might be one or two students there you can coerce into joining your revolutionary army."

He took my queen with his king. "Sure. Why not?"

We had obliterated each other's pieces, and our match ended in a draw.

"I apologize for not joining you at dinner," Yuri sputtered as we met in the hallway. He eyeballed the musclebound man standing next to my door. "I see your little arrangement appears to be working for you."

"Yes, so far." I took a five-ruble coin from my pocket and placed it in the guard's palm. "Thank you, Vasily. That will be all for this evening. You may resume your regular business."

"Thank you, sir. Shall I return tomorrow?"

I glanced at Grigori to get a sense of his demeanor. As usual, I could not detect anything from him. "Yes, please. I hope you enjoyed Dima's cooking."

"Oh, yes! It is very much better than what my wife prepares." He looked to both sides. "Please do not tell her I said that."

"Of course not. It will be our secret." I patted him on the shoulder.

Yuri pointed toward the staircase. "Shall we? I believe our carriage awaits outside."

The four of us trudged down to the ground floor, Grigori in the lead. Outside, Vasily walked away, toward the *konka* stop, I presumed.

Our neighbor approached the *droski* driver and started a conversation I could not catch. Yuri waved, implying we go to him.

"Do you wish to ride with the coachman?" I asked the boy before taking a step.

"Sure. Why not?"

That seemed to be his preferred answer this evening. We strode to the carriage.

Yuri confirmed, "The boy can ride up front."

"Excellent!" I responded.

This snug *droski* seat barely accommodated our adjoined hindquarters. The coachman handed us a woolen blanket, which the doctor spread over our legs.

We headed out Nevsky Prospekt as many people walked in the opposite direction to participate in the continuing White Night celebrations. It had been a long time since I rode in an open cart like this. It had become my custom to walk or take the *konka* everywhere I went within St. Petersburg. Personal conveyances such as this denoted wealth or power.

The doctor grasped my hand under the coverlet. The vision of his next few weeks flashed through my mind. Nothing interesting or intriguing stood out for me.

"This is going to be so much fun!" he gushed like a schoolchild. I felt happy for him that he could maintain such a sense of amazement after all the death and illness he had witnessed. Lights along the street reflected off his prominent forehead, which added to the festive atmosphere.

"Perhaps I should have brought gloves," I mumbled to myself as I pulled my hand away.

The doctor's head tilted toward me, altering the decorative images. "What was that you said?"

"Oh, nothing. Just thinking aloud." I cleared my throat. "So many people headed toward the waterfront."

"Yes. I feel as though we are sturgeons"—he clasped his hands and wriggled them away from his body—"fighting our way upstream."

We turned onto Liteyny, passing grand houses and buildings. A few blocks from the bank of the Neva River, the driver maneuvered into Zakharyevskaya Street. Several other carriages filled the road. He stopped in front of a three-story plain, brownstone mansion.

In front of the entrance a small crowd of protestors carried "Land and Liberty" placards. They shouted, "Remove the Tsar!" and "Rid Russia of the Romanovs!"

"People's Will," I yelled to Yuri over the loud chants.

"Yes, they will," he responded.

I imagined that someone of his station had no idea of the protests and unrest in the city. I had forgotten their existence until Grigori reminded me of the group. The boy hopped down from the *droski* and stood watching the activists.

Behind us, the royal coach approached, and the angry voices grew in intensity. A guard appeared, scanned the area, and motioned for others to line a path to the door. He reached up for Catherine, now the Tsaritsa. She took the soldier's hand in one of hers and scooped up the layers of her skirt fabric with the other, disregarding the mob's cries and chants around her.

As they reached the front entrance, Vladimir Stasov, whom I recognized as the host of the charity concert and from the hospital room, walked up. "Your Highness," he bowed, took her hand, and gently kissed it. With a smile, he held the door for Catherine and the two guards escorting her.

Yuri returned the blanket to the driver as we alighted. I grabbed the boy by the arm and followed the royal entourage inside. At the far end of the sitting room, Madame von Meck's young student played quiet parlor music. His blank expression and pursed lips suggested a desire to be elsewhere.

A dozen or so people dressed in fashionable formal garb milled about the grand chamber. Tables lined the walls, and heavy, wooden chairs formed rows for the guests. Atop the tables sat small stands with canvases, but one great easel near the piano held a cloth-covered piece.

Madame von Meck—in a garish and sprawling frilly frock bursting with baubles—breezed into the room and rushed to greet Catherine. "Your Highness." She performed a deep curtsy, and the crinoline hoops of her skirt clacked against each other. "Welcome to my humble abode." She straightened up like a ballerina in third position, her sweeping arm presenting and displaying the room with a final wrist flourish.

The Tsaritsa extended her hand to Nadya, who grasped and kissed it. "Madame von Meck, we appreciate your invitation. The Tsar and I are particularly interested in the great and talented artists of our nation. And, please, call me Catherine."

Madame von Meck's eyes ignited, and her face lengthened in surprise. "Yes! By all means. And you must call me Nadya." She genuflected again.

"Thank you, Nadya." The Tsaritsa responded in a monotone.

"Excuse me… Catherine," our hostess grinned like a little girl with a big secret, "I must go retrieve our… *other* guest of honor. I shall return momentarily."

The Princess gave a curt nod, and Madame von Meck exited through one of the sets of double doors.

"I believe *she* got what she wanted," Grigori observed.

"What is that?" I asked.

"It is obvious our hostess appears to enjoy collecting people. She now has acquaintance of the woman who sees herself as Empress." He crossed his arms. "The devil delights in squalid pride."

At times, I wondered how someone as young as my "apprentice" could perceive human nature with such sharpness. He had never met Madame von Meck before, and only once encountered Catherine. Nadya's behavior left little doubt of her motives.

"Let us take in these works of art," I suggested before moving to the nearest easel. The painting displayed three bear cubs and their mother frolicking among storm-broken pine trees at twilight. Next to it, the image of a plain-clothed girl stood in a storage room holding some sort of odd hook on a stick.

"What kind of artist creates this rubbish?" Grigori queried.

Yuri informed us, "I believe they are itinerants who travel about the country displaying their latest pieces."

"That explains why they must keep moving," the boy quipped.

Criticism dripped from his tongue with painless ease. I hoped this lad would learn not to spit into the well from which he drank sooner rather than later.

Madame von Meck returned, holding the hand of a fellow who appeared somewhere between thirty and forty years old. His green eyes darted beneath the dangling shocks of dark hair. A wispy mustache and shaggy goatee covered most of his puckered lips.

"*Byon zhyur.*" Nadya pronounced French with Russian undertones. She moved toward the covered painting on the large easel at the end of the room. "*Mesdames, messieurs, s'il vous plaît.*" Her flailing arms indicated the chairs as people began to sit. A house servant escorted the Princess to the front row, and a grinning hostess beamed at her prized guests.

"Achille, if you please." Madame von Meck turned to the pianist, and the young man played a few more measures before ceasing the serenade. She then addressed the assembled guests, "I have invited you here today"– her eyes traveled to a few of the people, ending with the Princess, and a grand smile–"to enjoy the works of our traveling artists, and–in particular–a new, and quite timely, portrait of our recently-departed national treasure, a musical genius for the ages, Modeste Petrovich Mussorgsky." A few people applauded politely. "*Monsieur* Repin, another illustrious Russian master, began shortly before the composer's death and completed the work just last week." Nadya stepped to the concealed canvas. "*Mes amis, je vous présente…*" and she tugged at the muslin wrapping, flicking her wrist, to reveal the portrait.

Silence.

INSTEAD of an homage to one of the country's most beloved composers—perhaps a youthful, vibrant version of Mussorgsky seated at a piano playing one of his many popular works, or even leading an orchestra with a baton—Repin chose to paint the ailing man sitting for a portrait. While an honest and true depiction, it could not be considered flattering. His auburn hair looked unkempt, flying off at strange angles; the nose depicted like a reddened potato. A rather plain, dark green housecoat with a wide, red lapel appeared unwashed and disheveled. Only the sidelong glance of bright, shiny grey-blue eyes gave life to the otherwise dreary work.

After a few soundless seconds, someone coughed. Both Nadya and Repin craned their necks, gazing about the non-responsive crowd. Madame von Meck stood and began clapping, with others joining a few moments after. She turned to the painter. He snapped his chin upward and disappeared through the doors from which they entered.

"More rubbish," quipped Grigori. I did not disagree with him on this.

People strolled to the refreshment tables. The young pianist commenced a Bach partita. Madame von Meck approached the Princess.

"Your Highness—Catherine—may I get you something to drink or eat?" A pretentious grin crinkled her face powder.

"Thank you, but no," the Princess stood, assisted by a guard. "I only eat food prepared by my loyal chef." She turned to a blond man nearby, who stood and bowed. "However, we can share a bottle of sweet sherry, but only if it has never been opened and you take the first drink." She returned the all-too-practiced smile.

Nadya froze for a moment before responding, "Of course, of course! This way, please," and she indicated one of the sets of double doors.

"A great loss," Stasov declared. He moved to view the fairly realistic portrait, and the portly poet Apukhtin—whom I also remembered from the charity concert—stepped next to him. "A great loss to us all."

"Such a tragedy, do you not think so, Volodya?" The big man pulled a large red silk handkerchief from a pocket and dabbed at his sorrowful eyes. "So soon after the loss of Dostoyevsky. How many other deaths must we suffer this season?"

Stasov focused on the two-dimensional depiction of his old friend. "It is incredible!" he muttered, "Simply incredible!"

I scanned the room for Grigori and located him next to the piano. He chatted with Nadya's young fellow while the musical performance continued to flow. I approached the portrait once Stasov and Apukhtin wandered off.

"Your thoughts?" Yuri prompted me.

We had both been present for the composer's demise. Attempting to access Mussorgsky's mind after death appeared to have diminished my ability to sense others' futures, which presented both positives and negatives.

"I only met the man in hospital, and I do not believe the blind should judge colors." I snapped my fingers. "Now, wait. We did see him perform at the Conservatory. He did not look well then." My head waggled side to side.

"It did him no good that *someone*"–the doctor's eyes shifted to Grigori– "smuggled the poor chap liquor, which I *strictly* prohibited."

I glanced over and observed the two young fellows engaged in a lively conversation, with Grigori's fingers pointing up, down, and various other directions. Achille nodded every so often, the blank expression unwavering.

"And your thoughts, sir?" I returned the inquiry.

He shifted his weight onto one foot and tucked the opposite fist under his chin. In that pose, I imagined someone who enjoyed the male physique might find him rather becoming.

As he sniffed the air, his nose wrinkled. "I understand the current attitude of painting has shifted to an impressionistic style, but I much prefer a more accurate reflection of real life. This portrait appears to attempt to bridge the two approaches, failing at both." He faced me. "My opinion, as you requested."

Having observed several centuries of art throughout my time, I watched as painters improved their techniques until they learned how to represent perspective, light, and shadow accurately. Recent advancements in photographic science allowed for more widespread use of cameras to record family likenesses. Rather than standing or sitting for hours, posing, while a portraitist captured commissioned settings, people only needed to hold still for a second or two. Fearing the loss of patronage, visual artists chose to compete by presenting their imaginative interpretations of selected scenes, something that could not be obtained with a mechanical box and glass plate.

"I much prefer a painting, no matter how misrepresentative, to a cold, emotionless photograph," I responded.

Yuri's head nodded. "I can certainly agree with that, but I would rather have a more sentimental rendering of the composer."

"The world will be a sadder place without him," I mused.

"Rodya, how good to see you." Catherine's voice purred in my ear.

"Your Highness." I turned and gave a respectful bow.

She giggled and put a hand to her breastbone. "Oh, there's no need for you to do that with *me*." She stretched out her arm and presented the royal hand. "We have known each other for far too long. In fact, you probably know more about me than my Sashka."

Without question, I had inside information regarding this ruthless tigress that most people did not. No amount of silk wrappings could bury this woman's aspirations to jump above her own head.

When I took her hand in mine, my brain exploded with a blur of startling images. At the limit of my view, several weeks ahead, I saw Catherine, dressed all in black, a mourning veil covering her head. She walked before a funeral caisson draped in flags. A mass of mourners behind the royal barrow filled a bridge and several blocks after that. This onslaught of grim impressions initiated an impulse to pull away, but her grip held firm, as if she grabbed my wrist with both hands.

"Is something the matter?" she asked.

One of the most difficult aspects of my condition involved withholding bad news from those to whom it would befall. My mind had to function in an instant to contrive a believable falsehood. After kissing the back of her hand, I withdrew my own and coughed into it. "Just…" Cough, cough. "A touch of hypersensitivity. This room wants for dusting."

Her head swiveled about. "Yes. Nadya's staff should have seen to a more thorough cleaning for such an event."

"Catherine!" Madame von Meck's voice rang out, her waving, gloved hand appeared above the crowd.

"What a pity about Mussorgsky," the Tsaritsa clucked. "If you will excuse me, it appears the hostess wishes *more* of our company." She took a step then turned back to me. "Please schedule a visit for next week. We shall be calling upon Prince Yusupov at Moika Palace. Our cousin Nikolai seeks a blessing for his daughter's marriage from my Sashka." Her heavenward eye movement suggested annoyance. "Perhaps we can meet there. You and I have much to discuss. Oh, could you bring your charming young associate with you?" She turned and promenaded toward Nadya.

My young associate? Moika Palace? The combination of those two items reminded me that as we walked past, Grigori had a strong reaction to the location. Perhaps a portent of some future event. Also, of late, he began expressing sympathy with the People's Will anarchists. Perhaps it would be his hand that brought down Tsar Alexander. What a dilemma.

"Rodion, are you feeling unwell? You appear quite pale," Yuri tapped my shoulder. "May I test your pulse?" He held out a hand.

In that moment, the thought of another person's touch terrified me. Even though I had sensed the doctor's next few weeks earlier in the evening, I did not want to tempt the chance of discovering yet more bad news.

"Thank you, no. Just a passing thought." I clasped my hands together at the waist. "I shall be fine in a moment."

My throat constricted and my breathing diminished. I could feel cold sweat on my neck and forehead.

"On second thought," I gasped, "I believe I have need of some fresher air. I would like to leave now."

"Yes, of course." He held up his open palm. "I understand."

"I apologize if I have disrupted your evening plans." A futile swallow could not dislodge the lump entrapped in my throat. "Should you prefer to remain, I could catch a tram."

"No, no. I brought you here and I will see you home." He wrapped an arm about my shoulder. "Especially if you continue to have concerns for your personal safety."

With gentle pressure of his torso, he guided us out of the house and into the street. While I harbored no emotional attachments to the doctor, his protective behavior fostered my comfort level with him.

The shock of future events just revealed to me eclipsed any apprehensions about my own wellbeing.

Yuri asked, "Where is Grigori?"

I looked about but could not locate the boy.

"Ah, I see him." The doctor pointed to the crowd of protestors. Grigori stood chatting with some of the People's Will members. I feared the alder-tree resisted the proper bending I have attempted to provide.

Someone barked, "Propok," in my ear. I recognized the voice as the one who tackled me on the White Night. When I turned to look, no one stood close enough to me to have made that accusation. As if I did not already have enough reasons to be troubled. I could feel my heartbeat accelerate as I began to tremble.

Yuri ushered me to his hired *droski*. "You remain here, and I will fetch the boy." He wandered into the throng.

As I sat waiting for their return, horrific images played again and again in my mind, alternating with the attack outside our building. If only I possessed some means to block them. So many questions to resolve, and all of them led to and through Grigori, the one person from whom I could not sense.

The doctor climbed into the narrow seat beside me, Grigori jumped up with the driver, and our cart moved off. Horse hooves clacking on the cobblestone resounded in my ears.

"Your thoughts seem very far away this evening, Rodion."

Closer than he knew. Should my premonitions prove correct, we sat just behind a young assassin.

"I apologize, Yuri. I only wish I could discuss my thoughts with you, but it would not be prudent at this time."

He nodded. We rode the remainder of the trip without speaking.

During our return home, we traveled in the same direction as people moving toward the waterfront for White Night celebrations. They might as well party while they can. Dark days for all of Russia will fall in a few weeks.

When we reached our building, I hopped out of the cart and walked up to my apartment without saying anything, not even a "Thank you" to Yuri, who had been so gracious to invite us to ride with him. I hurried to my den and settled, arms folded, motionless in my reading chair.

As Grigori entered, he sputtered, "That was rather rude. Not saying 'thank you' or 'good evening' or anything to our neighbor. What is bothering you?"

I turned my head away because I could not look at him, given the burdensome secret thrust into my mind by Catherine. "I wish I could speak of this with you, but I cannot. Please leave me."

"Something happened to you at that rich woman's house." He approached. "Your behavior is most strange. I have concerns for you."

"Only because I provide meals and a place for you to live in St. Petersburg." I levelled a finger at him. "Without me, you would still be starving with your poor mother out in Siberia!"

He blinked a few times. "It seems some morsel of bad news reached you this evening, and you are having difficulty accepting it."

"Yes!" I glared at him. "I did learn several things that have me very much upset. As we left Madame von Meck's home, a voice—a voice I recall from a few nights ago—shouted my name in my ear. I remember that voice as the one who assaulted me on the street upon returning from White Night."

"Hmmmmm."

"I am concerned about your ongoing association with those People's Will revolutionaries, and I have to wonder if you had any part in that attack on my person."

Grigori placed a palm on his breast. "Are you accusing me of something?"

"Did you tell some of them who I am and our address?"

His head dropped. "A few people have asked me where I live and how I support myself."

"And you gave them my personal information?"

"I saw no harm in that. We all know each other's business." His gaze returned to me. "I realize, now, that it might have led to negative consequences."

The boy knew how to transgress and how to keep secrets. "I also saw you trying to recruit Achille into your little army of radicals."

"Achille?" He squinted. "Who is that?"

"Madame von Meck's piano student."

"Oh, him. His name is Claude. Only the hostess calls him by that other name."

"Claude," I echoed. "Did you manage to convince him to join up?"

"No. He wants to travel the Continent with her and feels he needs to play along with that bourgeois life." He stood and started toward his room but stopped at the doorframe. "I still feel like something deeply disturbed you this evening. Did you get news of someone's impending death?"

My heart froze and I gripped the front of my jacket. "How do you *know* that?"

The left side of Grigori's mouth curled up, reminding me of many malevolent people I met during my time. "I know more about you than you know about me. And I know you need to go across the hall and apologize to our neighbor." He pointed out the door before retreating to his room.

"Yes," I said to the otherwise empty den. "I believe you are correct in that."

My mind whirled with potential possibilities. In all my lifetimes, I never once made any attempt to alter the course of history. Despite years of plague, wars, and tyrants, the touch of my hand could not be detected on the world's rudder.

But this time, I had foreknowledge of a great ruler's impending death and the probable perpetrator. Tsar Alexander planned to visit the Moika Palace to call upon a cousin. Grigori felt something upsetting when we walked past that same building. He previously sensed residual dread at the site of an attempted assassination.

The coincidence dominated my thoughts because this tiny spark possessed the potential to spawn a great conflagration. I needed to find a way forward. The next few weeks might pass like centuries, given the intelligence I bore. Time is the best doctor, they say.

Yuri opened his door a few seconds after I stopped knocking. "Rodion. Would you like to come in?" He ushered me through to the sitting room. "What is on your mind, dear neighbor?"

"First off, I need to apologize for my unpardonable behavior this evening."

"Please, sit with me." He pointed to a chair as he sat. "There is no need for you to make amends. We are good enough friends—I hope—that it should not affect our affiliation."

"Thank you, my friend." I sat. "Please understand that if I could reveal the contents of my concerns, I would." My eyes met his. "I know that you also become privy to certain information—bad news, if you will—that you might need to refrain from delivering. I am seeking guidance from you as to how to handle such... subtle situations."

He stroked his chin with one hand. "Yes. Our teeth are rarely strong enough for *that* nut." He stared off into a corner. "As a healer—and one with a long career ahead—you have the opportunity to choose your clients. However, a doctor does not have that option. We must take those presented to us. How do you make *your* determination of which people to see?"

As much as I trusted Yuri, I could not disclose my power to see into people's futures. He might be tempted to abuse the privilege in discerning which of his patients would live or die. Experience has shown me that even respectable and sober men fall prey to unearthly abilities. "I imagine through assessment skills, similar to yours. As you say, I am not beholden to take anyone as a client, and I choose to see only those whose life forces remain robust."

"Then, you do not cure anyone."

"Not in a physical way. I provide a service to those who can afford it. Most of my healing time is spent listening to clients complain about their spouses, children, vexations, politics, and such subjects. They feel better after verbalizing their inner thoughts. There is healing in that, I suppose."

"And Grigori is your apprentice?"

My body shuddered at the mention of his name. "The boy's mother delivered him to me on that pretense. However, he chooses to spend his time elsewhere. He assists Master Korsakov at the Music Conservatory, and, lately, he has been cavorting with some of those People's Will anarchists. In fact, I just learned he provided my information to those devils, and they accosted me upon my return from the White Night celebrations."

"A delicate balance to maintain, to be sure." The doctor nodded a few times. "But to answer your original inquiry, I have found it best to reveal only what is absolutely necessary, keeping the bad news to yourself, if at all possible. Use utmost diplomacy. Shall I brew some tea?"

My tongue clucked. Diplomacy. No more useful than tea in solving the world's problems.

TEA.

Thinking about the beverage stirred memories of Grigori's attempt to poison me with it on our first morning together. He placed some "inheritance powder," otherwise known as arsenic, in my first cup to test his speculation I might be immortal.

This presented one option for the current situation: I could do him in with his own weapon. However, he did mention exposing himself to small doses so that he could build up a tolerance. Perhaps he could foretell when others might endeavor to kill him.

Another option: I could throw myself in front of a train, as Anna Karenina did, but that would probably not bring the relief I sought. It might hurt for a while, but I would continue to live, still left with that monumental decision.

Of course, one choice always available would be to just do nothing and let events unravel as they may. I chose that option for generations. Look how the world turned out.

I sat in my den, steeped in contemplation, when Dima interrupted my thoughts. He presented me a fancy gilt-edged, citrus-scented envelope.

Tea? I balked at the personalized invitation from Madame Panaeva. She requested my presence to meet with her poetic friend, the one with uncontrolled eyes and only one arm, who has come to visit once again.

"How shall I respond, sir?" the servant asked. "Her messenger is waiting."

Perhaps a bit of distraction would be good for my distressed soul. "Let her know that I shall be in attendance. Thank you, Dima."

This would also provide an opportunity to tell Vasily I no longer require his services. As I have discovered the background of my attacker, having a personal guard seemed unnecessary. I could stop off at the Turkish bath after the terrible tea.

Following my morning ablutions and a midday meal, I ambled to the street outside. Favorable fortune allowed me to ride the *konka* without encountering any other humans.

"You remember my very good friend, Yulia Zhadovskaya, do you not, Rodya?"

I bowed a polite distance then took her ashen hand, kissing it as quickly as possible. From our brief contact, I knew the next few weeks of her life consisted of poetry readings and gentleman callers. "A pleasure to see you again," I lied as I straightened.

One of her eyes pointed toward me as she winked. I could only hope she did not notice my shudder.

"Would you like some tea, or, perhaps"–an eyebrow arched–"something a bit stronger?" Our hostess held a bottle containing some brown liquid, which looked like kvass.

"I should like to read you a poem I wrote in your honor." Yulia's enigmatic smile rattled me anew.

"The stronger stuff, *please*," I responded to our hostess. It might help me get through the remainder of this uncomfortable interview.

A staff member poured and served the liquor in cut crystal sherry glasses. I took a quick gulp.

With one eye on me and the other aimed toward a piece of paper she clutched in her only hand, Madame Zhadovskaya recited:

> I remember the look–I will not forget that look!
> It burns in front of me irresistibly:
> There is a shine of happiness in it,
> There is poison in it of a wonderful passion,
> The fire of longing, inexpressible love.
> He worried my soul so much,
> He gave birth to so many new feelings in me,
> He bound my heart for a long time
> Unknown and sweet anxiety!

At least I had the consolation of knowing I would not appear in her days to come for the next few weeks. Despite the lady's daunting appearance, her words had an ability to stir the soul.

"Lovely, Yulia! Just lovely!" Avdotya gushed.

The poet peered at me. "And you, Mr. Propok. Did you enjoy my writing?"

I took a moment to sip some more kvass and concoct a response that complimented her talents without any hint of flirtation. "You have the ability to capture an impassioned moment with such magnificent narrative."

She blushed. "Oh, Mr. Propok... you flatter me so..." Yulia fanned herself with the sheet of paper.

It astounded me that so many gentlemen found her asymmetric appearance appealing. Some other factor must arouse them that I could not perceive. Many women possess beauty, but only the Devil likes their temper. Yulia seemed the antithesis.

"Rodya, have you continued *your* writing?" our hostess inquired.

"I confess, due to urgent business of late, I have not had the opportunity for such pastimes." I stood and took her hand to get a sense of the future. Nothing of importance stood out for me other than her citrus-scented perfume. "However, I continue to urge *you* to begin the task of writing your memoirs as soon as possible."

"My!" She withdrew her hand. "Do you know something of my health that should concern me?"

"Ah, no." It took me a moment to realize she had perceived me in my role as healer rather than fellow author. "I meant to say it might take you a while to complete."

Her hand went to her neckline, and she turned away. "Because of my age?"

"Not at all." If she desired a discussion of age, my collection of centuries would overwhelm her mere six decades. "You have lived an adventure-filled life. Much of that time has been in the company of very important and talented people. Certainly, you will have many magnificent experiences to record."

"Which is—again—a matter of my years." She turned back to me with a raised jaw. "However, I have come to believe it is not how *long* you have lived, but *how* you have lived that matters."

Those words struck a jeweled dagger through my heart. Given my predicament possessing foreknowledge of the Tsar's approaching death, *how* I live this coming month might make a great deal of difference for a great number of people.

The remainder of the afternoon passed with polite conversation about the weather, the White Night celebrations, and the dispositions of several writing circle members not present. Now and again, I observed Yulia staring at me with her left eye, which generated enough anxiety. Several times, she used the right one.

After leaving Madame Panaeva's home, I walked to Znamensky's. The evening air smelled more of dinner than dung. Upon entering the Turkish bath, I told Gavrilo I sought Vasily.

"You and everyone else!" His large belly jiggled as he laughed. "I believe he is with a client just now and will be finished presently. If you wish to wait..." The gruff manager indicated a few chairs along the wall.

Several minutes later, a nervous-looking man dashed through the foyer toward the way out, his head snapping left and right as he passed. *Tchaikovsky*, I remembered.

"Good sir," the proprietor boomed, "I believe Vasily is awaiting you in *there*." He pointed toward the same stall where I first met the young man.

As I entered the small, steamy room, Vasily made a slight bow. "It is good to see you again, sir. I did not anticipate that you would come to my regular place of work."

"I am not here for a rubdown. My visit is regarding resolution of discovering the perpetrator in the attack against my person for which I originally subscribed your services."

"And how I have enjoyed serving you, sir. The additional earnings have allowed our family to acquire a few necessities previously beyond our means." A broad smile brightened his face.

"It has been my pleasure to provide you with the means." I gave a cursory nod. "However, as I no longer fear the danger, your services are not needed. I wished to tell you in person, rather than writing you a note."

"Just as well, sir." He glanced down. "I cannot read."

"I hope you are not terribly disappointed with my news."

"Oh, no, sir. I have been happy to earn some extra money, but now I will be able to spend more time with my loved ones." He smiled again. "All is well, sir. All is well."

"Thank goodness for that. I had worried you might have been upset by this change in status."

"Not at all."

"Very well. I shall be on my way, then." I extended my hand to him.

"Hold up, sir. This time has been blocked for me to spend with a client." Vasily slapped the top of the table. "As you have been so generous with me and my family, it would be my honor to provide you with my services."

"Thank you, Vasily, but I have no need of —"

"Pardon me for interrupting, but all I planned to offer is the standard Turkish bath massage. Nothing more, sir."

I reflected upon these recent stressful times. The thought of giving myself over to someone I trusted for a bit of physical healing sounded very good, indeed.

A quick search in my pocket revealed, "I did not bring enough money for such treatment."

"Not necessary, sir. You have already given me far more than I could have asked for."

Even better.

"Please, place your clothes on the pegs while I retrieve the kettle." He started toward the door.

"Kettle?"

"Yes. From our samovar. I have just brewed some fresh tea. It is very healthful. You will like it." Vasily exited.

Tea. No escaping it.

Upon returning home, I found a note from Master Rimsky-Korsakov requesting we meet the following morning. I assumed the subject would be Grigori.

After dispatching an affirmative reply, I retired to my den to finish reading *Anna Karenina*. A serialized version published in *The Messenger* did not include the last section, Book Eight. Only the three-volume set incorporated this additional material.

With Anna gone, Kitty's husband Levin became the central figure. Following the death of Nikolai, his sickly brother, Levin—previously an unbeliever—contemplated religious beliefs. He expounded, "If I do not accept the answers Christianity gives to the problems of my life, what answers do I accept?" As an example, he described a man inappropriately seeking food from toy and tool shops.

He contemplated, "In infinite time, in infinite matter, in infinite space, is formed a bubble-organism, and that bubble lasts a while and bursts, and that bubble is Me." Levin, troubled by unmoving stars' power over the principles of people on Earth, looked to other belief systems. Following an examination of the various interpretations by Jews, Mohammedans, Confucians, and Buddhists, he concluded, "I have no right to decide, and no possibility of deciding."

In that moment, I fully understood his uncertainty. Witnessing the deaths of thousands, if not millions, due to wars, plagues, and geological disasters, dispelled whatever nominal beliefs I maintained of a personified deity. My parents never took me to church, and I may not have even been baptized. I could not fathom the idea of a heavenly figure who caused—or allowed—the deaths of so many of their own followers.

The phrase, "It is not how *long* you have lived, but *how* you have lived that matters" resounded in my mind. I have lived long, and I have lived well, for the most part. Every so often, one person *can* change the course of human events, but I have no desire to be that person. Because I must change locations from time to time to keep people from learning my secrets, widespread notoriety might be deleterious. Too many folks asking too many questions for my comfort level. Although, a mother—or her son—in Siberia learned of my healer accomplishments somehow.

I heard the front door open then close. Sprightly footsteps on the wooden floor indicated my young boarder.

"Grigori!" I shouted from the comfort of my chair. "Come to the den."

The boy appeared in the doorway, unbuttoning his coat as he entered. "Yes, Mr. Propok?"

"How was your day? Gymnasium? Conservatory?"

A frown preceded his response. "I believe I am still a few months ahead of my school class. Afternoons with Master Rimsky-Korsakov pass quietly." He glanced at the closed book in my hand. "What are you reading?"

"Oh, this? Tolstoy's latest, *Anna Karenina*."

"Typical bourgeois fairy tales?"

The first impulse, "No," almost escaped my lips. However, when I considered the tale of the unscrupulous characters that populated the work, I decided upon, "Somewhat. The heroine throws herself in front of a train at the end. Does that bring some redemption?"

He tilted his head one way then the other. "No, not really."

"You might enjoy his next book. It will be about death."

He nodded. "That sounds more of interest."

My head bobbed as well. "Somehow, I thought you might like that. Grigori"–I patted the book's cover–"do you believe in God?"

"No," came the abrupt response. "Do you?" The gleam in his dark eyes challenged my very existence.

"Not at all. It is a concept I have grappled with for a very long time."

"That is good… because I feared you might want my company at worship." His lids narrowed. "A minute ago you inquired into my daily activities, yet you have refrained from asking this before. Did you have a specific concern?"

Rubbing at my chin did nothing to remove the difficulty of probing. "I received a request from Master Korsakov to meet with him in the morning. Has he been satisfied with your work?"

"As far as I know, he has. Frequently, he tells me how much he appreciates my speed and accuracy at copying scores for him."

"Yes." I scratched at a temple. "I wonder what concerns him."

Grigori squinted. "Do you think he has a problem with *me*?"

"Why else would he request a morning appointment, rather than the afternoon?"

"He spends most of the hours before noon in his office, as far as I know. After luncheon, he gives me music to prepare while he takes classes."

My eyebrows rose, and I sighed. "I can only hope it is not something I have to make excuses for."

"How do you mean?" He glowered. "Have you made excuses for me before?"

"No, but I do not want to get into the habit of defending you."

"I see no need for that." The boy crossed arms with balled hands in front of his chest. "I believe I am sufficiently capable of explaining myself to whomever disapproves of my behavior."

"You are but a boy, Grigori. Most people do not expect one so young to have such a mature appreciation of how this world works."

He nodded his head four times. "It would be to their detriment to underestimate me."

My thoughts went to occasions when I did not properly consider the boy's disconcerting, precocious sophistication. Detrimental, indeed.

Grigori pointed toward the entrance. "Where's Igor?"

I cocked my head. "Who?"

"You know, the large fellow who stands guard outside. I did not see him when I came in."

"Ah." I chuckled. "His name is Vasily."

"He seemed more like an Igor…" Grigori muttered.

"And I terminated his station here because I now know that the attack upon my person came from an identifiable source." I stared at him.

He looked away. "That is too bad. I rather enjoyed his presence. I felt safe with him around."

"Do you not feel safe with *me?*"

"Not as much." He blinked a few times. "You see, *I* am not immortal."

"It concerned my belongings more than my wellbeing, you know."

"Either way, he represented additional protection."

From what would he need protection? I recalled his use of the word *bourgeois.* "Do you feel safe with your People's Will comrades?"

"Yes, I do. You may see them as radicals or insurgents, but–to me– they represent the future of this nation. The House of Romanov is doomed."

I hoped my widened eyes did not give away the privileged information I struggled to conceal. While I have been unable to sense *his* days ahead, I had no idea whether he could intuit *mine.* No evidence existed to determine one way or the other. Conversation with Grigori regarding my foreknowledge of the Tsar's death could wait a while.

"I know very little about your People's Will group… other than what I read in newspapers. What is it they stand for? What do they want?"

"The Empire exists for the taking of resources from poor peasants and hoarding this wealth for the royal family and its disciples."

Which included many of my patrons. "And how do they propose to remedy this imbalance?"

"We have issued a proclamation calling for the execution of Alexander because of his crimes against the people."

My head shook without command. "That is quite a radical notion."

A sly smile spread across his face. "Not in light of what happened a century ago in France."

Although I lived far from Paris at that time, I remembered those days with trepidation. After the successful rebellion in British America, the masses in several other nations took a hard look at their ruling class and realized some restructuring might not be such a bad idea. "And you agree with this proclamation?"

"Yes. I had no idea of the inequitable conditions when I lived in Pokrovskoye with my mother. Now that I have had a chance to observe how the wealthy live in *this* city, built on the sweat of my brethren, I find this unbalanced economic structure unfair and corrupt."

I wish I could believe these rabblerousers instilled the boy with such nonsense, but it probably would have developed, nevertheless. Life in St. Petersburg introduces one to affluence and squalor alike. "You could follow *my* lead and take money from the wealthy by performing services," I suggested.

"I do not wish to become a parasite, like *you!*" His eyes burned with passion.

This accusatory outburst led me to wonder why he continued to remain in my home. A long inhale preceded my next question. "And you believe that removing our emperor will bring justice and equality for everyone?"

"Yes! Yes, I do."

"But he ended serfdom. There are no more feudal lords or imposed slave labor."

"It is not enough!" Grigori barked. "He has allowed this revolting inequality to flourish, and he must *die.*"

Which prompted me to ask, "If they directed you to kill the Tsar, *would* you?"

His head dropped. After a few seconds, he responded, "Given the opportunity and the means… yes. Without hesitation."

The stickiest lump ever formed in my throat that no amount of tea could dislodge.

WITH all the unsettled issues whirring in my mind, I found it difficult to sleep. No matter which side I tried to lie on, my eyes refused to remain shut. When slivers of pre-dawn sunlight invaded my bedchamber, I gave up any hope of slumber.

After my morning toilet, I stumbled into the dining room. The rose-scented aroma of tea infused the air. A hot cupful and some warm kasha with slabs of butter helped to restore some of my lost energy.

"Dima, where is Grigori?" I shouted, as if the man could hear from wherever he lurked while not attending me.

The servant entered, assessed my face, raised an eyebrow, and replied, "The young master departed rather early this morning."

Just as well. I didn't know if I could handle seeing him so soon after last evening's intense debate. He admitted that if commanded to assassinate the Tsar, he would discharge his duty with delight. Perhaps he hung noodles on my ears to provoke a reaction, but from what little I knew about the boy, I judged his threat as sincere.

Images from my last encounter with the Tsaritsa revealed her leading a state funeral procession in the next few weeks. My gift of prescience—a gift I wish I could, at times, return—provided me with this dilemma of knowing about the emperor's demise. My association with Grigori—whom I would also like, at times, to return—portended the potential deliverer of our Tsar's death.

A tap on my shoulder roused me. "Sorry to interrupt your deep thoughts, sir, but I wish to ask if there will be anything more you desire from me."

"Yes, Dima. I am to visit Korsakov at the Conservatory this morning. Could you lay out some clothes for me?"

He pivoted away and strode to my room. I continued to stew on my situation between lumps of buttery buckwheat.

Once dressed, I exited the building and stepped into Nevsky Prospekt. I could have ridden the Sadovaya or Ekaterinhof streetcar but chose to walk instead. With my head so full of thoughts, I did not want to take the chance of coming in contact with other people.

The warm, lemony sky distracted me somewhat, and I had to remind myself to be careful when crossing at intersections. I traversed the long canal via short Bank Bridge, its two pairs of gleaming griffins glaring down at me in judgment. "You have survived here many decades, much longer than *I* have dwelt in St. Petersburg." I glanced up into the darkened bronze eyes of one of the beasts. "What unspeakable secrets do *you* guard?" No response.

"Come in," rang the cheerful answer when I knocked on Korsakov's office door. Inside, the music master removed a stack of untidy papers from a wooden chair next to his desk. "Rodya. Thank you for obliging me. Please, sit down."

I dusted the flat, cracked leather cushion with my hand before taking a seat. "Korsakov, your request surprised me. I hope young Grigori has not been too much of a trouble for you."

"Trouble?" His forehead wrinkled. "No trouble at all. As a matter of fact, because of the boy's assistance, I am further along with *Snow Maiden* than expected. The work should be finished by year's end. I thought it might take much longer." He bowed his head and grasped his temples with a hand. "Once I have completed *that*, I need to begin transcribing Mussorgsky's *Pictures* while I still retain memories of it."

"It would be a shame to lose such a marvelous work." The only musical piece I ever felt moved me at all.

Korsakov returned his gaze to me. "As far as your young friend, due to his diligence, I have increased his daily wage to a half ruble and could not imagine working on my endeavors without him."

I paused before asking, "Has Grigori spoken to you of… politics or a group called the People's Will?"

He squinted at me. "We hardly converse. Any speech between us is in regard to music. Nothing more."

"Ah. I presumed your request to meet in the morning might have something to do with his deportment because I know he works with you in the afternoon."

"No, no. Not at all." He glanced up into a corner of the room. "The cause for my invitation is someone else entirely." Korsakov drew his upper teeth across his lower lip. "Tchaikovsky. Pyotr Ilyich. Do you know him?"

Although no one had introduced us formally, I had watched him perform at the charity concert, and Yuri alerted me to his presence in the Turkish bathhouse. "Not directly, no."

"He is quite the tempestuous fellow, you know. I have concerns about his future here, and I want to provide him with the best chance possible for success." He tapped his fingertips on the desk a few times. "Until recently, Nikolai Rubenstein has been the source of his support and guidance, but the poor fellow has taken ill and will—most likely—leave this world behind before long."

"That is sad to hear. Is he someone you want me to visit?"

"Oh, no. As much confidence as I have in you, I believe he is beyond your talents as a healer at this point. His brother Anton—despite instructing Tchaikovsky—has little patience for the poor chap."

"I see. What is it that you think *I* can do?"

"Oh, yes. I nearly forgot." He tapped the side of his head. "Nikolai recommended Pyotr Ilyich to compose a symphonic piece for the Tsar's upcoming silver jubilee."

An event that will not take place. I closed my eyes and sighed.

"Is something the matter, Rodya?"

My mouth formed a smile my heart could not support. "No, Korsakov. I have other weighty subjects on my mind just now." The smile fell. "But I know nothing of music. What possible contribution could I make to this project? I understand Madame von Meck bestows patronage to the composer. Can she not provide the desired encouragement?"

"While it is true that Nadya subsidizes Pyotr Ilyich, she admires him from afar and has no plans to meet him." Korsakov threw a few fingers in the air near his eye. "Strange, yes?"

Many things about Tchaikovsky appeared so. "Yes, indeed."

The master nodded. "Now, I understand your hesitance. It is not your musical knowledge I need. Our creative friend requires… oh, how shall I say this?… reassurance to keep him on the straight course. As a healer, your confidence in him should provide the encouragement he needs."

"Is he ill?"

"Not at all. However, he sees ailments in every corner. This grand composition is one I believe in, and I will pay you handsomely for your services."

Due to my fear of leaving the apartment, I had not seen my clients for the last week or so. This additional income would make up for that decrease in earnings. "All you need me to do is attend him as healer? I don't see how that would help."

"Rodya, I know the man. He is easily distracted, and I want him to complete this composition in time for the jubilee. There needs to be someone urging him deeper into the forest for more firewood. I believe *you* are the person for this."

If only I could tell him there would be no celebration and no need to hurry. Then again, the additional earnings would help rebuild my shrunken coffer. Under regular circumstances, I would not take a client without having sensed him first. However, work persisted as a tenacious wolf that would not run away on its own.

"I appreciate your belief in my talents. When would you like me to start?"

He stood, took a scrap of paper from his desk, and handed it to me. "Here are the particulars. Tchaikovsky lives on the Fontanka Embankment with his brother Modest. I told him to expect you this afternoon."

"This afternoon?" I whined. "What if I already have appointments scheduled?"

Korsakov stared down at me. "Do you?"

"No, actually." I stared down at the floor.

"Good! It is settled." He slapped a pile of paper on his desk. "Would you do the honor of joining me at the midday meal? Our kitchen prepares a rather tasty poultry roast for the faculty. You will love it!"

I do not eat meat. I do not enjoy music. However, I do require rubles.

"I do not understand why you ate none of the roast," Korsakov remarked as he escorted me to the street. "It was delicious!"

"Nikolai Andreyevich, I cannot make this any plainer. I refuse to eat the flesh of other animals."

"But that wasn't an animal." He pointed down. "It was a chicken!"

I wanted to slap my forehead and scream, "Chickens *are* animals!" but it might be rude to contradict the man who would be paying my income for the next week or so. "I really enjoyed the potato *piroshki*. Very filling." I patted my belly.

Korsakov slipped a gold ten-ruble coin into my palm as he opened the door of a waiting *droski*. "As you wish, Rodya. *You* are the healer. I shall provide you another payment when Tchaikovsky completes the composition." Once I had stepped into the little carriage, the master turned to its driver. "Fontanka Embankment. Tchaikovsky's," he shouted, as if the older looking gentleman had difficulty hearing. When he turned to me again, the music master tapped one of his ears with a finger and winked.

How kind of him to send me off this way. I would not have to walk the long distance to the riverfront, and I would not be subject to other people's prospects. The horse trotted along only slightly faster than walking. At this unhurried pace, it would take a while to reach our destination.

I found it difficult to believe that Grigori could make himself so invaluable to Korsakov. As I observed before, he looked to other men for guidance. I should have sent him directly back home with his mother and never accepted him as a student. However, I could not read his future, which fascinated me. I assumed I could learn from him and felt I could be enough of an influence to adjust and improve his manners. I failed at gaining his respect. I failed at discovering more about this mysterious boy from Siberia. If only I could learn what he would be doing these next few weeks.

While certain the Tsar would soon perish, Grigori might not necessarily be the instrument of dispatch. I could not–and would not–change the course of history, but I might prevent the boy from committing such an act. If I could return him to Pokrovskoye, it ensured someone else would accomplish the assassination, relieving me of harboring a murderer.

I would have to devise a way to get him back to his mother. Perhaps I could write and ask her to send a request for her son to return home. I do not believe he would go on his own, and I would have to travel with him on the train to make sure he arrived safely.

The *droski* halted along the bank of the Fontanka River, across from a park. The driver hopped down and opened the door for me. I had but two coins in my pocket, the gold ten-ruble Korsakov just gave me and a one-ruble coin. I presented the ruble, but the fellow glanced down and held up a hand in refusal.

Once I stepped to the ground, I retrieved the piece of paper Korsakov had given me and walked to the address. Inside, I climbed the grand staircase to the proper level and stood outside the indicated apartment. I could hear strains of "At the Gate" played on a piano.

A handsome, clean-shaven 30-year-old man I did not recognize opened the door but a few centimeters. He looked at my face, then cocked his head and examined me from shoe-to-hair. "Yes?" came the inquiry with one raised eyebrow.

"Good afternoon. My name is Rodion Propok. Master Rimsky-Korsakov from the Music Conservatory sent me here to meet with Tchaikovsky." I extended a hand, but the fellow did not take it.

"*I*… am Tchaikovsky," he replied and stretched to full height.

"Pyotr Ilyich Tchaikovsky," I reaffirmed.

"Modest Ilyich." The man made a tiny bow. "At your service. Do come in."

He opened the door, and I followed him through an ornate entryway. Hall tables with porcelain statuettes lined both walls. At the end, I could see the full-bearded composer seated at a Becker pianino, banging at the keys with vigor. His head bobbed up and down in time to the music.

"Petya!" Modest yelled. "Petya! There is a gentleman to see you."

The folk tune stopped mid-phrase. "What, dear brother?"

"You have a caller."

The composer's gaze lingered on me for a second. "Are you here to replace my little pigeon, Lyonya?" He picked up some disarrayed pages from the piano's top. "I require your services immediately as I must complete this composition with all haste. How quickly do you transcribe?"

I wondered what Korsakov told him, if anything, regarding my visit. The true nature needed to remain confidential. "I think there may have been some misunderstanding, Mr. Tchaikovsky. Master Rimsky-Korsakov directed me to attend you as healer, not music copyist." He should have sent Grigori, not me. Perhaps he harbored reasons for keeping the boy to himself.

"A healer? What nonsense!" He stood, sliding the bench away. "Does Korsakov believe I am ill?"

Unprepared for such a question, I needed to concoct a response that did not insult Tchaikovsky yet allowed me to remain in his company. I required rubles.

"Wait!" the composer spouted. He pointed at me. "I recognize you. I know I have seen you before."

"That is possible," I replied. "I attended the charity concert for Mussorgsky. Perhaps you remember me from there."

"No. No. That's not it. More recent than that. I know I saw you somewhere…" His hand went to his chin as he searched his memories. "Ah! Now, I know. I remember seeing you at –" He stopped mid-sentence, glanced to his brother, then at the floor. "No. It must have been someone else.

I sensed he did not want his brother to know of his visits to Znamensky's. Just as well. Nevertheless, we both received services from Vasily.

"Yes. I believe you were correct." He snapped his fingers. "The charity concert. And your name again?"

"Rodion Propok." I stretched out my hand, and the composer took it. As we shook, I got a vision of his next few weeks. A handful of trips to the Turkish bath, work on this composition, and arguments with Modest. Nothing suggested illness or inability to complete the work.

"Petya," the brother interrupted. "I am taking Kolya to the theater with me. We are rehearsing *The Benefactor* today." A bright-eyed boy slightly older than Grigori appeared. Modest wrapped an arm around him. "I hope you will be fine with me departing."

"Yes. Of course. I am looking forward to the premiere. We could all use a good comedy these days." He faced me. "My dearest brother excels as a dramatist."

Modest kissed the composer on the cheek. "Don't get into any trouble with your guest, Petya." Pyotr Ilyich snapped his head away. The playwright grabbed the boy's hand and muttered, "You always liked Anatoly better," on the way out.

After the door latched, I asked, "Who is Anatoly?"

"Modest's twin." One end of Tchaikovsky's mouth drew up. "And I *do* prefer him."

"And who is…?" I pantomimed patting the head of the youngster.

"Kolya?" came the response in the form of a question.

I nodded.

"Oh, he is my brother's pupil. He cannot hear or speak. Modest studied something called 'sonic speech' and the boy's parents engaged my dearest brother to tutor him a few years back." He waved an arm about. "This is their flat, and they allow us to live here as long as instruction continues. Kolya is quite intelligent, and I believe he has learned to read and write in several languages."

"Impressive." That is, compared to what little progress I have made with the so-called apprentice left with me.

"Now that Modest has gone, I can frankly state that I recognize you from Znamensky's. Am I correct that I have seen you there?"

"Yes. My neighbor suggested taking the baths. I attended with him."

Tchaikovsky glanced toward the ceiling. "The tall, balding fellow?"

He possessed a superior memory. "That is Yuri. He is a physician."

"A physician," the composer mused. "Well… why did Korsakov not send *him* to putter over me?"

A good question. "I believe it has more to do with supporting your composition than examining your health, sir."

He slapped one hand into the palm of the other. "An amanuensis would have been more of a practical assistant."

Korsakov should have sent Grigori, but he chose me. "You can inquire of the Music Master at your next meeting."

"Indeed, I shall! You are as much use to me as a tuft of wool from a black sheep." He sat on the piano bench with his back to the keyboard. "Well, Mr. Propok, how is it that you can *help* me?"

Indeed. I required the income but had no idea how I *could* help him.

AS I stood contemplating a response to the composer's query, I observed him assess me with his vibrant blue eyes, from top to toe, much the way his brother's did a few minutes before. Perhaps he assumed I found pleasure with other men because he had seen me at the Turkish baths. My formulated, diplomatic reply must address both issues. Necessity inspires imagination, so they say.

"Perhaps you could tell me something about your current project, Mr. Tchaikovsky. That way, I might be able to formulate an approach to assisting you."

"If we are to work together, please call me 'Petya.' And may I call you 'Rodya'?"

"Of course." I grinned. All this polite chatter. If we wanted to observe proper protocols, he should be calling me, "Mr. Propok." After all, I am several hundred years older. However, I shall maintain the agreed upon informality. "Please describe your work for me."

"Yes. Well…" He stroked his beard with one hand. "My good friend Nikolai Grigorevich Rubenstein suggested I compose a piece for the impending twenty-fifth anniversary of Tsar Alexander's coronation. We discussed a few ideas and settled on the glorious Russian defeat of Napoleon Bonaparte and his failed attempt to capture Moscow."

I remember the military escapade well. The French forces fought their way to the capital only to find it deserted and charred. Without supplies or help from locals, the few troops who endured evacuated as winter set in. The Russians did not drive out the invaders through any armed engagement. Napoleon's men retreated with no shots fired. Tolstoy wrote a rather accurate depiction of this campaign. Perhaps Tchaikovsky planned to set *War and Peace* to music, a rather ambitious undertaking. I had to put a hand to my mouth to cover the amusement that entered my mind. Visions of soldiers twirling muskets and prancing about to ballet music distracted me.

The composer scowled. "Is there something humorous concerning the war or my composition?"

Apparently, the hand failed to conceal my expression. "No. Not at all. Please continue."

"My plan is to use counterpoint—weaving French and Russian tunes together—as a means to represent the battle. I call it *The Solemn Overture*."

"I see. Earlier you asked if I would be replacing someone you referred to as a pigeon. Lyonya?"

"Ah, yes. His given name is Alexsey, but I refer to him as my little pigeon. He has helped me transcribe my compositions. Unfortunately, he could not join me here in Peter. That is why I surmised Master Korsakov sent you to me."

"I can understand the confusion." My head bobbed a few times. "However, I know almost nothing about music."

"Then I ask again: How is it that you can *help* me?"

My mind had yet to derive a plausible response to that question. Korsakov requested me to provide support and guidance for this uneasy fellow so that he would complete such a massive undertaking in time for the upcoming jubilee. Neither of them knew the event would not occur as planned. This whole situation would be much easier if I did not have such a desperate need for money. It had become easier to drive me with a ruble than a whip.

"Working so intensely and rapidly can lead a man to exhaustion. Perhaps I can watch over your health as you complete this monumental task."

"Like a mother?" His voice raised in pitch. "I do not need another mother. I have managed for many years without one."

"No, more like... a concerned friend."

"Or a watchdog." Tchaikovsky squinted. "If I stray from the path, would you bare your teeth and snarl at me?"

"If that is what is required to assist you. Master Korsakov believes in your talents and has every hope of seeing your grand composition to its completion."

Petya pointed toward the Conservatory. "Then *he* should attend me, not you!"

A perceptive observation. I would have to consider my words with more care in our conversations. Especially if I wanted to rebuild my financial situation and have enough funds to pay for the rail fare to Siberia. "I believe your selection of prospective assistants to be rather limited. Would your brother be able to function in such a capacity?"

"No. Nor would I allow him." He smacked one palm onto the other. "He has his own pursuits: mentoring the child and staging his dramas."

"And Gavrilo, the Turkish bath attendant?"

"That fool! Between his horrible breath and his horrible humor, I would achieve nothing."

"Well... it seems we are fated to work together, Petya."

He surveyed me again. "How much would I have to pay you to just disappear?" His hands drew together then flew apart.

I grinned. "There is no sum great enough to deter me from my task, sir. I have my orders, and you cannot bargain away your ministering angel."

He slapped his flank. "I expect you will stick to me as a bathhouse leaf!"

"If that is what it takes to compel the completion of this piece, then so be it."

"Bah!" he exploded.

"Come, we are wasting time. Should you not be working?"

Tchaikovsky cocked his head and pursed his lips. "Do you have the acquaintance of one Nadezhda von Meck?"

Most people in St. Petersburg knew the wealthy widow financed Tchaikovsky's welfare. "She is one of my clients. Why do you ask?"

"The lady provides me the funds to create, yet she never desires to meet or attend my performances."

"She tends to be rather reclusive, and I am aware of your professional relationship." I could not determine his reason for this interrogation. "Did you wish *her* to provide the necessary motivation?"

"Aside from subsidizing my comforts, I doubt she could understand me any better than a random stranger. We only communicate through exchanged letters." The composer coughed into a clenched fist. "When she heard about this undertaking, she encouraged me to create a joyous and celebratory masterwork. I wrote her that I am not a conductor of festive pieces and anything I composed for this very purpose would be very loud and noisy, lacking artistic merit, without warmth, without love." He crossed his arms over his chest with a thump.

My task appeared daunting. However, I reminded myself that I have survived much worse situations. "Perhaps you can demonstrate some of your overture for me."

"I'm not sure what good that will do." He swiveled around to face the keyboard and began playing "*La Marseillaise*" very quietly. "This tune represents the French forces approaching Moscow. A small ensemble will play it from the side of the stage so that it sounds distant. It repeats and gets louder as the army approaches."

At the time of the Russian invasion, I remember living along the balmy shores of the German Sea, part of Napoleon's French Empire. From what I recall, General Bonaparte detested "*La Marseillaise*" and chose "*Le Chant du Départ*" as the anthem. Something inside told me that I should keep this information to myself.

"The hymn 'Troparion of the Holy Cross' follows to represent the Russian people." He played a few seconds of the piece. "After that, I intersperse the French theme with several Russian folk tunes, ending with 'God Save the Tsar.'"

Oh, heavens! His sense of musical history seemed quite distorted. "God Save the Tsar" had been composed a few years after the event he proposed to memorialize. "Fascinating!"

"Yes. While this commemorative composition does not suit my customary style, several stars in my constellation encourage its completion."

"I must confess I stand with those who desire it." Given the circumstances, I needed to reassure him, but at least my feelings aligned with the others.

He swung back to face me. "Have *you* any ideas to contribute, Rodya?"

This question caught me unprepared as I had not expected to function as consultant. When I started considering recent musical experiences, memories from the charity concert sang in my mind. I recalled the amazing suite performed by the guest of honor. "Mussorgsky's *Pictures* concluded with a section of flourishes that evoked the pealing of church bells in a celebratory fashion. Perhaps you could include something like that."

"*Church bells?*" He gazed to the ceiling. "Church bells. Yes. They would have rung the chimes to proclaim victory." He hummed what sounded like "O Lord, Save Thy People," swinging his extended arms in rhythm. "I like that. Very good! Perhaps you will be of some use after all."

I could not think of anything to say other than a bland, "Thank you."

"Let me demonstrate my appreciation by inviting you to a performance of *Swan Lake* at the Mariinsky Theater tomorrow evening. I have several seats available in my box. Feel free to bring a few friends."

Dancing. With or without twirling muskets. I may well tolerate it better than theatre or opera because there would be no dialogue or singing. I could invite Yuri and Grigori.

34

THE next morning, I wrote Grigori's mother and asked her to send a post requesting her son to return home on some pretext of her invention. I could only hope she responded without delay so that I could begin convincing the little beast to go back to Pokrovskoye before the Tsar's impending death.

When Yuri returned home, I invited him to dinner and the ballet. Dima prepared his exquisite cabbage rolls, which the two of us enjoyed. Grigori grumbled about the absence of meat.

The doctor and I dressed in our best outfits, he in a tuxedo and woolen overcoat with fur lapels, me in my dark suit over an embroidered shirt. Our young friend wore what he had brought with him.

Riding the *konka* the theater would involve transferring lines, making our arrival time uncertain. Yuri hired a carriage for us, and we rode in style.

I had expected to see a large crowd of people waiting to get into the building, but only a handful of others queued up. If we had been the only ones in attendance, I might have wondered if Tchaikovsky gave me incorrect date or time information. I exchanged questioning glances with Yuri.

Inside, the composer spotted us and hustled toward us. "Ah, Rodya. I'm glad you could make it." He surveyed our little company. "And who are your friends?"

"This is my neighbor, Yuri." I indicated the tall fellow next to me.

Tchaikovsky's eyes grew big then shrank to their initial size. "I believe I recognize you. Where have I seen you before?"

One side of the doctor's mouth curved upward. While physical relationships between men transpired publicly—the Tsar's brother Sergei brought his lover to the charity concert—it appeared the acknowledgment of such affairs remained a matter of privacy.

"Yes. Now I know." The composer looked down at Grigori. "And who is this restless youth?"

"My… apprentice." I hesitated to acknowledge the relationship, given my failure as a mentor. You cannot break a wall with your forehead. "He also assists Master Rimsky-Korsakov at the Conservatory."

"I see. And what do you do for the great master, young man?"

Grigori assumed his full height. "He is composing an opera, and I copy out musical parts for him."

Petya glared at me. "And he sent *you* to help me? Kolya should have provided me with *this* lad's talents."

"You and I are in total agreement, sir." I nodded. "Korsakov's decision still confounds me."

Shaking his head, Tchaikovsky led us down the aisle to a private box on the left-hand side of the stage. He opened the gate and ushered us in. "As you see, there is room for a few more." Six cushioned chairs awaited their charges. "Invite others to join you, if you like."

"Petya, I thought you invited us to a performance of your ballet." I waved my hand at the nearly empty chamber. "Why is there no audience?"

He grinned like a child with a secret. "This will be a performance, yes. However, it will be a rehearsal performance. We may stop and start a few times to review problematic sections. I hope you enjoy. I must go prepare now." He skittled off through a side door.

Even better than I expected. No overwhelming crowds to deal with.

"I suppose we did not need to dress up so." Yuri frowned and indicated his formal attire.

To which I responded, "No. I suppose not." I turned my head so he could not see my grin.

Grigori waved and called out to a young man who entered the auditorium. "Claude!"

I recognized the fellow as Madame von Meck's pianist, whom she called, "Achille."

"Come join us in the composer's box," Grigori invited. "Oh," he turned to me with a smirk. "I suppose it would have been better if I asked you first."

I nodded. "Yes. But all is well. I know the lad. Please have him sit with us. You will have someone to converse with." Although I feared my little anarchist might use this advantage to recruit Achille/Claude into the revolutionary army.

House lights dimmed, and Tchaikovsky stepped to his podium. The orchestra played a lush underscore as rows of dancers tiptoed and gyrated across the stage. Several times, the performance halted. The choreographer screamed at the performers regarding their lack of form or attention to the step sequences. The composer screamed at the orchestra for not following him or playing the wrong piece. He also took the choreographer to task for altering pre-arranged movements. A few times they screamed at each other for an uncomfortable minute or two.

When the white swan chose to give up her life at the end, I wondered whether I should consider my own transformation. As much as I have enjoyed this wondrous city, my sense of things to come has always served me well.

At the conclusion of the ballet, I realized it contained more memorable melodies than all the operas I have ever attended. That haunting piece accompanying the swan flight persisted in my consciousness, and I even hummed a few bars to myself as the three of us exited the theater.

During the ride home, Yuri imparted his analysis. "It surprised me how much of the music had been cut from the original version I saw in Moscow a few years back. Also, the white swan got promoted to Queen, and the evil Baron did not return in Act Four."

"I preferred the Black Swan. She was the best," Grigori expounded, which did not surprise me, as I had observed his preference for malevolence.

As we approached the Kazan Cathedral, our carriage halted before a crowd of rowdy people obstructing the way. They carried placards similar to the ones we saw outside Madame von Meck's home the night she unveiled Mussorgsky's portrait. "Land and Liberty" and more calls to remove the Tsar.

Our driver opened the carriage door. "I am sorry, gentlemen, but I will travel no further. You must continue your homeward journey on foot. It is but a few blocks." He waved us out from the vehicle. Once we all alighted, he dipped his fingers into a vest pocket and retrieved a few coins. "Here, sir." He handed them to Yuri. "This should make up for the shortened trip."

"Well," chimed the doctor as he deposited the reimbursement into his own pocket. "It appears the anarchists are out tonight." He indicated the road away from the protestors. "Shall we?"

"I wish to remain here," stated Grigori. "Please find your way home safely. I shall follow in a short while."

He idolized these zealots. They proposed to initiate a revolution that would kill the Tsar and transform Russia's trajectory. I felt certain nothing I said could change his mind. "Please be safe yourself."

As we strode off, Yuri observed, "At least the evening air remains sufficiently warm for walking." He carried the warm greatcoat folded over his arms.

One of the protestors leapt past us and addressed me. "Comrade Propok." He wore the black wool coat associated with the group's members. "Stay a moment, healer," he ordered with outstretched hand. "We would like to have a few words with you before you disappear."

We halted and the doctor inquired, "Do you know this man?"

I waited until my rapid breath and heartbeat slowed to near normal before responding, "We have not been properly introduced, but I recognize his voice." I had not forgotten the sound of that fellow who waylaid me outside our residence.

He clutched my wrist, allowing our flesh to connect. I could see only a week into his future, which allowed me to relax. A violent life would end in violence. No crossing the meadow for him.

"Let them go." Grigori stepped forward and pulled the interloper's hand away. "They are not our enemies."

"As you wish, young master." The ambushing fellow made a mock bow and swept his arm off in the direction of our travel. "You two may pass." Once he had regained his original posture, he added, "But do not return here this evening."

When I looked to Grigori's eyes, he turned his head. Despite connections with this group of revolutionaries, I felt thankful he achieved our safety. Perhaps he felt some guilt about arranging my attack during the White Night celebration. Whatever the cause, my heartbeat and breathing calmed.

Yuri peered over his shoulder as we walked away. Should this explosive group succeed in removing the Tsar, they might also establish a new form of government as well, one that did not favor the people I knew and served. Perhaps the moment for me to leave St. Petersburg had arrived. Every vegetable has its own time.

If I could save all the money Korsakov planned to pay me, I would have enough for the train tariff to Pokrovskoye with enough left over to transport me to my next home, wherever that may be. It would be best if a letter from Grigori's mother arrived in the next day or two so that I could begin the process of convincing him to head back to Siberia.

We reached our building without incident, and the doctor held the door for me. As we climbed the stairs, he remarked. "You have been very quiet. I can only imagine events of the evening disturbed you in ways I could not conceive."

How perceptive and quite correct. "Yes, my friend. My thoughts lay far away." Farther than he could conceive. Farther than the borders of this great land.

He tugged a watch from a pocket and glanced at it. "The hour is not too late. Would you care to join me for a libation before bed?"

At first, I thought he might be attempting to seduce me. I grasped his wrist to ascertain his designs. No. He had set aside any ideas of physical intimacy with me, and his intentions appeared platonic. It might be pleasant to spend some time with my neighbor—someone who helped me during this difficult time—before I left. They say an old friend is better than two new ones.

"Yes. Thank you. I believe some tea—or something a bit stronger—would be most welcome." I pulled my hand away. "But just one drink. I must visit a client in the morning."

"Just one drink. Of course, Rodya." He smiled, tilted his head down, and blushed. "As you wish."

His reddened face confirmed my understanding of his intentions. "I very much appreciate the offer."

A few days later, an envelope waiting in the mail plate caught my attention. Addressed to Grigori, the handwriting appeared familiar. His mother had written, as requested.

When the boy returned late in the afternoon, I retrieved the letter and extended my arm to him. "Grigori, there is mail for you."

He held his head at a few different angles before responding. "Who would send me a letter *here*? No one has my address."

"I believe it is your mother's hand."

"And how would you know that?" He squinted.

A sharp pain at the base of my neck made me wonder if we were about to have another tension-filled chess match.

"She wrote me a while back inquiring into your progress." I swallowed the little lump that had formed.

"Oh, yes. I have forgotten you two corresponded. Please remind me how you answered her."

"I mentioned you went to gymnasium each morning and assisted the music master in the afternoon. As far as your apprenticeship, I wrote you attended several clients with me."

"Hmmmmm. That sounds reasonably believable." He scratched at the back of his head. "It is difficult to accept that she wrote asking after me. It is my firm belief she never wants to see me again. My guess would be she probably intended to make sure I would remain in St. Petersburg a while."

My eyebrows shot up. "You think your mother left you here without expecting you to return?"

"Oh, yes. My parents cannot afford to raise me in *that* little village."

"Really? How does your father earn his keep?"

The boy's glance went to the ceiling, then the floor. "He raises and sells horses." Grigori blew air through his flapping lips.

"Don't you have brothers and sisters?"

"Mother and Father had seven other children, yes, but they all died." He spoke with the dryness of reporting weather.

Seven dead children! That poor woman. Learning of this tragedy made me wonder how she could have fostered her only surviving child with *me*. That Grigori believed his mother did not wish him to return felt untruthful. Perhaps she wanted to give him the best chances for a successful life.

Perhaps she wanted him out of the house, as the boy suggested. As I handed him the envelope, a heavy sigh escaped my mouth.

I observed as he broke the seal and pulled out the letter. His eyes darted left-to-right, over and over as he read. As he refolded the paper, his head bobbed up and down.

"Well?" I prompted.

"She wants me to go back to Pokrovskoye because my father has died."

My request stated she devise a reason for Grigori to return home, but I had no idea whether such distressing information bore any veracity or no. He spoke without any discernable emotional tone in his voice. As if reciting a train schedule or the latest horse prices.

"How sad," I offered. "Quite upsetting news, no?"

"Oh, no. Not at all. I hated the old man. He wanted me to follow him into his trading business, but I had no interest."

Almost every father wanted his son to continue his line of work. "That would be frustrating for both of you."

"To let him know how I felt, I set one of his horses free. He thought someone had stolen it."

I cannot imagine why he would share this story of mischief with me. Dima would have to count the silver later.

"When will you return to your mother?" I hoped the question did not sound too dubious or formulated.

His side glance suggested suspicion. "I have no plans to go back there."

"But your father died, and your mother wants you to come home."

"Well… that's what she wrote." He looked away. "But I suspect it is not true."

The lump at the back of my mouth returned. "How can you *say* that?"

He tilted his head. "In fact, I have a feeling *you* put her up to this." He might as well have pointed an accusatory finger at me.

I imagined chess pieces on the floor between us. He slid one of his bishops to an aggressive position.

"What?" I sputtered, hoping for adequate authenticity. If only I could protect my king by arranging all the pawns with one move. "How could I? Why would I? What…?" My shoulders hunched as I struggled to maintain restraint.

Grigori's eyelids narrowed. "I believe you want me gone from your home. I have not lived up to your expectations, even though I have provided you with more than sufficient money to pay for my lodging and meals. Meatless as they are…"

"I will be the first to admit this situation has not worked out the way I had intended, but for you to accuse me of orchestrating your departure is… well… preposterous!"

His piercing dark eyes stared into mine. "Yes. I had a feeling you would say something like that."

What impudence from this diminutive demon! If we had been playing a proper game of chess, I would have felt like swooping the pieces from the board onto the floor in frustration. Before saying another word, I took a few deep breaths. Experience taught me that to respond would be better than to react. "I am not sure how to answer your accusation."

"There is no need for an answer." He blinked. "I believe I know the truth."

Very few times in my long, long life have I felt my blood turn icy. While I still could not read the boy's future, it seemed he could sense *my* thoughts. We stood for a few moments in silence.

Grigori reached toward me, letter in hand. "Here. See for yourself."

I took the paper and read what his mother had written. She said nothing about her husband at all. The writing expressed how much she missed him and wished he would return. Grigori challenged me yet again for some perverse purpose. I stared at him with as blank an expression as I could muster in the moment.

"What? It's not like I put arsenic in your tea again." He rested both hands on his hips, elbows pointed outward.

I wanted to project as much calm as possible so as not to give in to his trickery. After a few shallow breaths, I asked in a measured tone and tempo, "What do you want from me?"

The edges of his mouth curled upward. "You cannot possibly provide for me what I desire. I know you are unable to read me the way you look into others' minds, and that frustrates you. The last few days, my observation of your actions tells me you embrace a powerful secret. Tell me. What is this information you have withheld?" He folded his arms across his chest.

I could not disclose my knowledge of the Tsar's death and my suspicion that he might be the assassin. Perspiration moistened my neck. "There are things…" I paused for a bolstering breath and time to calculate a reply. "…I cannot reveal to others. My words may alter their behavior, for better or for worse, and I believe this is one of those situations."

"I see." He hugged himself. "Is this because you have some knowledge of my impending actions?"

So many questions I could not, should not, answer. "All I will say is that I believe it would be best for everyone if you returned home."

"St. Petersburg *is* my home now."

My head turned toward the east. "I meant Pokrovskoye."

"Yes, I know. I have no desire to go back to that trifling, provincial town. This city holds my future. Of *that* I am certain."

Reflecting on incidents at the memorial in the Summer Garden when he first arrived and near the Moika Palace a few days later, I agreed with him. "Maybe at some point in future years, but at this time, I feel you need to leave. The sooner the better."

His darting eyes suggested troublesome sentiments. "I would prefer to remain here, even as your 'apprentice.'" He snorted. "If you both wish me back in Siberia, perhaps I should consider that option. Even a crawfish is a fish when your hook has no luck." The boy returned the threatening bishop to its original position.

"Please. Please give it some thought. I wish I could say more, but I fear I might divulge potentially devastating information." Sweat trailed down the side of my face.

"I see how much distress this situation has caused." Grigori turned away. "While I do not agree with you about me leaving"–his eyes darted about the room—"a clock may soon strike the hour for me to close this chapter and begin again with my parents."

Given his propensity for misrepresentation, this unexpected transformation might just have expressed what he believed I wanted to hear. But toward what end, I could not determine. Better to extinguish the spark before flames arise. For the moment, and in my best interests, I chose to accept his words as sincere.

The conflagration in my mind faded to embers. I could hear crawfish whistling on the mountain.

Over breakfast, Grigori announced, "I have decided to return to Pokrovskoye."

I scrutinized my tea with audible sniffs. Yuri informed me that when heated, arsenic imparted the aroma of garlic. The boy had filled the cup from the samovar before handing it to me.

He smiled. "You needn't worry. It is just tea. Nothing else."

After a quick sip, I inquired, "What changed your mind? Did something happen of which I have no knowledge?"

"Nothing has changed. I made the decision last evening after our conversation. I have determined to make it *my* choice rather than yours." He glanced downward. "Or my mother's."

"I see," I said, even though I did not. "When are you planning to leave?"

"The schedule shows a train departing tomorrow morning for Moscow, where I shall board the Trans-Siberian to Tyumen."

Had I a mouthful of tea, I would have spit it out in surprise. "Tomorrow!? That is too soon. I have much to accomplish the next few days." Most of all, I needed to finish my business with Tchaikovsky and visit my clients to let them know I planned to leave. However, I did not wish Grigori to know of my own determination.

He looked up at an angle. "I don't remember inviting you to join me."

"Well, I planned to accompany you home to make sure you got there safely." I took another sip of tea.

"After all the things you have witnessed me accomplish during our time together, do you really feel I cannot take care of myself, Mr. Propok?"

"But… but… I assumed…" I sputtered.

"There is no reason for you to hover over me. Like a mother." His gaze turned to my face, and he patted a pocket. "I still have my magic stone should I require protection."

I recalled how he displayed that dark lump of rock outside the Summer Garden, claiming it possessed powers he could wield.

I felt it not in my best interest to tell him I planned to leave St. Petersburg permanently. "I wish to escort you. I am certain your mother would appreciate that."

His head rotated a few centimeters left and right several times. "If you believe it is best, who am I to say?" He held his open palms up.

I felt the urge to roll my eyes at this sudden shift in compliance. "Can you give me a few days to complete my immediate duties?"

"I suppose I could, but I thought you wanted me out of here as quickly as possible."

I lowered my chin to my chest. Neither of us spoke.

His assertion rang true, but I still needed time to set several situations in order. My mind gyrated with myriad thoughts requiring contemplation.

Once Grigori departed for the gymnasium, I refilled my teacup from the dull, dented brass samovar. Dima had not polished it for quite a while, but the device still served us well. Aside from my morning tea, the servant used it frequently to prepare evening meals. A well-worn, practical, and versatile apparatus. Much like myself, I reflected. Not to mention this amazing city. After a few centuries, we have both lost our luster and acquired a few dents.

With regard to finances, I have secured a nearly sufficient sum to afford our rail fare plus adequate funds to sustain me while I relocate to my next place of residence. As morning is wiser than evening, I planned to consider my geographical options once I have returned the boy to his family.

The boy. This moniker hardly feels fitting for one who appears wiser than his mere decade on this Earth. In many ways, his advanced attitude bears a similarity to my own accumulated experiences. We both concealed wisdom and understanding behind deceptively youthful façades.

I hoped to learn from him, but that has not come to pass. I hoped to encourage him to be less angry and vitriolic, but that, too, has not come to pass. These two failures weighed heavy upon my breast.

I have fostered a fear of him, which, in the end, made little sense and seemed rather odd. He did attempt to harm me—unsuccessfully—on more than one occasion that I knew of. Most recently, the attack outside. The first time with tea. I stared into the nearly empty cup.

Having foreknowledge of the Tsar's imminent demise overwhelmed me. This People's Will group Grigori befriended openly conspired to remove the Emperor. They could be grooming him to perform the deadly deed. And if he were the instrument of their insidious plot, no logical reason existed for me to interrupt the flow of history, should that be pre-destined to pass. I never made such an attempt before.

At first, I did not want to suffer such a crippling outcome for the boy if I could somehow rearrange the chess pieces. His mother had left Grigori in my care, and I felt a fiduciary duty to protect him. As time passed, I realized the ultimate futility of this enterprise, and my motivations metamorphosed into self-preservation.

I worried how harboring a potential assassin might implicate me, disrupting my disciplined and efficient life. But now that I planned to leave St. Petersburg, I saw no reason to worry about such foreboding reflections. However, my conscience, my integrity, my soul, forbade me to stand by without acting in response.

Yet, Grigori's presence makes me tremble, as if he were a wolf in the woods. Something about this little imp leaves me uneasy and unsettled. If only I could have discovered the seed before it sprouted. He is so stubborn one could chop wood upon his head.

Nevertheless, I have made my decision to depart, and I shall need to follow through with the action. Before anything, I must meet with my clients to inform them of my withdrawal from St. Petersburg. Also, a few more rubles would, indeed, help to pad my purse. However, the one person I needed to see the most—the one who paid me the best—I could not see at all.

Lady Catherine, now the Tsaritsa, provided me with plenty of gold in the past. Having knowledge of her husband's death would make a visit quite uncomfortable. The last thing I would want would be to speak without intention and refer to the upcoming event. I do not possess patience sufficient to console her avalanche of grief.

As plans stood, I would spend the morning with Tchaikovsky. When I stepped into the street, I inhaled the bouquet of St. Petersburg: boiling cabbage, frying onions, and horse manure. My walk to the Fontanka Embankment seemed shorter than before. Perhaps the knowledge of my impending departure minimized my accumulating frustrations with the people, and city, surrounding me.

The younger Tchaikovsky, Modest, greeted me with a dispassionate expression. "Ah, Mr. Propok. Please, do come in. My brother has not yet returned from wherever he goes on mornings when he stays out late the night before."

My first thought went to Znamensky's Turkish bath, a place where the composer often retreated. Perhaps he found inspiration for his music there. I could not imagine what sensual delights Vasily delivered.

Modest led me to the parlor, where his charge, the young Nikolai Konradi, a few years older than Grigori, sat pecking at keys on the piano in a haphazard order with one hand, the other resting on the music holder.

The sequence did not remind me of any tune I knew, but the result sounded more pleasing to me than some performances by others.

"Kolya!" Modest screamed. As the boy could not hear, he continued playing. Modest stepped to keyboard and slapped at the fellow's hand.

I winced in sympathy. A breathy gasp escaped my mouth as I inhaled by reflex.

The music stopped. Flurries of gesticulations followed.

Kolya turned and stood. He assessed me with his soft eyes and extended a hand.

"Mr. Propok, may I present my student, Nikolai Konradi." Modest made a few hand movements near his own ear. "There is no need to speak as he is deaf."

After the cruelty I just witnessed, I hesitated to take the recently slapped hand, but when I did, torrents of disturbing images flooded my mind.

THE Konradi parents allowed Modest and his brother to live in this luxurious apartment on the Fontanka Embankment as long as their son received lessons and his interpersonal communication skills improved. They might not have been so happy to learn his trusted linguistic coach pilfered half of Kolya's allowance. In addition, I witnessed scenes of the adult man placing his hands on the boy's body in ways inappropriate to their student-teacher relationship. Touching the backside of Kolya's knee pants, a shirtless hug from behind, protracted kisses on the lips, staring into each other's eyes. I found it odd the boy harbored no ill feelings regarding such exploitation. Any form of amusement as long as he doesn't cry, I suppose.

I wondered if Petya knew of this scandalous behavior. And if he did, what he had done to address it. My short time around the composer demonstrated a preoccupation with his own person and work, oblivious to proximate goings-on. It would not surprise me if he had no knowledge of his brother's fiduciary duty violations.

Kolya pulled his hand from mine, and I turned my head so that neither of the other two people in the room could observe an expression of disgust on my face. Learning of these repulsive abuses made me want to leave at once. However, I still required funds for the upcoming travels, and I needed to remain as long as possible, no matter how offensive the instructor and his actions.

When I turned to observe Kolya, he smiled at me with one raised eyebrow. A pleasant, happy expression suggesting interest in my person. Knowing what I did of his distasteful demeanor, this created even more discomfort for me. It felt as though my throat constricted, making breathing difficult. I wheezed.

"Are you not well, Mr. Propok?" asked Modest.

Hearing his voice froze me in place. Following a deep, grating breath, I replied, "Just a momentary irregularity. All is well, sir. All is well."

"I hope you will not mind waiting for my brother on your own." Modest smiled with one raised eyebrow, causing me to nearly choke on my own saliva. "You see, Kolya and I must visit his parents to demonstrate the boy's most recent accomplishments."

I would not want to be in *that* room. I did not even want to be in *this* room. The sooner I could leave, the faster my nerves could subside. "Perhaps I should leave as well. I can always return —"

The front door slammed and Petya marched into the parlor. "Propok! Just the man I wanted to see."

Having knowledge of his brother's actions, this presented yet another dilemma as to whether I should disclose such information in hopes of rescuing the suborned lad. In all my centuries, I have not come to anyone else's rescue, and saving Kolya would do little, if anything, for me.

His introductory phrase impressed me the composer possessed some important information he wished to impart. Unsure of his intentions, I knitted my brows and blurted, "Yes?"

"You have been most helpful, friend. Your encouragement and presence have assisted me at every moment." He made a slight bow. "My composition is finished, and it will premiere at the Tsar's jubilee. I no longer require your services." His hand indicated the hallway to the front door.

There is no good without bad. No longer would I suffer the presence of brother Modest and his hapless pupil. However, I had been counting on the additional funds to tide me over until I could begin earning money on my own in my new—yet undetermined—locale.

One marginal matter required addressing, though. "Before I go, sir, I should like to state, again, my opposition to your use of gunshots to punctuate the final measures of your brilliant work. I feel they detract from the emotional height of the moment and suggest more of a circus or carnival-like scene."

"Hmmmm, yes." He nodded. "Begone, now."

I felt like a discarded undergarment with this sudden dismissal. Tchaikovsky could be mercurial, but to be ordered out in such a capricious manner soured me on the man. At least I could rest assured the premature death of Alexander II would preclude the introduction of this lumbering and dreadful musical opus.

As I walked toward the hallway, I heard loud banging on the piano in chunky chords. Treble, bass, treble, bass, treble, bass.

Such an extraordinary household. A composer, a playwright who teaches the deaf, and a victimized student. Perhaps I should be glad to be free of its deleterious influence. Although Modest has had more success with his charge than me with mine, I would have never employed instruction methods similar to his.

The air along the embankment smelled particularly salty. Perhaps the wind had shifted. Consulting my pocket watch, I realized a few hours remained before my first appointment of the afternoon. Given that no *konka* served this area, I strolled back to Nevsky Prospekt and headed toward The *Passazh*.

Every time I departed a town in the past, I felt some exhilaration, some sadness, and some apprehension. My interactions with others as a healer allowed me to build relationships in ways most people never experienced. This time, I stumbled into several situations where some knowledge of the future proved overwhelming. My decision to leave would help me avoid beholding a potential downfall by the House of Romanov as well as abuse of a deaf boy. I felt uneasy and unsettled about the choice to gamble on a new hometown, yet I remained sure it would be the correct course of action. As the centuries passed and humankind progressed, our world grew brighter with novel inventions and clever devices, yet dimmer in philosophy, values, and sentiment.

Despite the anthology of talented artists who populated this bedeviled city, I had grown disconnected from its scene. I thought back to the night Grigori's mother presented the little monster, when I allowed my curiosity to get the better of me. If only I had chosen the proper and wiser path of dismissing them straightaway. The introduction of this boy detoured my life onto a route I had never considered. If only I could retrace my steps and begin anew. Unfortunately, history proceeds in only one direction. We cannot return to the moments of our regrettable decisions to choose a different course.

After passing through the gates of The *Passazh*, I strode to the small café where I brought Grigori for lunch after first introducing him to the Music Master. I sat sipping some borscht and nibbling a bublik as if I had all the time in the world. Yet, the Tsar's death approached, and I needed to accomplish several more matters before I could relax again.

Throughout the afternoon, I visited several clients, which gave me the opportunity to conduct final sessions and inform them of my departure. When I returned home in the early evening, the aroma of roasting potatoes greeted me. This reminded me I shall need to inform Dima of my imminent departure. He has served me well the last few years. Aside from managing my rooms in a very tidy order, as well as handling our young visitor, he produced the most delicious meals. In all likelihood he would be able to hire on with another gentleman, perhaps my neighbor, Yuri. The doctor spent many evenings at our dinner table complimenting the servant's culinary skills and devouring his cooking.

I crossed the hallway and knocked on the door. Yuri answered wearing a brocade silk dressing gown.

"I am so sorry. Are you entertaining?" I burbled.

A wide grin crossed his face. "Not at all. Just relaxing before a visit to Znamensky's later. Would you care to join me?"

While the thought of Vasily working over my stiff and stressed body sounded appealing, I dreaded a potential encounter with Tchaikovsky. "Thank you, no, but I shall have to pass this time. My evening plans are... already... planned." I could not think of a better response, and I let my nerves get the best of me.

"Yes, of course," the doctor responded. He raised his nose and sniffed the air. "By the by, do I smell the aroma of roasting potatoes?"

For the first time all day, I laughed. The unanticipated release of tension felt marvelous as well as therapeutic. "Yes, my friend. Would you care to join me? There is a particular matter I wish to discuss with you."

I sat alone at breakfast the following day. Dima placed a bowl of steaming kasha on the table.

"Have you seen Grigori this morning?" I questioned as I plopped a lump of butter onto the hot cereal.

"Our young master did not return home last evening, sir." The servant spun about and headed back to the kitchen.

The boy had never stayed out all night before. Even when we attended the White Night celebration, he returned before sunset. As he made clear previously, he can take care of himself. However, I preferred to return him to his mother alive and in a healthy state.

Upon completion of my morning ablutions, I headed out to speak with Rimsky-Korsakov regarding payment for my services with Tchaikovsky. When I reached the street, a carriage displaying the royal seal stood nearby.

A tall man with dark hair dressed in a fine suit approached me. "Mr. Propok?"

When someone knew my name and I had no knowledge of his, it rattled my confidence. "Who inquires, sir?"

He made a slight bow, which diminished my dread. "Mikhail Mikhailovich Dolgorukov. You are healer to my sister, Catherine Mikhailovna."

I did not know she had siblings. It never came up. "Yes. Yes, I am."

"The Tsaritsa requests your presence."

The person I did not wish to see because I might accidentally divulge my knowledge of Alexander's approaching death. I strolled off down Nevsky Prospekt.

Mikhail grabbed my arm as I passed. When I grasped his hand to remove it, I saw his days at the palace, attending his sister, conveying correspondence, and comforting the grieving widow.

"Please allow me to pass, sir." I requested. "Master Korsakov awaits me at the Conservatory." In fact, Korsakov had no idea I planned to visit, but I needed to suggest something plausible and imperative.

"Your appointments can wait, Mr. Propok." He withdrew his grip. "Perhaps I should have said, 'My sister *demands* your attendance.'" He opened the carriage door and bade me enter.

It appeared I had no choice in this matter, and I acquiesced. The maroon velvet seats appeared timeworn, with small tears and holes from years of use. Even with all the royal riches, the mere brother of the Tsar's second wife did not merit a well-appointed carriage in good condition.

The fellow sat opposite me and rapped twice on the roof. I sank as far as I could into the thin padding so that my face would not be visible. At first, I had no desire for others to see me, but I soon realized whatever reputation I thought I needed to protect would disappear in a few days. Gazing through the window, I observed people along the street straining to get a look at us.

At the foot of Nevsky Prospekt, we turned onto the palace grounds. As much as I dreaded seeing Catherine, riding in a royal carriage elevated my mood. I hoped my next incarnation aligned more closely with the ruling class.

Mikhail led me through a series of hallways to a chamber I had never seen before. Grander than the previous apartments, this sitting room had taller ceilings, excessive gilding, and more than one interior door. The furniture appeared plump and cushy. In the center stood a small table with the deck of square cards Catherine had so enjoyed contemplating.

"Wait here," Mikhail instructed before leaving and shutting the door to the hallway behind him.

Left alone with my thoughts in this sanctimonious sanctum, I wondered how many of the country's poor could have been fed and clothed with the money the royal family spent on just this chamber. While I could not condone the People's Will methodology for effecting change, I sympathized with their motivations. They appealed to Grigori's appreciation for anarchy. Similar sentiments have resulted in a bad end for other modern European monarchies.

A door opened behind me, and I turned to see Catherine in a gold-trimmed gown. She raised her chin in my direction.

"Your highness," I sighed as I bowed.

"Dear Rodya." The hint of a smile appeared. "There is no need for such formality. I am still the same Catherine you have always known." She stepped toward me and took my hand with her ring-encrusted fingers.

As soon as her flesh contacted mine, my mind overflowed with tearful and upsetting scenes. Grief over her husband's death, scrambling to retain any semblance of the power she had struggled so long to achieve, abandonment by the House of Romanov. I struggled to maintain a calm expression in light of these disturbing images.

"Have you been well, my lady?" I faced down as I pulled away.

With a sidelong glance she responded, "I believe you should know the answer to *that* question, my dear, even though it has been quite a while since your last visit." Catherine glided to the table and picked up the cards. "Shall we have a go?" The tilt of her head suggested an ulterior motive.

I reached for the deck. "Shall I shuffle for you?"

As I approached, she pulled away. "They are all set, thank you."

She began turning up cards, and a few recognizable images appeared. The path, the heron, the fox, the scythe, the snake.

"What do you make of *this*?" she inquired, passing a bejeweled hand over the display.

My eyes darted from picture to picture. With any other person, I might have explained that bad times lay ahead, most likely brought about by underhanded friends or family members. While interpreting the Gypsy cards might not have been my specialty, this arrangement appeared rather obvious. I wondered if Catherine had placed the cards in this order to produce a personal and sharp message.

"Dearest Catherine —"

"I'll tell you what *I* see," she interrupted. "I see a man whom I have entrusted with my *life*." She paced about the room as she continued. "Someone I allowed into my private chambers, a man I have treated as an equal. A fellow who has vital, important information about me and my family that he deliberately withholds. For what purpose, I cannot determine." The Tsaritsa, beads of sweat dotting her face, turned to confront me. "Speak, healer. Speak!"

I could feel my own perspiration weeping from several places. Concocting a credible response required all my diplomatic skills. "What makes you believe I have held back knowledge regarding your health, Your Highness?" My head rotated away from her as I spoke.

"When we last met—at Madame von Meck's event—I could tell you knew... something about *me*. Your expression changed; however, you regained composure within a second or two, but long enough for me to recognize the situation. I concluded you held back information I wish... no... *need* to know. As you did not request time to consult me since then, I compelled you to attend. These are just flowers. Berries will come soon."

Sweat flowed in rivulets. If only I could escape as quickly as possible without angering her or revealing what I foresaw. It might have been easier to bite my elbow.

I thought about the speech I gave Grigori when he asked a similar question. "There are times, my lady, when I cannot reveal the substance of what I have discovered. My words may alter your behavior, for better or for worse, and I believe this is one of those times."

She stood, unblinking, staring at me. Although wife of the Emperor, she had no power, even over the pig. No order, no threatened torture could open my lips.

"But Rodya…" She relaxed her posture and softened her eyes, an obvious shift in attitude, a modification of strategy and approach. On several occasions she had attempted to sway me with her body; however, she never deciphered my indifference to people of the opposite sex, or any sex for that matter. As Tsaritsa, that kind of behavior reflected even worse upon her. "You can tell *me*." Her eyelashes fluttered in flirtation.

My feelings for her shifted from sympathy to pity. A prince's daughter, who served as lady-in-waiting while also performing royal concubine functions, had achieved her goal of marrying the Tsar. Yet she still attempted to peddle her female charms when she could not get her way.

"I am sorry, my lady, but I cannot, shall not, will not —"

"Enough!" Catherine barked and marched to a shelf by the door. She rang the same crystal bell from her previous rooms, and her brother appeared from the hallway. "Mishka, please show the gentleman out." Catherine turned to me with narrowed eyes. "Mr. Propok, I wish never to see you again." Following a grand turn and a flourish of fabric, she disappeared through the door from which she had entered.

For once, we bore the same sentiments.

Mikhail Dolgorukov accompanied me back to the coach that transported us here and opened the door. "Shall I have the driver convey you to the Music Conservatory, Mr. Propok?"

That had been my intended destination. However, following two days of rejection by former clients, I had no desire to make it three in a row, as the gods adore trinities. In addition, I wanted no further favors from the royal family and decided to return home. "No, thank you, sir. I shall walk."

39

WHEN I reached Nevsky Propspekt, a *konka* heading east pulled in front of me, and I hopped on. After a few minutes of fresher air, my mind cleared. Leaving behind all the problems polluting my thoughts, the realization hit me that I needed to replace the additional ten rubles I might not receive from Korsakov for assisting Tchaikovsky with that appalling composition. I decided to stay aboard until Sadovaya Street and visit Suvorin at *Novoe Vremya*.

"Friend!" he shouted as I entered his book-strewn establishment. "I have not seen you in a while. How did you get on with *Anna Karenina?*"

I chuckled. "Good enough, but I liked *War & Peace* much better."

"More intrigue? Larger cast of characters?" he guessed.

"Both true, but I found it difficult to sympathize with Anna. Almost felt like throwing *myself* under a train."

The publisher guffawed.

I continued, "Count Bezukhov's personal and family struggles captured my interest more deeply."

"Yes, yes. Several other people have expressed similar views." He nodded. "And what brings you here, today, friend? Are you seeking a new Tolstoy? Sorry to disappoint, but he has not yet completed a new work."

"*The Death of Ivan Ilyich*."

"*Who* died?" Suvorin scrunched his face, making his straggly beard look even more like fringe on a *babushka*'s shawl.

"No one that I know of. It is to be the title of Tolstoy's next book."

"Ahhh… And how did this information come to *you* when *I*, his publisher, have not even heard?" He straightened his spine and looked away.

"Madame Panaeva invited me to attend her writing circle. Tolstoy read the opening of his draft."

Suvorin's eyes bulged. "You… met… Tolstoy? In person?"

His protruding eyes reminded me of Yulia Zhadovskaya, and I shuddered. "Yes, along with Turgenev, Goncharov, and… Chernyshevsky."

"Not Dostoevsky?"

"No. Avdotya said Dostoevsky quit the group because he and Turgenev disagreed about too many things. I wish I could have met the author."

After all, I gleaned my name from one of his characters.

"And how was Tolstoy's writing? Good? Bad? You must tell me!"

I hunched my shoulders. "He read only the barest part of the opening. Not enough to develop an informed opinion."

"Ivan Ilyich…" the publisher mumbled to himself as he scribbled on a piece of paper.

My throat felt dry. "I must confess I am a bit parched. Do you have more of that kvass?"

"Of course!" He stood, retrieved a bottle from the cabinet, and poured two glasses. "So… again, I ask, what brings you here today?"

A good question. I just planned to go home and nurse my emotional wounds, but spotting the streetcar made me jump onboard. Contemplating my financial woes made me consider selling the writings I had penned. Hence, the visit to this cozy office. After a quick sip of kvass I asked, "If I wrote a book, would you publish it?"

Suvorin had taken a mouthful and gagged, spilling brownish liquid all over the counter. "If I had a kopek for every person who asked me that question, I would live in a palace today." He wiped at the wet spots with his long, flowing sleeves. "What makes *your* book worth printing?"

An issue I had not considered before. I could only imagine how many aspiring authors had written books and wished for publication. After a few seconds of deliberation, I realized, "Many of my clients are well-known residents of St. Petersburg, and —"

"You wish to divulge their secret lives?" He licked his lips. "That would be quite profitable. Yes. Yes, indeed."

I could see imaginary rubles piling up before his glazed eyes. "I am not sure I would be comfortable revealing personal matters I learned in private, in confidence."

"Even if I pay you beforehand?" His fingers twittered.

He seemed to like the idea. Perhaps a bit too much. My clients disclosed information to me believing no one else would learn of it. It would be a breach of confidence to make these intimate details known. However, I needed money and would not be around to suffer the consequences. If Suvorin paid me more than Korsakov owed me, I saw no reason to approach the Music Master for the remainder of my fee. "How much are you offering?"

"Perhaps I should examine your papers first, friend."

"Of course. I shall return soon with my manuscript." I downed the rest of the kvass and strutted out of the shop. With no *konka* in sight, I strolled home, accelerating my pace the closer I got.

Inside, I found Grigori sitting in my den, reading.

He looked up when one of the floorboards squeaked. "Ah, Mr. Propok. I have been waiting to speak with you."

"Where were you last night?" I didn't mean to sound parental but could not think of another way to ask.

"I attended a protest and stayed with one of my friends. This morning I went to gymnasium and told them I would be leaving. After that, I informed the Music Master." He patted the book. "This is very interesting reading. I am surprised you have such volumes in your library."

He held my copy of *The Idiot*, Dostoevsky's manifesto on morality and religion. I imagine he enjoyed the anarchist sentiments. "One of my favorites. I am glad you are enjoying it as well."

"Particularly the anti-Church arguments. You know I am not a believer."

"Yes, I remember our previous conversation."

"I should like to leave tomorrow." Grigori stared at me. "Would that be possible?"

If I could get sufficient funds from Suvorin, we could depart this evening. "I believe we might accomplish that. However, I must visit the *Novoe Vremya* offices to speak with its publisher. Would you like to accompany me?"

"That pro-Tsarist drivel?" he snapped. "Why would I want to go there?"

A good question. However, I wanted to keep the boy as close as my shirt. "I understand how you might feel about the newspaper, but I am planning to sell my writing to earn money for our journey."

His head popped up. "You write?! I thought you only read other people's books and other people's minds."

A deep breath helped me avoid a mindless reaction to the insult. "I have kept notes on my clients and also my experiences in St. Petersburg. The publisher believes I could realize quite a bit of money from this."

"Did you write anything about *me?*" His eyes bulged.

Oddly enough, I did not reference Grigori in my notes at all. However, given his unpredictable nature, and the darkness of his soul, I could not predict the correct response. This seemed like a good time to just eat bread and salt. "No, I did not mention you."

Grigori turned his head to several angles before responding. "Yes, I shall accompany you, but if I do not feel comfortable, I shall leave straightaway."

"Of course. Just let me gather my papers." I opened the locked drawer where I had stashed the draft. After setting it on top, I secured the bundle with a crisscross wrapping of string.

As we walked up Nevsky Prospekt, I considered asking Grigori about his recent activities but then realized he would only be in my company for another few days.

"Ah, Propok! Back so soon?" Suvorin greeted us as we entered. He looked down. "And who is your little friend?"

I imagined Grigori bristled at *little friend*. "My… apprentice. I asked him to join me. I hope that is not a problem."

"No, of course not." He reached for the bundle. "Let me take a look at your writings."

I handed him the manuscript. Suvorin placed it on the workbench and untied the string. As he read, his lips wiggled, parted, and the tip of his tongue became visible. After examining the first page, he flipped through and stopped every so often to peruse various sections. His head bobbed as he absorbed my story.

"Very interesting," he mused. "*Very* interesting."

That put a grin on my face. "I am glad you like it."

"Hmmmmm. I did not say I liked it." He smoothed his stringy beard with one hand. "I said I found it very interesting."

A most awkward burden to begin the bargaining. "So… what will you pay me?"

"Normally, I would not purchase the incipient work of a new author, but because you are my friend, and I believe people will want to read the intimate details you provide, I would consider… say… ten rubles."

The same as Korsakov's wages. "*Ten rubles*?! Is that an insult or a joke?"

"Neither." He folded his arms across his robe. "Simply my offer for your manuscript."

An additional ten rubles would not last me for long. "How about twenty-five? I believe that to be a more reasonable price."

Suvorin snickered. "You think more of your work than I do. If you will not accept ten, I suggest you take your pages back." He shifted the pile toward me.

Grigori stepped forward, one hand in a pocket. "Give Mr. Propok fifty rubles." He glared, eyes wide, at the publisher.

I choked at the number. Much more than I requested. Fifty rubles might last me a few months.

"Fifty… rubles?" Suvorin intoned.

The boy nodded four times.

"Yes. Fifty rubles sounds fair." The publisher jerked upright, as if under the control of another, and walked in the manner of a rigid automaton into his back office.

"How did you *do* that?" I questioned Grigori.

"I will explain afterward. For now, take the rubles, and let us leave."

Several minutes later, the little negotiator and I walked down Nevsky Prospekt. Five gold ten-ruble coins jangled in my pocket.

"How did you induce Suvorin to open his treasure cave and pay me fifty rubles?"

Grigori patted his pocket and nodded his head.

"The magic stone?"

"Yes, and I believe you should give me one of those coins for commanding such a good price."

That seemed fair. I would still have forty rubles, more than I had bargained for. I fished out a gold piece and handed it to the boy.

He scrutinized it as if judging a diamond, turning and examining the coin in the sunlight. "Good. Now, I wish to murder me some meat pies!"

AFTER Grigori purchased and devoured three grease-drenched meat pies, we stopped at *The Passazh,* where I purchased a nesting set of three suitcases for travel.

"Why do you require so many valises?" he inquired when we arrived home. "Do you expect to be away for a long time?"

Not wanting to reveal the true nature of my journey, I needed to formulate something he might believe. The dull and dented urn caught my eye, and I pointed at it. "I should travel to Tula and purchase a new samovar."

"That would be the place," he shot back with one raised eyebrow, implying his awareness of my perjury. The lad's perceptive nature allowed him to unravel knots tied by fools.

Grigori went to his room, I imagined to pack his belongings. I hoped he took his collection of powder packets with him. The next occupant of this apartment might not be as resistant to poisons.

The decision of what to take and what to leave behind felt daunting and overwhelming. I had acquired more apparel and personal belongings than I could pack into three nesting suitcases.

A pair of tawny kidskin gloves on my dresser communicated they wanted to accompany me to my next destination. Over the centuries, men protected their hands with thick leather or metal. However, as modern fashions changed, gloves began to disappear. I rarely wore them, but they cost me a few rubles. Roughly the same color as my own skin, thin and smooth, they felt cool to the touch. Allowing sentimentality to wash over me, I pressed them into the pockets of a pair of good trousers before folding and packing them into the larger valise.

One thing I decided to bring was the set of *Anna Karenina* volumes, as they might command a good price at a later date. I added several changes of clothing and stood the luggage next to the door.

Grigori emerged from his room carrying the knapsack he had brought from home. I planned to use the smallest case for my toiletries, but I offered it to the boy to promote peace.

"Thank you, no. I have not acquired anything here I wish to bring with me."

It astonished me that someone could live with so few possessions. I had filled my apartment with many useful items. However, I would need to acquire countless new items in my next location, wherever that might be. Yuri agreed to employ Dima, and they should be able to sell what I left behind with little difficulty.

Grigori snuck up behind me. "Are you sad to be leaving your home?"

"Pardon me?" I wondered if his question intended to elicit the truth that I planned not to return to St. Petersburg.

"If I understood correctly, you have not left the city since your arrival a few years ago. Does it make you sad to leave?"

The thought had not occurred to me, but his accusation stood correct. "I guess I never considered such a sentiment, but it is true."

"I have lived here only a short time, but I am sad to leave. However, I am certain that I shall return." Grigori settled fists on his hips. "In fact, I believe I will die here."

"What?" At times his provocative words proved shocking and upsetting, but I believed he spoke them all with intention.

"Not any time soon," he rejoined. "I imagine it will be at least thirty years from now. There is much to accomplish in that time."

Again, a phrase meant to provoke. "How can you be so certain of your future?"

"There are things I know that you do not." The barest corner of his mouth turned up.

If only I could have developed a technique to see his future the way I saw others. It might have saved me indeterminable trouble and anxiety. "I may be sad to leave as well, but I feel that we shall both be happy upon returning."

"I might get back here before you, you know." His sidelong glance suggested he deduced my plan.

"How can you *say* that?" It began to feel like yet another chess match. "You are to return to your family home, and I shall come back in a matter of…"

"Hours? Days? Weeks? Months?" He pummeled questions. "Years, maybe?"

His aggressive attitude startled me. "I am not sure what you mean, Grigori."

"Of course not, Mr. Propok. Of course not."

I felt the need to take a few breaths before continuing. "You have made it clear you wish to remain in St. Petersburg. Have you no desire to see your parents again?"

His head shook a few times. "No. Not really. More than anything, I wish to retrieve a few… items before returning."

"Well, if that is all you are going to do in Pokrovskoye, would you like me to wait with you, and we could travel back together?" It seemed only polite to offer, even if insincere.

"Mr. Propok, I know you have no intention of staying in that little remote village. I have even less desire, but there are several things I had forgotten to bring with me. Besides, you need to travel to…"

Seconds passed before I realized he wanted me to finish the thought. "Ah… Tula."

"Tula, yes. To get a new…"

When he did not complete the phrase, I offered, "Um… samovar."

"Of course. As they say, one should never bring their own samovar to Tula."

My heart stammered as I fathomed my own previous pointless existence. As I kept reminding myself, in the past, I avoided taking actions that might change the course of history. However, in a short while, I would perform a task that, while not changing the overall path before us, might save—or enrich—one young person's life. And I could not even discuss the matter or let him know of my motives.

"Yes, it would be pointless," I agreed. My conscience churned with turmoil as I perpetuated this lie. He knew I would not return yet did not confront me. Divining his motives proved difficult.

Perhaps bored with the discussion or wanting to have one last look around, Grigori returned to his room.

During my time in St. Petersburg, I had the honor and privilege to meet and work with so many of its artistic and creative denizens, as well as social luminaries and a particular royal family member. When Suvorin publishes my memories, I could only imagine how my former clients' sentiments toward me might change. Having gained their confidence, they revealed personal information I consequently made public. If the same thing happened to me, I knew for certain it would prove disconcerting. However, I arrived with an assumed façade and name, making it nearly impossible to locate me once I left town. Better take a scythe to the grass before any dew settles.

I considered several destinations for relocation after I returned Grigori to the safety of his family. While I had not yet lived in several major European cities, the New World felt a blank slate to me, and the remaining continents seemed foreboding or too challenging due to major cultural and anthropological differences. Perhaps I should focus my energies on the current situation and deliver the little devil to his sainted parents before making any permanent decisions.

Having lived with Grigori for quite a while now, I could not imagine the type of people who might have brought such a dark spirit forth upon this Earth. From what he told me, it sounded as though he had little, if any, direction from them. When he informed me of his belief that his mother brought him to St. Petersburg to rid their home of him, I should have given more weight to that view.

Of my own parents, I remember very little. They sent me off to work at a young age, and I hardly saw them. Back in those dark times, I labored for long hours in a filthy shop to earn my own keep. Pumping the bellows for the glassmaker exhausted me, but I learned a trade. I remember seeing mother and father for the last time at my journeyman initiation ceremony, where the master drove a pin through my earlobe to denote my new rank. This memory caused me to fiddle with that ear, attempting to locate the hole that had long healed over.

Knocking on the door interrupted my woolgathering, springing me forward a few centuries.

GRIGORI scurried to answer the door. "It's Yuri!"

"Good neighbor," I greeted him. "What brings you all the way here?"

We both laughed.

The doctor coughed into a balled fist. "Rodya, if you have a few spare minutes, there is a subject which I need to discuss with you."

"Of course." I opened the door wider for him.

He hesitated. "Uhhh… if you will, could we meet in my apartment?"

I glanced back at Grigori, who smiled, suggesting he found the situation amusing or he harbored ulterior motives I could not fathom.

"Sure," I responded. "We just completed packing for our little journey."

The doctor escorted me to his study. "Tea?"

"Thank you, no. We shall be leaving soon. What is on your mind, friend?"

Yuri paced for a minute or so, the clack of his heels filling the room. "I am not sure how much you know about your apprentice."

"Grigori?"

"Yes. I have had the opportunity to observe him when you were not around, and I think you should know —"

"I am aware of his activities with the People's Will," I interrupted. "For such a young person, he has become rather politically active."

"Yes, yes. I have witnessed that as well. However, what you might not be aware of is —"

Rapping at the door interrupted Yuri, who went to answer.

Grigori entered carrying my luggage and his knapsack. "Mr. Propok, have you angered the Imperial guards in any fashion?"

"Not that I can recall. Why do you ask?"

"Several of them are stationed outside our building, and I hear heavy footsteps on the stairway."

Yuri ordered, "Bring those pieces in here. You two remain in the study and stay quiet. I shall investigate."

Loud pounding sounded at the door. The three of us glanced at each other in turn.

I wondered if Catherine might retaliate for my not providing her the information she wanted. Most likely, she sent her guards to take me to the palace for interrogation. I had no wish to see her again nor have information tortured out of me. My heart raced, and I could feel perspiration forming around my collar.

Grigori and I sat where we could hear the conversation.

Yuri opened the door and asked, "May I assist you gentleman?"

A deep voice resounded, "Do you know who lives in that apartment?"

"You mean the *znakhar* across the way?" the doctor responded.

As much as I detested hearing the word, it illustrated Yuri's feigned ignorance of his neighbors. I stood and moved to the doorway so as to hear better.

"We are not seeking an adult, sir, but rather a boy of about ten years of age."

I turned to look at Grigori, who sat looking out the window.

"A boy, you say?" Yuri paused. "This building is for adults only, officer. There are no children living here."

"But we have this address and apartment as the place we could find him," the deep voice rejoined.

"Well, let me consult the maid. She might know something about this boy you seek."

Yuri appeared with a finger to his lips. "I am afraid the guards are after Grigori." The doctor turned to him. "Do you wish to surrender?"

Grigori's lowered brows and pursed lips suggested he had no intention of giving himself over to the soldiers. "I wish to exit this building without engaging the Tsar's minions, if you please."

Our neighbor turned to me with wide eyes, and I nodded. "If you are extremely quiet, you can slip out the back way," he whispered.

"There is a back way?" Grigori inquired. "We have but one door to our apartment."

"You also have a view of the street, which this set of rooms lacks. Go down the rear stairs while I detain the guards."

I moved to pick up my luggage.

"Rodya, wait." Yuri stepped to me and gave me a big hug before kissing me on both cheeks. "Please take care of yourself."

I knew him to be sentimental, but I considered the hug and kisses unnecessary. "Thank you, Yuri. You do the same." I did not want to seem ungrateful even though I felt discomfited from such unexpected affection.

"We are waiting!" came the call from the front door.

"Just a moment!" Yuri yelled. "Go!" he advised us, pointing through the kitchen to the back door.

As Grigori and I made our way out, I heard Yuri saying, "I am truly sorry, officer, but my maid has no knowledge of any boys in this building. If you like, you can come in and look around."

"Let us make haste," I whispered to Grigori.

He exited first. I intended to close the door gently, but it stuck. When I pulled harder, it sprang and produced a distinct bang.

"Come on, men!" I heard the guard shout.

Grigori and I shuffled down the rickety wooden stairs. We huddled in the shadows under the lowest landing. Clomping bootsteps drew closer from above. When they reached the ground, two soldiers turned west, and two headed east.

If we proceeded out Nevsky Prospekt, we would need to cross the Anichkov Bridge to reach the train station. Were I looking for someone on the run, that might be a good place to search. If only we could have been one of the mermaids in the bridge's brass railings and swam our way to safety.

Emerging from under the staircase once the guards had disappeared, I recalled the much smaller Lemonosov Bridge on nearby Chernyshov Street. It might be a bit out of the way, but the guards would probably not look for us there.

"Let us go," I directed.

"You're headed the wrong way," Grigori argued. "We must cross the Fontanka." He pointed to Nevsky Prospekt just as a carriage full of guards passed headed toward the river.

"Find that boy!" one of the soldiers yelled.

Grigori turned to follow me and stated, "Perhaps you have the better reasoning."

We walked at a steady pace, not wanting to draw attention to ourselves. Carrying several pieces of luggage slowed me down.

"Why are the guards looking for you?" I managed to ask between huffing breaths.

"How should I know?"

As if I would have believed any answer he provided.

When we reached the embankment, I looked about but saw no guards. We hustled across the short, stone structure and headed toward Ligovskaya Prospekt. Crowds concealed us on the large avenue that led to the same spot we would have come had we followed Nevsky Prospekt, just outside the train station.

"Pull down your hat. Cover your face." I surveyed the area. "Now what?"

"As they are looking for a boy, perhaps you should go ahead to assess the situation." He set his knapsack down. "I shall wait here."

"How can I trust you will follow?" Grigori said he wanted to return home to retrieve some personal items, but I had no indication of his sincerity.

"If I believe it too difficult to board the train proper, I shall devise a way." He nodded four times. "Believe me, I wish to leave more than you want me to."

I would have to trust Grigori in this. His previous exploits demonstrated devious ways, but he got what he wanted most of the time.

"All right, but if you do not join me in my compartment before the first stop, I shall take the return train and assist those guards with finding you."

"Where will you be seated?" he asked.

I had yet to purchase tickets. "You are a smart lad. I shall leave it to you."

Grigori smiled.

Attempting to appear as normal as possible under the circumstances, I struggled with my three suitcases to the terminal. A pair of Imperial guards stood scrutinizing pedestrians. My shoe caught a raised cobblestone. I stumbled, and the smallest case slipped from my arm.

One of the soldiers approached. "Let me assist you with that, sir." He grabbed the box and held it to his chest. "You haven't seen any boy children about, have you?"

The perspiration began to flow faster. Fortunately, my overcoat concealed the moisture. "Why, no, officer. I am traveling on my own." I pointed. "May I, please, have the valise?"

"Oh, yes. Of course. Sorry to bother you, sir." He placed the case on my arm. "You may pass. And do watch your step."

"Thank you, officer. Thank you."

I waited until the guard moved off before looking to where I left Grigori. He had vanished. I started back toward Ligovskaya Prospekt in hopes of finding him before the troops.

"Do not move so quickly," the boy whispered from behind. "I saw the soldier inquire about me."

"Yes. How do you propose to get onboard?"

He squinted. "I have a plan. A very good plan."

Perhaps it might be best if I had no idea what he intended to do lest a guard question me. "Do not describe it." I shook my head. "I have no wish to know."

"Certainly not. I had not intended to divulge it in any case. I shall join you once the train has passed into open country and the guards have left."

"When the wolves are full and the sheep safe?" I asked.

"Exactly."

A voice called out, "There's a boy!"

Grigori disappeared.

I approached the platform and reached into my pocket to retrieve a handkerchief. Instead, I found a folded piece of paper. The inscription, in Yuri's hand, read, "Open when you are alone." He must have slipped it into the pocket when he hugged me. While prone to foolishness, now and again he proved clever.

"Moscow! Moscow!" cried the conductor. "All aboard for Moscow!"

ONCE I got aboard the train, I found an empty first-class compartment near the end of one car and purchased a ticket. The porter assisted in stowing my suitcases, and I sat looking through the window. People moved about outside next to the car, but I saw no sign of Grigori. I left the sliding door open so he could locate me.

With a startling jolt, the carriage moved, and I watched the terminal disappear into the distance as we maneuvered out of the city. Once we crossed the American Bridge, scenery changed from city to farmland. The first stop, Chudovo, would be in about an hour. I hoped Grigori could find his way to this room before then.

Every time I left a city for good, I experienced sadness and regrets. My neighbor, Yuri, became more than just an acquaintance, and if I had remained, our friendship would have surely strengthened. My days in St. Petersburg brought much delight, as I got to meet many of the artists I admired for their talents. Over the centuries I met several people whose names lived on long after they died. Even though I spent less time here than in other places, I departed with many more memories than ever before.

"Excuse me, sir," came a gruff voice from the doorway.

An Imperial guard stood at attention.

My heartrate increased, and my palms developed sweat. "May I help you, officer?"

He slipped thumbs under his wide, black belt. "We are searching for a boy of about ten years of age who might have stowed away on the train." The guard pointed to his head. "He wore a *kartuz*. Have you seen anyone fitting that description?"

"I have not seen anyone matching the image you have described since I boarded. I wish I could be of more help." The first part held truth, but the second did not.

"Sorry to bother you, sir." He moved on.

Between the exertion of evading guards and gentle rocking of the carriage, I drifted off.

When I woke, Grigori sat opposite me. He had closed the door and lowered the blinds.

"Good morning, Mr. Propok. I hope you enjoyed your rest."

"I believe it is well past midday, Grigori. I am happy to see you found me. Your presence confirms you managed to evade the Imperial soldiers."

He smiled. "I have discovered many spaces on a train in which to conceal myself. Information I shall use again in the future."

I had no idea how long I slept. "Have we reached Chudovo yet?"

"That was a while back. We're almost to Okulovka."

"Are you hungry?"

"Not anymore." He rubbed his belly. "I purchased a few meat pies."

My stomach grumbled. "I suppose I had better find the food cart." As I stood, my legs wobbled, and I grabbed the doorframe for support. "Sooner rather than later, it seems."

Grigori reached into his bag and pulled out a wrapper. "Here, I brought you this."

I took the fist-sized package from him and opened it. Inside lay a warm, cooked potato. "Thank you." I believed it the first time he brought me anything. I took a large bite. "Mmmmm. Not too much salt," I mumbled as I chewed.

He retrieved a bottle. "Also, for you."

"Kvass?"

He nodded.

I opened it and sniffed. "Did you add any... *special* ingredients?"

He laughed. "Why, Mr. Propok, I believe you understand me."

In St. Petersburg, it felt as though everything I did and said distressed or displeased him. Onboard the train, he demonstrated a caring and jocular disposition. Of course, I had every right to be distrustful of his behavior, as everything he did seemed to have concealed motives. Grigori chose to remain in my company even though he had an opportunity to run off on his own. That encouraged me to interpret his actions in a positive light.

It saddened me that I never got to know this side of the boy while we lived together. Perhaps the thought of retrieving his forgotten items brought him more joy than I could comprehend.

After nightfall, we huddled on our benches and fell asleep. At least I did.

I woke with the sun, peeked around the blind and saw the spires and domes of Moscow. The train slowed as it pulled into Nikolaevsky Station.

We gathered our belongings and stepped out onto the same platform where Count Vronsky first espied Anna Karenina. I gawked about and smiled at seeing the scene with my own eyes, but my indulgent nostalgia ended when a woman screamed.

An attendant rushed to her. "What happened?"

She pointed down to the tracks. "That boy. He leapt in front of the moving train."

I followed her finger to see the figure of a mangled youngster who looked very much like Grigori. A tattered *kartuz* lay nearby. I hoped this would not be another "bad omen," as in *Anna Karenina*. When I re-examined the platform, I could not spot him. I could feel my heart pounding.

"What are you looking at?" came a voice from behind me.

I turned and shuddered to find a hatless Grigori. "Where have you been?"

"I just went to —"

"A young person who looks very much like you jumped onto the tracks and got hit by an oncoming train."

"How sad," he condescended.

"Sad? That is madness! Boys do not just leap in front of trains." My head tilted and my eyelids narrowed as I looked at Grigori. "You… did… not…?"

"Mr. Propok! I would never. What you must think of me to suggest such a thing." He took a step toward the edge of the platform and looked down. "He does bear a slight resemblance."

An Imperial guard pushed through the crowd, stood next to us, and glanced down. "Sergeant! I believe that is the lad we have been looking for." He pointed to the body on the tracks.

My palms felt moist, blood throbbed in my ears, and I felt the urge to flee. I withdrew from the crowd and Grigori followed. The two of us headed toward the platform where we could board the train to Tyumen.

"You know, I can get home by myself." He pointed to another plat-form. "If you wish to catch the Tula train, it will be leaving soon. You could save yourself many days of travel."

How clever of him to attempt to get me to leave him on his own. The train ride to Tyumen would take a day and a half. Despite his recent ami-cable comportment, I did not come all this way to have him carry out some deceitful scheme.

"I appreciate your consideration, Grigori. However, I intend to deliver you to your mother, no matter how many days it takes." I approached the newspaper seller and purchased a copy of *Moscovskie Vedomosti*. Its coverage of world events might give me inspiration for my next destination.

He moved to the standing train. "Depart. Don't depart. As you like, Mr. Propok."

"Shall we board?" I stepped up with my luggage. A staff member greeted us, and I purchased third-class seats.

"Third class?" whined Grigori. "We shall be riding this bone shaker for days. Do you expect me to sit so close to those peasants on splintered benches and sleep sitting up?"

"Do you wish to pay the additional tariff?"

He shook his head.

"The only reason I paid for a compartment from St. Petersburg was so that you could hide from the authorities. They believe they found their target. Besides, how did you and your mother travel to St. Petersburg?"

"Third class..." he muttered.

We rode through the Russian hinterlands toward the east in a creaky, crowded passenger car that reeked of garlic and boiled cabbage. Alternating swaths of tall trees and broad grasslands dominated the observable landscape. Seven kilometers to heaven, they say, and all through forest.

The newspaper kept my attention and discouraged conversation. By the time I had finished page two, the sun had set, and we hunkered down for the night.

At dawn, the train pulled into Kirov, and we disembarked to purchase items for the remainder of our journey. Grigori bought a few meat pies, and I found some fresh produce.

Most of the day I sequestered myself behind the newspaper, absorbing reports from foreign lands. Other passengers boarded or departed. None of them spoke to us, and we did not speak to them.

Around sunrise the following day, the train pulled into Tyumen. We grabbed our gear and stepped off.

"This way," Grigori instructed.

I followed him to an open space where several carriages stood. He spoke with one of the drivers and motioned me to join him.

The ride to Pokrovskoye took about an hour, and the road wanted for repair. By the time we arrived, my tailbone screamed in pain from all the bouncing and jostling about.

Our carriage stopped in the center of a quaint town, next to the Intercession of Our Lady Church. Such a contrast from the taller stone buildings of cities. Most of the wooden structures looked very old and in as good a condition as the gravel wagon path.

The driver held the door for us, and I rubbed my tender backside as I stepped down onto the unpaved street. He dropped our belongings then sped off.

"Follow me." Grigori headed away from the middle of the village.

I gathered my cases and followed him along the dusty, earthen streets. Pokrovskoye reminded me of many small towns I visited along my extended way. A church and administrative offices in the center with house-lined roads spoking outward.

He pointed to a squat, unremarkable, gray building. "That is the bath-house where I was born."

Villagers passed us, but no one said anything, nor did they look our way. As an outsider, that seemed proper, but Grigori lived here, yet no one acknowledged him. We walked nearly a kilometer before arriving at a small farmhouse situated next to a large fenced, grassy area.

"This is my parent's home." He stepped to the door, opened it, and called out, "Mother!"

Anna Vasilyevna appeared with the wide grin of a person whose grandmother tells fortunes. "Grishka!"

This time I could see her handsome face. On our first encounter, the evening we met at my apartment in St. Petersburg, rain had dampened her hair and scarf. She hugged her son and kissed his head.

"Mr. Propok. How good to see you again. Please, come in. If I had known you were coming, I would have made myself more presentable." She shuffled the folds of her long dress around to shroud her body.

"Where is father?" asked Grigori.

Anna's smile drooped. "My son, I did not wish to alarm you, but he died a few months back. That is why I wrote and asked you to come home."

I recalled how Grigori first told me the letter contained the news of his father's death, but when he let me read it, the correspondence made no mention of this.

"That is not what you wrote, Mother."

"No. I did not want to say because I was afraid you might not return if you knew."

But it seemed he did know.

"When your father died"—she glanced down and clasped her hands—"I wanted you to come back and take over the horse trading, but —"

Grigori crossed his arms and stamped a foot. "I have *no* interest in horses."

"But I knew you had no interest in his business." She looked up and pointed toward the meadow. "I hired a man to manage the raising and selling."

"A goose is not the pig's friend." The boy might as well have spat at his mother's feet. "I wish to go to my room." He disappeared.

Anna sighed. "No matter how much you feed a wolf, he still looks to the forest."

I could only imagine the difficulties in raising a child like Grigori. He treated his mother with only slightly more respect than he showed me, but not much. And, from what he told me, all her other children had died. Only this one remained. Quite a quandary.

With the boy out of the room, I had the opportunity to ask, "Madame, did you write Grigori based on the request I sent you?"

"Mr. Propok, the only communication I ever received from you was in response to my original inquiry about my son's progress."

"That is extremely odd. I sent you a letter asking for you to —"

"What is all that rubbish in my room?" Grigori howled as he returned.

"My dear, when we thought you were not coming back, your father and I used it for storage. Do not worry yourself. We can remove those items, and it can be yours again."

"Did you touch any of my belongings?" His eyes bulged.

Anna rested her hands on her hips. "We may have moved a few things about, but most everything is where you left it."

"I am very unhappy." He reached into his pocket.

I observed this maneuver before, most times resulting in pain or suffering of others. Compassion urged me to say something before anything grave transpired. "Grigori, are you going to show your mother the magic stone?"

"Magic stone?" Anna sounded amused, as if the boy had filled her ears with countless fantastic tales in the past. "What nonsense."

The glare he turned on me could have melted lead, but I took the risk of angering him if it would save his mother's life.

Anna approached and grasped my arm. "Mr. Propok, thank you for taking care of my little Grishka. I hope he learned much from you and that he was not too big a bother."

I glanced at her hand. When I touched her, visions presented a simple life. Cooking, cleaning, taking care of her son, nothing remarkable.

"It has been said the best teacher learns more from the student than the student learns from the teacher." My attention turned to Grigori. "Your son has taught me a great deal."

"Why, thank you, Mr. Propok." Grigori extended his hand. "When I return to St. Petersburg, I shall certainly look you up."

He never offered to shake hands before, and his anger abated all too fast. In the presence of his mother, he tended to exhibit good manners. However, I remained vigilant.

When our flesh met, he looked up into my eyes, and a blizzard of images flashed through my mind. I could see him as an adolescent, falling in love for the first time and, soon after, taking on a religious mantle. I had never been able to see that far ahead into someone's future before. Beyond that, I saw him befriend Alexander's timid grandson, Nikolai, who would become Tsar in his own right. Fostering favor with his wife by assisting her son with the blood disease inherited from their British cousins. Far too many carnal encounters with young women and snipping locks of their hair. Snip, snip, snip, snip, snip. The alder-tree would not bend, after all. And one fateful winter afternoon in the Moika Palace courtyard, Grigori would meet his end at the hands of a political assassin. His body lay untouched in the snow for hours with an obvious gunshot through the forehead.

My breathing halted. When it resumed a few seconds later, I stammered, "I… you… how?"

"Do not worry yourself, Mr. Propok. The cat knows whose meat it has eaten." The boy smiled. He cupped a hand to the side of his mouth and whispered to me, "Mind what you do with that information. And, please, do not sell it to your friend Suvorin before its time."

My brain stumbled after seeing all those disturbing images. "No. Yes. Of course not. No."

As much as I found the horrific images disturbing, none of them involved taking another person's life. Perhaps I removed him from St. Petersburg without proper justification. Oh, well. No sense in looking for improvement on good.

"Mr. Propok, I hope you can stay for supper." Grigori's mother invited. "I shall need to prepare more food at any rate with Grigori home."

The boy stood with hands on hips. "I believe Mr. Propok needs to leave if he wishes to catch his train."

His mother glanced at me, but I stood shock-still. "Not even for tea, Grishka?" she inquired with furrowed brow.

Grigori shook his head.

"Oh, that is too bad." Anna walked out of the room.

"Can you tell me what you saw, Mr. Propok?"

From the unexpected question, I gathered his inability to envision the future himself, and he required my talents to discover this strange story. Far be it from me to tell him what he did not, and—without a doubt—should not know. My head swiveled from side to side, expressing both my reaction to the visions as well as my response to his question.

"That is too bad," he murmured. His hand went into his pocket. "You will travel back to Tyumen?"

I continued to reel from witnessing the future phantasms in my mind, unable to process further conversation. "Yes. Tyumen."

The little devil nodded four times. "Because you are headed to Tula, yes?"

"Tula, yes." I echoed.

"Here." Grigori's mother returned holding out a sack. "I packed some meat pies for your return journey so you will not starve."

Without looking, I could feel the boy smirking at the gift, knowing my distaste for flesh. Not wanting to be rude, I took the offering and responded, "Thank you, Mrs. Rasputin."

I tucked the meat pies into a coat pocket, retrieved my luggage, hiked back to the center of Pokrovskoye, and booked passage to Tyumen. If there had been a cushion vendor, I would have purchased one for the rugged ride to come.

With each bump and jolt of the coach, assorted scenes from Grigori's future repeated in my head. By the time we reached our destination, my nerves felt raw and frayed. And to think, I permitted that boy monster to live with me.

When my carriage pulled into the station, a large crowd surrounded the newspaper kiosk. People shook their heads or wailed. Once I got close enough, I could read the large-type headline: "Tsar Assassinated!!!" I bought the last available copy for later reading.

The schedule indicated the train for Moscow departing in about an hour. I sat in the waiting room and perused the periodical I purchased.

The deed occurred a few days back, but it took time for the news to reach Siberia. As best as I could tell, it happened during our train ride from Moscow.

Alexander II of Russia Blown up by a Bomb Sunday Morning.
Arrest of the Assassins.

News of the long looked for successful attempt upon the life of the Tsar of Russia has been received. Alexander had been fatally wounded by the explosion of a bomb thrown by an assassin while he was out driving in the forenoon. At first it was supposed the report was a canard, for the emperor's assassination is so often announced and so often denied, since the nihilists began to compass his death, which was so quickly followed by a full account of the tragedy.

The carriage was moving fast, and the first shell struck the ground behind it and the end of the carriage was blown out. The coachman implored the Tsar to enter the carriage again, but he moved a few paces from the carriage to see to the wounded of his escort when the second bomb exploded. A Cossack and a passerby were killed on the spot. Cossacks and police had charged upon the knot of people from which the two bombs were flung. The assassins stood on the opposite side of the road. Several persons pointed to a man in the rough sheepskin garb of a peasant and declared that he had thrown the first shell. This was confirmed by the Cossacks, who saw him hurling it. Colonel of Police Archemoff seized him.

The man struggled desperately, and as the dismounted escort closed upon him, he shouted the People's Will motto, "Land and Liberty!" He drew a revolver, as though intending to shoot Grand Duke Michael, but his hand was struck down. In an instant, he was thrown to the earth and securely pinioned, the police putting on the irons and the Cossacks binding him with ropes. It is stated that the bombs were made of a thick mass filled with nitroglycerine.

The Tsar was carried upstairs on a litter beside surgeons in an ordinary. The most skilled men in the city were present, but the case was hopeless. His left leg was fearfully shattered—the greater portion of the foot and ankle having been blown off, and his right leg was nearly torn from his body. He was sensible, with brief intervals of unconsciousness, to the last. He had lost an enormous quantity of blood, and the shock had utterly prostrated him. The doctor's efforts to rally him were fruitless. At 1:30 p.m. the imperial family were summoned to his bedside, where prayers for the dying were being said by the Greek Patriarch and clergy. The leave-taking is said to have been most touching. The Tsar kissed them all and gave them his blessing. He bore the agony of his wounds with heroic fortitude.

The arrangements for the funeral of the murdered Tsar will be made on the most extensive scale, befitting the high rank of the dead ruler.

When the train to Moscow pulled alongside the platform, I boarded the second-class section and took a seat at one of the empty tables. I put my hand in the jacket pocket and discovered Yuri's note, which read, "R, last evening, several soldiers came to the hospital with arsenic poisoning. They claimed a boy threw something at them that dispensed powder. When I described your apprentice, they said that was him. -Y"

Perhaps Yuri provided our whereabouts to the officials. That would explain why the Imperial guards wanted to apprehend Grigori. His People's Will friends must have put him up to this prank. He might have been the very one they selected to throw a bomb at the Tsar's carriage.

My eyes followed the text of the newspaper, but my mind kept reviewing recent events. I had removed Grigori from St. Petersburg because I feared he might attempt this assassination. Against my better judgment,

I changed the course of history to protect him. After observing his true future, I had to wonder if my actions may have made things worse. As they say, a helpful fool can be more dangerous than any enemy.

No matter what I did, the Tsar would have died. Unless his son could gain control quickly, Russia might plunge into anarchy or civil war.

I have witnessed bloodshed on a grand scale many times. After some interval, equilibrium returned, and the world continued to spin. My actions never had any lasting, historic effect. Much like Shakespeare's King Lear, left with nothing but regrets.

Tomorrow, we arrive at Moscow, hub of most train routes in Russia, and I shall have to determine my next destination. Built on the remnants of timeworn horse-cart tracks, Moscow's narrow streets twist and convolute, opposed to St. Petersburg's grid of wide avenues and canals. Muscovites tend to stay home in the evening, whereas nightlife flourishes in Peter. Despite my distaste for the white stone city, I may have to remain a day or two before deciding where to travel next.

Given all I have witnessed, I should attempt to put my memories into writing and publish them at some later point. I sold Suvorin my previous manuscript to finance this excursion and must begin afresh. As it stands, I have centuries of memories to draw from.

The seat bobbled, rousing me from my ruminations. So much time passed since leaving Tyumen, I had not realized we pulled into Yekaterinburg. Across the table sat a flaxen-haired young man with a close-cropped beard and piercing blue eyes. He reminded me very much of an old, long-gone friend.

When I first apprenticed to the town glassmaker all those years ago, I met Michel, another trainee. Youthful and inexperienced, we developed a mutual and supportive bond. He went on to sit at the university while I continued to assist our master. During our years apart, I rose to journeyman status.

Years later we joined up again following his expulsion from medical training. He began working on a prophylactic against the plague, his "rose pill," as he named it, and titled himself, "Doctor." When time permitted, Michel revealed some of his apothecary knowledge to me, which kindled my interest in healing.

Despite taking his miraculous medication, I believed the plague finally caught up with me. Once I woke from that grim sleep, we never encountered each other again. I've known so many people in my long, long life, but every now and again, Michel's memory touches my soul. A tiny tear seeped from the corner of my eye as I realized how much I missed that camaraderie over the centuries.

I smiled at the fellow sitting opposite and held up the sack Grigori's mother provided me. "Would you fancy a meat pie?"

Other titles by Wayne Goodman:

The Last Great Hope
A Secret Service agent comes out of retirement to find a missing Kennedy child while dealing with his own coming out issues

Britain's Glory — Charlotte: The People's Princess
The granddaughter of King George III (and second in line for the throne) struggles to find her voice in a man's world

The Seed of Immortality
Two immortal Mahjong sharps travel around ancient China and have an audience with the first Emperor

Vanya Says, "Go!"
A retelling of Mikhail Kuzmin's *Wings*, the first Russian-language book dealing positively with same-sex relationships

Better Angels
A retelling of Bayard Taylor's *Joseph and His Friend: A Pennsylvania Story*, the first American Gay novel

Fortune's Lot
A retelling of Francis Latham's *Live and Learn*, the first English-language Gay novel

All the Right Places
Short stories ranging from the near future to the near past showing men interacting with other men to pursue love and companionship

Princess Aina: Queen Victoria's Yoruba Godchild
For Middle Grade Readers. The story of a young woman taken from Africa to live with the royal children of England

Tim-Tam & the Space Pirates: Race to the Phantom Moon
For Middle Grade Readers. Two non-identical school-age twins board a space pirate ship for adventure and plunder

www.ingramcontent.com/pod-product-compliance
Lightning Source LLC
Chambersburg PA
CBHW061211210726
48294CB00006B/1814